Spawn

ROBERT HOLLES

Spawn

HAMISH HAMILTON/LONDON

First published in Great Britain 1978
by Hamish Hamilton Ltd
90 Great Russell Street London WC1B 3PT

Copyright © 1978 by Robert Holles

British Library Cataloguing in Publication Data

   Spawn.
   I. Title
   823'.9'1F   PR6058.0/

   ISBN 0-241-89828-5

Printed in Great Britain by Bristol Typesetting Co Ltd,
Barton Manor, St Philips, Bristol

I

More than a hundred people were soaking up the afternoon sunshine in the grounds of the hotel at Bad Mondorf in Luxembourg on 12 June 1945, yet only the gardener tending the well-kept borders was at peace with his surroundings.

The others lolled about, shirt-sleeved, sprawled in deck-chairs, chatted all too brightly on the edge of the swimming pool, swapped rumours in front of the notice boards. These residents were largely men over thirty, almost all of them Germans, and the majority were going to claim that they were acting under the orders of their superiors, and that the penalty for disobedience was death.

The preliminary interrogation of Nazi war criminals was under way. Many of those sunning themselves were to appear at Nuremberg five months later, and a number would meet death by execution.

The interrogation teams worked around the clock. The team which was to investigate case No 26 (Category C) later that day, was made up as follows:

For the United Kingdom, and chairman, Wing Commander Harley. For Canada, Major Osinchuk. For the Soviet Union, Colonel Kirochenko.

These three interrogating officers sat in a stark and dusty conference room in the hotel, dominated by a long rosewood table. They occupied the head of the table, flanked by two interpreters and a stenographer. Each accused, and his lawyer, had free choice of any of the other half-dozen chairs around the table. There were no others in the room. Armed guards patrolled the hotel precincts at a respectful distance. The

1

internees had been thoroughly searched on arrival.

It was the third interrogation of the day by the same officers in the same room. The first—that of a young U-boat lieutenant—had taken twenty minutes. The second, that of the late Governor-General of Poland, Hans Frank, five hours. Both defendants had been committed for trial at Nuremberg.

The defendant who was guided to his place by an orderly at 7.45 p.m. was one of Germany's foremost scientists, a man with the gaunt and frail body consistent with a mind so preoccupied it frequently forgot to eat.

The interrogation proceeded as it appears in the official records of the Allied War Crimes Commission.

Harley : What is your full name?

Buechner : Heinrich Karl Buechner.

Harley : What was your profession?

Buechner : I was professor of medicine at the University of Leipzig.

Harley : Yes, but for a good many years you were director of the research institute attached to the municipal hospital at Magdeburg.

Buechner : That is correct, since 1929.

Harley : You are a very distinguished scientist?

No reply.

Kirochenko : You had an international reputation before the war?

Buechner : Yes, before the war, that is true.

Osinchuk : Professor, what was your particular area of research?

Buechner : Fertility.

Osinchuk : The fertility of women?

Buechner : The fertility of both men and women.

Harley : What would you say was the objective of your research?

Buechner : The objective? I would say the objective was to allow infertile women to conceive children.

Osinchuk : Seems a very laudable objective.

Kirochenko: You claim that you had a very high reputation before the war. Why did this not continue during the war?

Buechner: During a war everybody has other things to think about, such as their own survival. The only scientists whose achievements are praised during a war are those who can think of better ways of killing people.

Harley: Well, I don't suppose anyone would disagree with that. But I take it you continued with your original line of research during the war years.

Buechner: Yes, as far as this was possible. But I had no access to the work of others in my field of research such as Jelks in Canada or Matthews at Cambridge.

Kirochenko: This was the only problem?

Buechner: It was one serious problem among a number of others.

Harley: Professor, I am sure you are acquainted with the Nazi ideal of the pure Aryan.

Buechner: I have heard about this outrageous concept, yes.

Harley: Well, as this seemed to involve a very deep interest in genetics and sterilisation techniques, I should have thought that you might have been under some pressure to collaborate in some of the research which was going on.

Buechner: I do not see the need for this question. I have already made it clear in my statement that I was under a great deal of pressure.

Osinchuk: But you didn't go along?

Buechner: I am sorry, I don't understand the question.

Osinchuk: You didn't give in to these pressures.

Buechner: No, I did not.

Harley: When was it that you first came to know that a large number of experiments were being carried out on living inmates of the concentration camps?

Buechner: I learned of this about eighteen months ago. I was filled with wretchedness and disgust to think that such crimes were being committed by my own fellow-countrymen.

Kirochenko: But although you say that you refused to

co-operate, you were not sent to a concentration camp your-self. Why was that?

Buechner: I think it was because the S.S. believed that I would change my mind eventually.

Harley: Right, now let's get down to page five of your statement which concerns your relationship with S.S. Brigade-Commander Professor Hans Clauberg, who was a medical scientist like yourself.

Buechner: Clauberg was not a scientist. He was a sadist. He was given the title of professor by Himmler.

Osinchuk: But I understand you were a friend of his a long time before the war.

Buechner: We were medical students together at Leipzig. He was never a friend. Not even an acquaintance.

Kirochenko: When he became a Brigade-Commander he protected you and allowed you to continue with your work.

Buechner: That is totally untrue.

Harley: Professor Buechner, we are now going to explore that part of your statement which involves Hans Clauberg. You have chosen not to be represented but before we proceed any further it is my duty to inform you that it may be in your best interests to have the benefit of legal advice. If you wish to do so, I will adjourn this hearing and arrange for you to consult a lawyer.

Buechner: Please continue. I have nothing to hide.

Harley: Very well. Now you say in your statement that you were approached by Clauberg on the 15th of January 1944. Will you carry on from there in your own words, please.

Buechner: Clauberg came to see me in my laboratory in Magdeburg. He told me he required my assistance with an experiment on female detainees at the Ravensbruck camp.

Osinchuk: Jewish women presumably.

Buechner: Yes. This I discovered later. He informed me that he had been working on sterilisation techniques with drugs and he wanted me to test the effectiveness of these techniques by attempting to make the women pregnant. He

4

stated that Himmler had personally ordered me to assist him.

Kirochenko: And you agreed to do so?

Buechner: At first I refused absolutely, then I pretended to accept for humanitarian reasons.

Harley: Before we come to these reasons, why did Clauberg ask you to help him? He must have known about your attitude to human experiments.

Buechner: Clauberg had a special reason for asking me— he was jealous of my reputation. It gave him great satisfaction to think that if he sterilised women I could not restore them to fertility. He considered that this would lead everyone to believe that he was a better scientist than myself.

Kirochenko: In that case why did you finally accept? Did you want to prove that he was wrong?

Buechner: It is in my statement. I believed I could help these women. I knew that they were due to be exterminated and I thought that if I could keep them alive for as long as possible, the war might finish before they died.

Osinchuk: For how long did you manage to keep them alive?

Buechner: I told Clauberg I needed at least a year to test his theories. He insisted on a limit of six months.

Osinchuk: How many women did Clauberg supply?

Buechner: Twenty-four women were sent to me from Ravensbruck. They were kept in a hostel in Magdeburg.

Kirochenko: And you gave them treatment for fertility?

Buechner: I pretended to Clauberg that I was treating them by artificial insemination.

Harley: But in fact you were not?

Buechner: That is correct.

Osinchuk: What sort of condition were they in?

Buechner: Most of them were in the condition one normally finds in heroin addicts.

Harley: Did you treat them for drug addiction?

Buechner: To the best of my ability, yes.

Kirochenko: Is it not true that you agreed to take part in these experiments because you were afraid of being shot?

A*

5

Buechner : Nobody's life is worth such a degradation of the human spirit. I did not conduct experiments on these women.

Kirochenko : But you still managed to stay alive. That was very clever of you.

No reply.

Harley : What happened when the six months was up?

Buechner : Of course, after six months none of the women was pregnant. So Clauberg considered his theories had been proved.

Osinchuk : So what happened to the women?

Buechner : They were taken back to Ravensbruck.

Osinchuk : And you did nothing to stop them?

Buechner : What could I do to stop it?

Harley : Professor, I have to tell you that Clauberg tells a very different story in his own statement.

Buechner : That doesn't surprise me at all.

Harley : He claims that you willingly, and in fact enthusiastically, took part in a series of appalling experiments on these women.

Buechner : I would naturally expect Clauberg to claim such a thing. As he is no doubt destined for the scaffold it would give him the greatest pleasure to take an innocent man with him . . . myself in particular.

2

The imperturbable peace of the Wildenstein Gallery in New Bond Street on 3 March 1974, was almost indecently out of character with the mood of the nation. The Heath government had just fallen. In the dripping gloom of the streets outside, *Evening Standard* placards forecast the impending collapse of the British economy as the miners' strike moved towards a reluctant settlement.

Inside the gallery David Durandt, managing director of Heller Art International, had been studying one of the Mondrians on display for twenty minutes and his companion, Barry Eckstein, was beginning to feel twitchy and impatient. There were nine of the Dutchman's works on show. Three were for sale. The other six had been borrowed for the occasion from art galleries and private collections in Holland, Switzerland, the United States.

Eventually Durandt turned his large, florid features towards Eckstein. 'Come over here. Look, I want you to stand a bit closer.' He projected Eckstein by the arm. 'You can see what he's doing, he's illustrating the problems of the cubist techniques . . . you see, he begins to build up a sequence, then comes to a point where he knows he's arrived at a dead end, there's no way to develop any further, he has to go back to square one, so he does but he builds again on the wreckage, leaving the ruins intact . . . so you can see how the whole conception is moving forward through a series of blind alleys.'

Eckstein peered closely at the painting but saw nothing but an architectural jumble of blue, red and yellow lozenge shapes.

'Listen,' the old man said patiently, wanting Eckstein

to share his enthusiasm, 'you ever see the manuscript of a great poem which the poet has been working on? There are some in the British Museum. There is one by Shelley I remember. You can see a word crossed out and replaced by another, and perhaps another. You can watch the man's instinct happening in his head, saying, "No, this isn't quite right, there's something wrong there." It is the same with Mondrian in this picture. He allows us to watch him struggle to overcome his problems.'

'I guess I can see what you mean,' said Eckstein, nodding.

'This is one of his most interesting pictures,' said the dealer. 'There are six or seven others, all painted from 1911 to 1913. Five of them are in the Kroller-Muller Museum. You could not buy one in fifty years.'

'Are you going to bid for any of the others?' asked Eckstein.

Durandt glanced briefly at the three pictures which were for sale, then tucked his fingers in his bulging waistcoat.

'No, I don't think so. They were all painted after he came to New York in 1940. There are some artists who are like wine, they improve with age, but I don't think Mondrian is one of them. With the possible exception of his last work, the *Victory Boogie-Woogie*, which is in the Tremain collection . . . but then, he never finished it.'

'You mean if he'd lived, he might have spoiled it?'

'Very possibly.'

A grey-uniformed attendant appeared at Durandt's elbow. 'Excuse me, would one of you gentlemen be a Mr Eckstein?' The dealer motioned towards his companion. 'You're wanted on the telephone, sir.'

Eckstein followed the attendant back to the gallery office and picked up a telephone, raising a strong flicker of interest in the two girl secretaries at adjacent desks. 'Eckstein here.'

The voice of his chief, Richard Coulman, said, 'Get back here as fast as you can.'

'Right.' Eckstein replaced the telephone. As he walked quickly through the long room of the gallery he had time to notice that Durandt was once more deeply engrossed in Mondrian's pictorial essay on the problems of cubism.

The Heller Art International Corporation had established its London headquarters at No 17 Parlane Close—a tall Regency house in a quiet backwater off the Brompton Road—early in 1968. There was some surprise in the art world at that time as to why David Durandt, formerly an assistant curator at the Metropolitan Museum of Modern Art, latterly a world authority on Rembrandt and Rubens and one of the most successful art dealers in the United States, should forsake his interests in that country, take over a moribund Pacific Coast company which was on the brink of calling in the receiver, and launch himself on the European circuit at the age of seventy. The old man himself claimed he found it difficult, if not impossible, to resist a fresh challenge. This was true. But the nature of the challenge had little to do with any ambition on the part of Durandt to add to his reputation, or increase the size of the considerable fortune he had already accumulated by the judicious buying and selling of masterpieces. He had in fact committed a large slice of his own capital to the enterprise, and other funds were not long forthcoming.

About a hundred well-endowed businessmen, mostly from the state of New York, were approached with the following proposition : they would each put up a five-year bond of $10,000 to be invested in the Heller company. These funds would be used by Durandt to purchase works of art by established artists on the European market. Since the market was inexorably rising these works, carefully selected by Durandt, could be expected to yield a useful profit over a comparatively short term. Unlike most commercial companies, however, Heller Art International would not pay a dividend and its managing director would draw no salary. All the profits would go straight to the exchequer of the Israeli government.

Only seven of those who were approached declined; they were having liquidity problems and couldn't find the money at such short notice. The remainder invested with enthusiasm.

9

These stockholders had one thing in common with their managing director—all were passionate Zionists.

In the first four years of its life the reborn Heller company had certainly justified its existence, sending to Tel Aviv during that period the sum of $692,000. Yet this was only a small part of its usefulness. It had a further, more significant function of which the stockholders knew nothing.

In 1970, as the hijacking and kidnapping activities of Black September and other Palestinian action groups got under way and spread to Europe, the Israeli Intelligence Service decided that it needed much stronger counter-espionage facilities in the European capitals than it was possible to provide through their embassies, which were under strong surveillance from the host countries. Thus in April of that year Durandt, who was just becoming firmly established in London, was approached with an unusual proposition. He was asked to take under his wing a small number of 'trainee directors'. They would arrive in London at intervals, be seen in Durandt's company around the galleries and auction rooms, and then rotated around Heller Corporation offices in the European art centres—Rome, Munich, Amsterdam, Zurich, Paris. Each of them would be a trained, experienced intelligence man employed directly by Israel.

The art dealer huffed and puffed over the suggestion for quite some time. Although a fervent supporter of the cause he had never set foot in Israel, nor to the best of his knowledge had his forebears, Dutch Jews who had lived at the Hague for generations before emigrating to America in 1908. The promised land had its attractions for Durandt as a vague and distant ideal. He felt quite alarmed at the prospect of getting involved in the blood and guts of its survival. Others were better qualified. He confided these reservations to Colonel Shahan, the Israeli security chief who had been despatched to London to broach the subject, over dinner at the Chez Solange.

'My dear David,' said the colonel soothingly, 'we have no intention of sending you to Damascus . . . anyway you're much too valuable to risk. All I ask you to do is to provide a home for a small team of intelligence experts . . . you can pretend they are your colleagues if you like . . . but they won't interfere in your business.' As these sentiments failed to quell the uneasiness in the old man's eyes he added, 'Don't worry . . . these fellows will simply gather information and pass it on to Tel Aviv—we'll just be using your premises like a post office.' Finally, the art dealer solemnly shook the colonel's hand in acquiescence.

Having now obtained the working conditions he sought, Colonel Shahan bent his talents to fulfilling the second half of his brief—finding the people.

At this time the Israeli Intelligence Service was fully stretched on operations throughout the Middle East and very few of its personnel could be spared. Moreover it had been discovered from harsh experience that not many of the home-grown product were suitable for European operations. An agent who carries around with him the olive tan of the Mediterranean seaboard, and whose cultural background has emerged from the kibbutz and the Talmud, is not too difficult to pick out among the pale cosmopolitans in the hotel foyers of Hamburg on a drizzling afternoon in February. So it wasn't long before Shahan was to be found at the Washington headquarters of the Central Intelligence Agency—or more precisely in the office of Kirk Wrathall, chief of personnel under the director, Richard Helms.

Wrathall considered the colonel's proposal carefully—that Shahan should be allowed to approach CIA agents with Jewish antecedents and recruit six of them on a five-year contract to work in the European theatre of operations for Israel.

On the face of it the request seemed absurdly optimistic. No intelligence service wants to lose half a dozen of its skilled and experienced agents, even for a limited period. But after more detailed consideration among the inner council of the CIA the idea was seen to have its advantages. There already existed strong ties and a steady exchange of information between the two services. Shahan's arrangement would serve to strengthen them further.

Two weeks later the colonel was given a list of seventeen Jewish-American agents who might be approached, on the understanding that the contract would be for only three years and not renewable, that any information collected by these agents affecting the interests of the United States would be immediately fed back to Washington, and that if any of them got into trouble with the European police or security forces, the Israelis would have to stand the rap.

Colonel Shahan was happy to accept these conditions. Within a further twenty days he had selected and signed on his six volunteers. One of them, Richard Coulman, a 46-year-old veteran of numerous South American operations, was assigned to take charge of the group's London headquarters. On Coulman's own recommendation, Barry Eckstein was appointed his deputy.

The others—Tony Sachs, Tim Goldberg, Victor Greb, and Ben Lewis—were given a brief but intensive course of instruction on the intricacies of the art world by Durandt, then despatched to represent the interests of Heller Art International on the continent.

'I don't expect them to know it all,' as the old dealer confided to Coulman, 'but at least they ought to be able to tell Monet from Michelangelo.'

The ground floor of the house in Parlane Close contained Durandt's office and store-rooms; the floor above it housed separate accommodation for himself and the secretary, Angela Stringer, who had been with him for seventeen years. Coulman's office was on the second floor and the two floors above this had been converted into flats for Coulman and Eckstein.

Coulman was waiting in front of the lift cage when his deputy arrived.

He said, 'We haven't got much time. I've just heard from Greb in Munich. Reisener's just left from the airport on his way to London. It's a BOAC flight . . . No BJ 73. It's due to land at Heathrow at 1642. Get out there now and see where he goes. You've got about thirty-five minutes, okay? Here's his photograph, just to refresh your memory. I've put the rest of the details on the back of the envelope.'

Eckstein looked at his watch and said, 'I'm so glad it's not the rush hour.' He put the envelope in his pocket, turned away and walked rapidly through the door.

Among the knots of welcoming relatives in the arrival hall of Heathrow's European terminal, Eckstein was not conspicuous. He had the good actor's flair for adapting his appearance to merge with the social and sartorial attitudes of his surroundings.

A tall, almost spindly man in his late twenties, with straight, lank straw-coloured hair, he passed easily as one of the current crop of middle-class trendies, an effect compounded by the newish, knee-length Afghan coat, the faded levis. There was a touch of the scholar about him, in the hunched walk, the neat smoked-lens spectacles—but one who would normally expect to pass his exams.

Moreover, there was no hint of a semitic origin in Eckstein's countenance. This was now of some advantage, but he had suffered from it as a child. His father had once laughingly told him he was a *shmuk*, left on the doorstep, taken in out of pity. Eckstein had half-believed this for two years, until his mother had raked out a curling sepia photograph of an Irish grandmother and pointed out the obvious similarities.

He had driven furiously to reach the airport in time, but this haste was unnecessary. Owing to the implementation of the stringent new security precautions the departure of the BOAC Viscount from Munich had been delayed by sixteen minutes, and the airliner had spent an extra twenty in the stack.

Eckstein had to wait for two other planeloads of passengers to pass through before the travellers from Munich appeared. And he needed no second glance at the photograph to identify Reisener. The German was short—no taller than five-six under his black Homburg—and it was easy to assess him even at this distance as a man used to power and authority. It bristled out of him, his quick walk towards the customs barrier, he gave off fumes of impatience at being involved in something so unproductive as simply getting from one place to another, his life forced into neutral gear.

The customs officer who attended to him was quick to assess this bellicose personality, and his natural reaction was to rub its nose in his own formidable sense of self-importance.

He took some twenty minutes prodding about among the contents and feeling along the lining of Reisener's monogrammed suitcase, pausing now and then to take a casual swig of coffee from a mug at his elbow. Reisener was perhaps doubly unlucky. This particular official disapproved generally of the rich and powerful, and of Germans in particular.

Eventually he closed the suitcase with evident reluctance, chalked it, then turned to Reisener's sole remaining piece of luggage, a large aluminium canister.

He tapped it. 'Would you mind telling me what you've got in there, sir?'

'I have a customs clearance certificate for it,' said Reisener tersely. It was already in his hand. He passed it over.

The official examined the document with care. The goods were described as 'One flask containing medical specimens for analysis in deep freeze conditions (-192 C.).' The consignor was named as the *Director of the Heidenstam Institute for Medical Research, Munich*, and the consignee was *Dr John Stephen, Grasspool Clinic, near Ipswich, Suffolk*. The certificate bore the stamp of the Customs and Excise Department at King's Beam House, Mark Lane. He handed it back, then chalked the top of the cylinder.

'Will you turn out your trouser pockets, sir?' The tone was not that of a request. The German did so, fuming. A handkerchief, a few coins, a gold lighter which the customs man thoughtfully tossed up and down before returning.

'All right sir, away you go.' Reisener expressed his contempt in a final stare before he turned to follow the porter through

14

the barrier. His tormentor strolled across, mug of coffee in hand, to join a colleague at the next check-point.

'These bloody idiots up at HQ, they dish out bits of paper like confetti. How do we know what that kraut's got in there? Could be enough germs to wipe out the lot of us.'

His companion smirked. 'The war's over, Arthur . . . didn't you know? Trouble with you is, you worry too much.'

By this time Eckstein, lurking a few yards away beyond the barrier, had begun to develop an even stronger interest in the canister.

It was now more than a year after the capture, and subsequent slaughter, of eight Israeli hostages by Arab terrorists at the Munich Olympic Games of 1972. In the atmosphere of shock and confusion which followed this event the West German Federal Government, at the urgent request of the Israelis, rounded up and deported any recent immigrant of Arab nationality who might conceivably be suspected of having connections with the Palestinian terrorists. The Israeli Intelligence Service was permitted to include among this number two of their own agents, both Palestinian Arabs, who had been quickly flown out from Tel Aviv.

They hadn't much time to work—merely the ninety minutes or so taken by the Lufthansa jet to fly from Munich to Rome, where the Arabs were to be escorted to other flights back to their countries of origin. There were sixteen of them, an assortment of Syrians, Jordanians, Tunisians and Algerians, all students or immigrant workers, and most of them entirely innocent of terrorist activity.

During the trip the two agents circulated freely among their fellow-passengers, introducing a whiff of carnival into an atmosphere which was largely glum and silent. They claimed to belong to a militant Palestinian group working from South Lebanon, and to have been sent to Bonn to deliver a birthday present to a politician known to be among the leaders of the Israeli lobby in the Bundestag. While they were disappointed at the failure of their own mission, they expressed huge delight at the success of their brothers in Munich. They wandered about the gangway, mocking the others, inviting them to share in the celebration, and join the cause.

Shortly before the airliner touched down, they made a breakthrough. One of the deportees, a Jordanian who had sat tight-lipped throughout this jocularity, curtly told them to shut up. It was foolish and dangerous to discuss operations in public. When challenged by the exuberant pair, he quietly revealed that he had been in Munich for the best part of a year and had played a prominent part in setting up the affair.

The agents immediately treated him with the hushed respect accorded to a hero; they eagerly begged for further details. As the aircraft rolled to a halt, they were given the name of the link man in Munich who had made the whole operation feasible—Hugo Reisener. A fortnight later Victor Greb had arrived in Munich to set up an office for the Heller Art International Corporation.

3

Outside the terminal building, Eckstein watched from behind his *Guardian* as the Rolls, a Corniche finished in silver mink, moved past a taxi queue and stopped beside the German. The passenger who emerged from the back was a stiffly upright man in his mid-fifties, who was all suave cordiality as he stooped to shake hands with Reisener. There seemed nothing furtive about the encounter but Eckstein was experienced enough not to be disarmed. He knew that most of the evil in the world is hatched in the safest place of all—in public, by the broad light of day.

There was another man in the front passenger seat, his features indistinguishable to Eckstein through the misted window. As the chauffeur came round in front of the car and briskly loaded Reisener's luggage into the boot, Eckstein moved quickly to his own vehicle, parked at a hundred yards distance.

When the Rolls left the airport Eckstein was some fifty yards behind. He was surprised to see the chauffeur turn off to the north-east rather than pursue the M4 into the heart of London. Then he realised that during his year in Britain he had hardly ever left the capital and had almost come to identify it in terms of the country as a whole.

That year had been less than exciting for Eckstein—now he hoped he was about to get his teeth into something.

Eckstein, when on duty, always travelled in an Austin mini van with a souped up Cooper engine and a false number plate. The van was painted a dull gunmetal grey and in the present conditions, with darkness falling and a misty rain sweeping across the road, it was all but invisible. Moreover the additional guts under the bonnet gave it the necessary speed and acceleration to keep up with anything it was likely to encounter. Unless of course the car in front was big and powerful and the driver knew he was being tabbed and wanted to get away. But if he knew, there wasn't much purpose in the exercise anyway.

There were one or two disadvantages, though, one of them being that if the little van was asked to travel much faster than a hundred on a wet and greasy road it had an unfortunate tendency to aquaplane. Another was that although it was useful to be invisible to a quarry, it wasn't quite so handy to be unseen by everyone else—especially the drivers of articulated container lorries.

Eckstein was an only child and had frequently been a lonely one. His father was a police chief in Williamsport. Another thing that this father once told him was, 'You're like me. You've got an analytical mind.'

Like father, like son, in other words. Eckstein had thought otherwise and set out to disprove this cosy theory. He had therefore majored in music during his time at Columbia University and after graduating in that subject had auditioned for places at various music academies for further training as an orchestral violinist.

It was a senior examiner at the Curtis Institute of Music in Philadelphia who finally told him the news.

'You are unlikely to make a good professional performer, not because your playing is inaccurate. In fact one might say it's too accurate, but it lacks the imagination for a good personal interpretation. And this is something you can't learn if you haven't been born with it. I should know. When I was around your age I used to play the piano like an exercise in pure mathematics. That's why I finished up teaching. So you can go for teaching music or you can think of something different. Don't take this as the holy writ but it's my opinion.'

Eckstein returned to his room and played Isaac Stern's version of Haydn's first violin concerto. Halfway through the slow movement, he knew the man was right. But he didn't want to be a teacher. The old Bernard Shaw dictum occurred to him—*Those that can, do. The rest teach.*

If an analytical mind was what Eckstein had got stuck with, he needed to exercise it to the full as the Rolls glided through Rickmansworth and Watford. The evening rush hour was approaching its peak and stuff was coming from everywhere out of the twilight gloom and the squalling rain.

Quite often a couple of cars would somehow jam themselves between Eckstein and his target and he would have to squiggle through in the teeth of opposition coming the other way. Once he skidded violently from the path of a double-decker bus. A horsebox tried to crush him against the cab of a car transporter but he squeezed out like an orange pip. The Rolls ambled through a set of lights as they changed to red. The brick wagon in front of Eckstein hissed to a stop. He reversed a yard, went round it and across the charging bumpers like a demented wasp, the blare of frantic horn notes dinning in his ears.

Eckstein had come to believe, during his student days at Columbia, that his generation was losing its head. He saw no merit in the pop culture, hated what passed for its music and what happened at its festivals.

It wasn't repression that was blowing in the wind, but something more like a self-destructive anarchy. Pour in Marxism and Christianity according to taste, with a seasoning of Zen, stir gently until the mixture comes to the boil, then flavour with cannabis. Consume while hot to the frantic accompaniment of the Jimi Hendrix experience. All those absent from the feast to be labelled fascist.

Nor did Eckstein like what was happening in Vietnam, but he didn't blame it on America. Better of course if they hadn't gotten into the situation in the first place but now they were in they just couldn't give in and walk out. He saw the continual student demonstrations on this issue as expressive of ignorance and treachery.

19

These attitudes did little to detract from the young Eckstein's isolation. He was a gangling, almost scrawny youth, earnest and introspective. And he did nothing to improve his situation, at the age of twenty, by falling in love with a girl student who was up to the eyes in it all : the drug scene, flower power, Trotskyism.

Wanda, a girl with a soft, plumpish body and long black pigtails, was also a Jew. Her father was something big in shipping insurance in New York. Eckstein knew it was much more than a physical infatuation, although he wanted to investigate the secrets of that warm body more than those of any other he could recall. But he was also possessed by a reforming zeal. He passionately wanted to penetrate the spirit of this girl who shared the same antecedents, the same pride of race, and return it to the security of rational thinking.

For the first few weeks of their relationship they argued, politics and sociology, over countless beers and coffees . . . *yeah, I know that baby, sure, I appreciate that . . . but what you've also got to consider . . .* At odd moments she would offer small samples of the joys which lay in store. A hand on his knee while she explained a thought of Mao's. A holding of hands on the way to the campus bar. Sometimes, when she was high, she became more demonstrative, but he never took advantage of the situation on these occasions. When it happened, it was going to happen right.

But it hadn't happened after a month and he started to get alarmed. Had he given her the impression that he wanted a platonic relationship, for Christ's sake? Maybe she even thought he was a faggot.

Two days later he passed her in a corridor, between seminars. She stopped, took his hand, smiled up at him.

'Barry. Hey listen, why don't we make it tonight?'

Suddenly dry-mouthed with tension, he struggled for words. 'You mean . . .?'

'Sure, that's just exactly what I mean.'

He tried to sound blasé. 'Now I think that could be a great idea.'

'Will I come over to yours or will you come over to mine?'
'I'll come over to yours.'
'All right. About seven?'
'Great.'

At nine minutes to seven the Rolls turned into the car park of the White Horse hotel at Hertingfordbury. Eckstein drove past, pulled off the road, and wandered back in time to see Reisener and his two companions walk away from the car towards the bar entrance.

Reisener and the one who had greeted him at the airport walked ahead. The other man followed a yard or two behind, with a slight air of deference. Eckstein studied him with interest. About early forties, despite the greying sideburns. Strong neck muscles, the complexion that of worn leather. His locomotion a relaxed sort of prowl. Relationship to the other pair subordinate but protective.

The chauffeur, younger and stockily framed, leaned against the car and lit a cigarette.

Eckstein gave it five minutes, then wandered into the hotel foyer where he sat down, scooped up a few cashew nuts from a bowl, and idly chewed them. Through a glass partition he could see the German and his host studying a menu in a corner of the saloon bar. He considered for a moment wandering in and sitting down near them, trying to catch the conversation. But a glance at the features of the other member of the trio changed his mind.

Those were eyes which missed very little and forgot nothing. And there was plenty of time to go. Instead, he waited until they had moved into the hotel restaurant, then found the telephone and rang Coulman, who sounded impatient.

'Where the hell are you?'

'A couple of miles from Hertford. Listen, Reisener was picked up in a Rolls by a tall guy and another who looks like the security element.'

'Where are they now?'

'They've stopped here, at a hotel.'

'Are they staying?'

'I don't know. Maybe they just checked in for a meal. Richard, the Rolls number is CFH 1. Maybe you could find out who owns it.'

'That shouldn't be impossible.'

'Okay, I'll stay with it.'

'Do that.'

Eckstein, as he walked across the campus to Wanda's room, had already composed the sonata.

First the introductory skirmishings, skittish and contrapuntal, followed by the growing tenderness of the slow movement, a gradual fusion of the spiritual with the physical—then the quick burgeoning of the final, allegro movement—the appassionata—as the whole piece moved towards its inevitable climax.

But as soon as he saw the wavering pupils he knew that she was high. It was the first time he had been to her room and he was appalled by the shambles it was in, as if recently ransacked, with clothes spilling out of drawers, Marxist pamphlets scattered over the floor, a couple of empty beer cans under the bed. She poured him a glass of Southern Comfort.

'Did you ever really get stoned?' she asked. 'I mean, right out of your head?'

'Not the way you mean,' he said.

'You want to try it once in a while, just for the experience. But not with booze. Booze is evil. Why don't you try one of these?'

She offered him a box of blue capsules.

'Not for me. You go ahead.'

She swallowed a couple. 'If you keep telling me to kick the habit you ought to know what you're talking about. Come on, stop suffering. It'll make you feel good.'

'All right.' He took one and swallowed it, and felt no perceptible effect.

'Great,' she said. 'Now you can have the rest of the goodies.' She undressed in front of him, then stretched herself on the tangle of sheets and blankets of the unmade bed and gave him a lazy smile.

Eckstein stripped off his shirt and sat beside her, but with growing desolation as he realised the truth. She had decided to throw him a casual fuck out of pity, as a prize for perseverance. And he loved her. He couldn't bear to touch her. It was much the worst experience of his life.

'What's the matter? Don't you want me?'

'No,' he said. 'Not this way.' He left a few minutes later.

He discovered soon afterwards that for some months she had been making it with a coloured guy who worked in the university kitchens. The guy was over forty and had three children and his wife had recently left him so that Wanda could continue using him for her revolution. Not that this news made much difference to Eckstein. He still wanted to save her . . . and hated himself for it. But he didn't get another chance. She failed to return to college after the next vacation and three years later he heard that she had died of heroin addiction in Manhattan. By this time Eckstein was working for the CIA.

But the Eckstein who now peered through the windscreen wipers of the Austin mini van was ten years older than the diffident student and no longer had trouble with women. He seldom stayed with one for more than a month and never committed more than a quarter of himself to their scrutiny. He found that on a superficial level this technique was highly successful. When he left them, they were always floundering in search of the rest. This suited Eckstein perfectly.

At 8.10 p.m. the Rolls left the hotel with its occupants and it was almost an hour and a half later when it slowed and turned into a long driveway flanked by big chestnut trees. A sign read, 'The Grasspool Clinic and Health Centre'.

Eckstein drove on past, then turned and came back with no lights, parked by a clump of bushes on the grass verge, got out and stretched his aching limbs. It was cold and very dark but the rain had stopped. He groped in the glove compartment for a torch, climbed through the strands of a barbed-wire fence and moved quickly through the soaking grass along the line of the trees flanking the drive.

He spent the next half-hour studying the geography of the place. The drive curved for two hundred yards through parkland until it arrived at the forecourt of a large Palladian manor. More than a dozen cars were parked outside, including the Rolls. Eckstein watched as Reisener, flanked by his two companions, walked through the front entrance. The German was carrying the metal canister—clearly he didn't want to let it out of his possession. Lights gleamed from a score of windows all over the squat bulk of the house and from a group of chalets built under a nearby cluster of hornbeams. A conservatory attached to the main building was bathed in a rosy glow.

He almost fell over a wooden seat among the shrubs fronting a lawn. It was a good vantage point. Eckstein sat down almost gratefully, filled a pipe and lit it, pondering on the circumstances which had led him to this spot at this specific moment.

Not many days after the music examiner had given him the doleful news, Eckstein had wandered into the university careers office to assess the score on possible futures for music graduates with analytical minds who didn't want to teach. One of the handouts he picked up began, *We are privileged, as Americans, to live in a free and democratic society. But this freedom has been hardly won and can easily be lost. There are those, not only in other countries but also in our midst, who are striving to achieve, by subversion, the overthrow of our cherished institutions. The price of liberty is therefore constant vigilance, and this can only be maintained by a continual supply of dedicated young men from the universities who are willing to enlist and train as professionals in the security services. . . .*

Why not, thought Eckstein. Why the hell not? He recalled what the lefties had done for Wanda, as he jotted down the telephone number.

24

His year's initial training with the CIA affected Eckstein considerably. He now studied in an atmosphere which was entirely sympathetic, with colleagues who shared his attitudes and enthusiasms. The open wounds of his recent failures quickly healed, although the scars remained. He soon shook off his brooding introspection, and exuded a quiet confidence. When he finished the course, with the highest grade, Eckstein was ready to take his revenge for Wanda.

At the end of his training Eckstein was posted to the department of Cord Meyer, responsible, among other things, for the infiltration of the National Students' Association, and came under the direct supervision of Coulman, who assigned him to a post-graduate course in the theory and practice of education at the University of Michigan.

He found he had little time for formal studies. Instead, he spent hours sprawled in campus rooms, hot and sweaty with the fumes of pot, expatiating on the doctrines of Marx and Engels and the social attitudes of Marcuse. His hair merged with his beard in an ideological fuzz. The smoked lenses glinted with an earnest radical fervour.

Within a year he had become secretary of the universities' branch of the International Socialists, and his time was almost fully occupied with committee meetings and the organisation of demonstrations, sit-ins, walk-outs, and other expressions of protests at Michigan University and others all over the country. He was twice beaten up by police—once, in Chicago, rather badly—and spent a month in gaol for inciting conscripted soldiers to desert.

By the end of the second year Eckstein had produced dossiers on something like a hundred and ten of the leading student activists, noting their strengths and weaknesses, and their resources, together with a careful assessment of the depth of their fanaticism and predilection for violence.

None of these students was destined in the future to hold any responsible public office, or rise to prominence in industry or commerce anywhere in the United States. Even those who would eventually abandon their juvenile stance and say so publicly would retain a large question mark on their personal files. The CIA's computer has a large distribution list and the longest memory in the business.

Eckstein knew this and thought it was justified. He never ceased to marvel at the simplicity of it all. His comrades were so high on idealism, so low on pragmatism. They assumed as a matter of course that all pigs were middle-aged and wore uniforms. They were also blissfully unaware that power had everything to do with money, and those who controlled it.

Then something happened which made him feel uneasy— the killing of the students during the demonstrations at Kent University by national guards. Eckstein was enjoying a brief holiday in the Bahamas at the time. When he returned he mentioned his reservations to Coulman.

'Those kids were not on my list of activists,' he said, 'or anyone else's.'

'How do you know?'

'I've checked out the files.'

'Okay Barry, I feel the same way as you do. Some of these state troopers have got itchy fingers . . . but it wasn't anything to do with us.'

Eckstein returned to duty. A few months later he was the first agent to report the formation of the Simbionese Liberation Army, and he identified two of its founder members.

For this he received a personal commendation from the CIA Director, Richard Helms. But by now he discovered that his enthusiasm for the work was beginning to evaporate and he started to wonder who was betraying who.

He was about to ask for a fresh assignment when he heard of the Israeli recruiting mission. When Coulman revealed that he had been approached Eckstein immediately asked to be allowed to join him. It offered the promise of a cause he could support with enthusiasm in place of one which had begun to perish at the core.

One by one the windows of the building blacked out. There was clearly something of particular interest going on behind

26

that façade and Eckstein knew that in the course of time he would get to know the nature of it. But right now his feet were soaked and freezing and his pipe had gone out. It was time to retreat and consider. *Sufficient unto the day*, he thought, *is the evil thereof*. He stuck the pipe in his pocket, trudged back through a meadow littered with the sleeping mounds of cattle, and started the drive back to London.

4

Marianne Seal walked briskly through the Essex village of Broxfield on her way to the butcher's shop.

She was twenty-eight, a tawny blonde with wide hazel eyes and an enthusiastic curiosity about life which six years as a social worker had failed to dampen.

It was a bright March day, but cold. A sharp wind gusted across the pavements and Marianne had to keep pushing her hair away from her eyes. The village high street was still unspoilt. The sixteenth-century façades of the houses, some newly patched and pargeted, huddled together like tipsy old widows at a wedding reception. Not half a mile away were the two big commuter housing estates. But the village centre with the big medieval church listing over it, would be preserved in time for ever.

A woman in a Volkswagen pipped the horn and waved as she passed. Marianne remembered the face only vaguely as she smiled back. But this was what she liked about the place. People passing in cars pipped and waved although they hardly knew you—and not only the men.

She had been in Broxfield, on and off, for fifteen years— since her father, a bank manager, had bought a cottage there for week-ends and holidays. Her mother, a volatile but snobbish woman, had left him seven years earlier, while he was in the throes of a drink problem which caused his early retirement. Immediately after her departure he had made an astonishing recovery. He was not, it seemed, an alcoholic after all. A year later he had decided, much to Marianne's dismay because she adored him, to spend his declining years among

28

the British colony at the Spanish resort of Benidorm. And he'd given her the cottage as a parting present.

So the villagers had come to know her and treated her almost as one of themselves. They even excused her Nick, the American she lived with, although he was considered a strange acquisition for a girl like her.

There were four or five other women in the shop; several of them flashed Marianne a smile of recognition. Tim Bushell, the butcher, was an old familiar.

'Now, what can I do for you, my sweet?'

'Hallo Tim. Just a couple of lamb chops and about a pound of rump steak.' Nick couldn't live without steak. 'Oh, and I'd better take a chicken.'

Bushell rested his beer paunch against the counter as he sawed at the meat.

'Reformed any more teenage vandals lately?' He liked to tease her. She grinned. 'I'm doing my best.'

A couple of the wives from the new estate chattered about some impending divorce in the background.

'There you are then, my lovely.' The butcher slapped the packet of meat into Marianne's outstretched hand, then turned and called to a middle-aged woman who had just entered: 'I've saved a couple of bones for that bloodhound of yours.'

Marianne moved to the desk where Tim's wife sat behind a cash register.

'That'll be two pounds sixty, just. And how are you this lovely morning, my dear?'

'I'm fine, thanks Enid.'

Suddenly the shop emptied of customers. Marianne looked round.

'What's going on?'

'It's Janet Carter's new baby.'

The butcher's wife quickly passed over the change, squeezed out from behind the desk, and made for the door. Marianne followed her.

The other women were clustered round a glistening new Pedigree Princess pram on the pavement.

'Coochee coochee coochee. . . . Aaaah, isn't he a dear one . . . Is he a lovely boy den, is he?'

The mother, a local girl of eighteen who had been married in the parish church only three months earlier, stood with a hand rocking the handle. She was almost purring with pride and pleasure. Marianne squeezed into a vacant space behind the pram and looked down at the infant.

It was about a fortnight old.

The tiny features were flushed a deep rose-pink, the forehead wrinkled as if with some deep anxiety. Tufts of dark hair sprouted towards the apex of the scalp. The dark eyes shifted from one side to the other.

'Isn't you a dee-ah, den.' The butcher's wife extended her little finger and tickled the moist palm of the miniscule hand.

'Aren't you going to smile for Auntie Enid?'

Janet moved round to the side of the pram. She bent over the baby. 'Come on, give Auntie Enid a nice big smile.'

The baby's eyes stopped wavering and focused on the big comforting orb of its mother's face. The pursed rosebud of its mouth relaxed. The lips distended until a thin sliver of a toothless gum became visible. A gurgle of pleasure emerged.

'Dere, he's smiling. Isn't he a beautiful bo-oy, den?'

Marianne suddenly reached down, pushed aside the coverlet, picked up the baby, and hugged it to her.

There was a stone cold silence. The women looked at her in amazement, turning quickly to outrage.

The mother came rapidly round the side of the pram and almost tugged the infant from Marianne's arms. 'Who gave you permission?' she cried out furiously.

As she thrust the baby back in the pram it began to wail.

Marianne was bemused. 'I'm sorry . . . I . . . I just wanted to hold him.'

'Well next time you just want to bloody well ask!'

Janet briskly disengaged the brake on the pram and wheeled it forward. As she receded into the distance the silence was punctuated by the forceful howls of the now distracted baby.

The butcher's wife said, 'Well, I never,' and walked back into the shop. The other women dispersed, looking back reproachfully at Marianne.

Left alone, she felt suddenly close to tears. How could she have done such a thing? Even in her desolation, something nagged at her—she'd left her meat in the shop. She went in to collect it. Tim Bushell said cheerfully, 'You'll forget your 'ead one o' these days, darling.' His wife gave him a sharp glance from the cash register.

As she walked back to her cottage, Marianne felt appalled by her behaviour—yet the urge had been irresistible. She and Nick had been trying to conceive a child now for six months. Was her reaction now the culmination of her repressed disappointment over those six monthly intervals. Whatever it was, Marianne was uncomfortably aware that she didn't just want a baby any more . . . she had begun to crave one.

Inside the cottage, she set a log fire blazing in the ingle-nook hearth, then went into the cramped kitchen to cook for Nick, who was on one of what he called his 'traumatic expeditions' to London.

They had been together for three years. Marianne had met him—an American journalist seven years older than herself—at a theatre club in Notting Hill Gate while she was working in London. Nick had entered her life by way of accidentally knocking over her vodka and tonic and she had been impressed by the originality of his apology. 'I'm sorry, I just can't help it. My mother was an alcoholic.'

The question of marriage had somehow got deferred. When they first started to co-habit, Marianne had got caught up in the women's liberation movement. Marriage was just a seal of approval, a piece of paper, a social con-trick designed to trap women into servility. Nick didn't seem to care one way or another. Now, if he suggested it, she knew she would eagerly concur. But she didn't want to be the first one to mention the subject.

31

Nick came in an hour later, a small dark man with large round spectacles and a protruding forehead which seemed in earnest collusion with his jutting beard. A Bostonian, he had originally come to England five years earlier to research a series for *Holiday* and had stayed. He liked the slower pace of the British life style, admired their bland indifference to what was going on elsewhere, their distaste for high performance ratios, and their tolerance of misfits. And he had a special regard for their women.

The one he regarded the most called out from the kitchen : 'Did you have a good day?'

'No more lousy than usual.'

He made for the fire and hunched his body over it. Nick was always cold in an English winter.

'Sell any ideas?'

'The one about Nixon? The *Telegraph* magazine, I think, will bite.'

She came and stood in the doorway, watching him. 'Great, anything else?'

'The *Reader's Digest* want me to do a piece on some beetle that eats elm trees.'

'That sounds interesting.'

'I find it extremely boring, in every sense of the word.' He piled more logs on the fire.

'What happened about the play?' Nick wrote plays for the theatre, rather furtively, and sent them round the circuit. He had not yet had one produced.

'Some guy at the Royal Court promised to read it.'

'A producer?'

'No, I guess he was one of the scene shifters. He was very large, and he didn't speak English too good.'

He slumped back into an armchair beside the fireplace and picked up a newspaper. After a few moments Marianne came and perched herself on the arm of the chair. Nick became increasingly aware of something on her mind. 'What's for supper?' he inquired vaguely.

'Boiled bacon with courgettes.' It was Nick's favourite food.

'I thought we might as well open that last bottle of Matteus to go with it.'

'I thought we were holding that for your birthday?'

'Yes, but I'd rather have it now.'

She went and fetched the bottle. Nick watched her with slight uneasiness as she poured out two glasses, and handed him one. Then she came back to sit beside him, pressed one of his hands in both of hers.

'Nick, there's something I want to talk to you about . . . seriously, I mean.'

He put down the newspaper with apparent reluctance. 'Okay, but why don't we wait until we finish the bottle?'

'No, now. Nick . . . I've been wondering if there's something wrong with me.'

He pretended to appraise her, fondling her hair. 'You could do with maybe a couple more inches round the chest, but who's complaining?' He kissed her fondly on the arm.

'I mean about not having a baby.'

'Oh that? Don't worry, it's my fault. My jissom is too potent. When I was in the States I won the competition for the fiercest jissom in the West two years running. They told me the only way I could become a father was to mate with some top woman athlete. I guess the only chance I have is to roger someone like Billie Jean King.'

'Nick, this is serious. I'm really worried about it.'

'We'll just have to try that extra bit harder.' He squeezed her hand. 'Hey, what's the hurry . . . there are cases on record of females giving birth at forty.'

'You do want us to have a baby, don't you?'

'Sure I do, honey. You know that.'

'D'you know what happened today? I went down to the butcher's, in the village. There was a girl outside the shop with a baby in a pram. I was standing there looking at the baby . . . and then I picked him up . . . I just wanted to hold him for a while . . . Nick, I just couldn't help myself.'

He stared at her, saw that her eyes were misted over. 'You did what?' He drained his glass, reached forward and refilled it. 'Jesus . . . and I figured I had problems.' He got up and stood with his back to the fire, frowning a little behind the spectacles.

'Maybe there's something you ought to know,' he said. 'The reason you haven't clicked so far is because your lover's jissom is no fucking good.'

She glanced at him in alarm. 'No, I'm sure it's something to do with me.'

'Then hear this. When I was in the States I was shacked up for two years outside of Milwaukee with one Christine, a female of the species.'

'Yes, I know. You told me.'

'Something I didn't tell you. She wanted an infant just as bad as you do. So we never used anything—for two years. That's why she eventually blew, because I couldn't ring the god-damn bell.'

'Oh, Nick. You never told me that before.'

'I'm telling you now. And I'll tell you something else. We were married. Which is why I don't have any further interest in that institution—I figured it could happen a second time round.'

'Not with me. Anyway, that doesn't mean anything. She was probably on the pill or something without telling you.'

'That doesn't sound like my little Christine.'

He stood there looking doleful, and suddenly vulnerable as he wiped the mist from his spectacles with the end of his sleeve. Marianne moved across and hugged him.

'Nick, it's probably something quite simple. Why don't we go and see a gynaecologist?'

He gave a small, wry grin.

'You mean we have some choice?'

'Oh, Nick.' She snuggled against him, joyously, then kissed him gently on the lips as he ran his hands up below her sweater.

'I'm sure we're both going to regret this decision,' he said. Finding himself rapidly becoming tumescent, he slowly unbuckled the belt of her jeans and reached down to caress

34

her thighs with small, circular motions of his fingers.

'We're going to make one final attempt,' he said.

'Nick, the food's ready.'

'Fuck the god-damned food.'

5

'What's inside that canister is the sixty-four billion dollar question.'

Coulman was a small, slim man with handsome, greying hair just beginning to bald, a deep voice. He could have doubled easily for a top-level accountant or an executive on Madison Avenue. At fifty-five he was close to the end of his useful time as an intelligence agent, but hoped for an Indian summer in the cause of Israel. He had made his name, and earned his promotion, in South America, where he had occupied a number of executive posts for I.T.T. He sat in his office, playing with a pocket calculator.

'It could be a controlled temperature flask,' said Eckstein. 'They use them for the transportation of medical specimens, bacteria, that sort of item.'

'You think there might be bad germs in there?'

Eckstein leaned against the desk and stretched his long legs. 'There could be. Just off the top of my head . . . suppose Reisener got hold of some of the stuff they use for experiments in bacteriological warfare—maybe a stiff dose of anthrax for the sake of argument. Then he sends a couple of guys up the Post Office Tower or some such place and threatens to scatter the stuff in the breeze over London . . . unless.'

'That could be worth the whole Gaza strip,' Coulman acknowledged. 'But why London. Why not Tel Aviv?'

'More security problems. Not so many people. Less pressure internationally.'

'I still don't believe it.'

'Well, there's plenty of other possibilities. For example, say

36

you get together a list of fifty prominent Jews over here, and you send 'em all a letter on the same day with some of the stuff inside. No metal, no explosives, so they don't get checked on the way through. And there are some strains so virulent, all you have to do is touch them. Then if it spreads, the chosen people aren't going to be too popular.'

'I suppose it's a possibility,' Coulman mused. 'Among other things Reisener is on the board of governors of the Heidenstam Institute for Medical Research in Munich. According to Greb they have a bacteriology department.'

'I do have another theory,' said Eckstein.

'What's that?'

'Reisener is hooked on caffeine. Wherever he goes he has to take a couple of gallons of hot coffee with him.'

Coulman screwed up his face in pain at this inappropriate levity.

'Of course,' he said, 'there could be a simple answer. Since Reisener was taking a trip to London, somebody at the research institute asked him to deliver something by hand, like maybe a piece of diseased tissue, for examination by some expert over here.'

'You mean it could be we've just got suspicious minds, Richard?'

'That's right.'

They both thought about the implications for a while. Then Coulman said, 'The guy who runs this clinic, this Dr Stephen. He's a gynaecologist. So maybe it's some kind of foetus he's interested in. Could be he sent it over to Munich for analysis in the first place and now they're sending it back.'

'With Reisener?'

'Sure. He could be over here on some other business.'

'Unlikely,' said Eckstein. 'Reisener isn't the kind of guy who runs errands.'

Coulman foraged among a few scrawled pages of notes on his desk. 'Then there's the other character . . . the guy who owns the Rolls. His name is Fox-Hillyer . . . Charles Moresby Fenton Fox-Hillyer to be precise.'

'That figures. He looked like a member of the upper crust.'

'Yeah. He's in *Who's Who* and the *Dictionary of International Biography*. Was once a Brigadier in the British Army until he retired in sixty-five. After that he wrote a couple of books. One of them was about Hitler—*The Man Who Changed The Face of Europe*. There was quite a hassle over that one. He claimed that Hitler only killed 300,000 Jews instead of six million, and this was the only blot on an otherwise first-class record.'

'I'll have to read it,' said Eckstein.

'That might be a good idea—seriously.'

'What else does he do with his time, this Fox-Hillyer person?'

'I haven't figured that out yet. He's not short of bread. He's on the board of five companies. He also owns a couple of thousand acres of farmland in Hampshire and a stud farm at Newmarket.'

'Just imagine, Richard. We're squandering the best years of our life for peanuts.'

'I know. But we don't have the conscience of the rich.'

'One of the first things you told me, Richard, is that a conscience is a liability in this profession.'

Coulman smiled blandly. 'That's right. I used to have one when I was your age. After a while I sent it to the cleaners and it never came back. They said it was beyond repair, covered in cigarette burns and stains that wouldn't come out. I got along much better without it.' He glanced at his notes again. 'By the way, this Fox-Hillyer—he's also got a big place in London, over in the Bloomsbury area.'

Eckstein ambled across to a window, and looked out at a traffic warden below, casually pinning a ticket on a small green Fiat. He stifled a yawn. 'Did you get any ideas about the other guy in the car?'

'Not up to now but I'm working on it. He sounds like one of Fox-Hillyer's good and faithful servants.'

'Well, what do we do next?' Eckstein carefully filled a pipe.

38

'I'll be doing some more research on Fox-Hillyer. The best thing you can do is get a good night's sleep, then get down to the clinic tomorrow morning and stay around. You'd better run through Greb's tape from Munich on the Reisener situation before then just to refresh your memory, okay?'

'Will do.'

Coulman went out.

Greb's voice emerging from the cassette was irritatingly bland, a drone which did not concern itself with emotions or shades of meaning. Eckstein tried to ignore this. He had met Greb once or twice and rather liked him. After all, the man wasn't trying to read a poem.

'. . . we haven't been able to discover much about Reisener's activities before the war except that when he left the University of Cologne in 1929 he joined his father's firm, Münchener Flug-industrien as an apprentice on the shop floor, and by 1934 he was a junior director. The firm was involved in the business of manufacturing electrical and other components for civil and military aircraft and was a main supplier to the Fokker and Heinkel companies. It wasn't the largest in the business but seemed to be highly profitable. It's still in business under the name of Münchener Elektronishe Montage but now makes microwave circuits. The main factory is in the Forstenried district of Munich and Reisener owns most of the shares.

'He was something of an academic prior to the war and he contributed to a number of scientific periodicals, notably *Flugtechnischer Maschinenbaukunst* and *Flug International*. He was married in 1935 to Gertrud Schell, the daughter of a professor of zoology. She was killed in a bombing raid on Mannheim in 1944. They had no children. I wouldn't know if this is important but Reisener was involved in a paternity suit in '34, just before his marriage, with a woman called Freda Weingartner. Sounds like a Jewess, maybe. Anyway, she didn't appear to get any joy.

'He seems to have been pretty fond of the ladies because a

39

couple of years later he was cited in a divorce action with a colonel's wife.

'Another interesting point is that Reisener joined the Nazi party some time in the mid-thirties and around this period he wasn't getting along too well with his father who tried, unsuccessfully, to get him thrown off the board in '37. Could it be that Reisener senior didn't like the Nazis. In any case he lost out. Son remained as sales director and in '38 he took over the company when his father committed suicide.

'From talking to one of the former factory employees I got the impression that Reisener always had an aggressive personality. He could blow up suddenly like a tornado, this guy said. He told one of the charge hands once, "If you offend me again I'll show you what will happen to you." And he broke a tea biscuit into little pieces in front of his nose, then stamped the crumbs into the floor.

'By the time the war started the firm was expanding rapidly, and Reisener spent a lot of his time hobnobbing with the Nazi hierarchy at rallies and dinners. He was known to be a personal friend of Heydrich at this time . . .'

Eckstein switched off as Durandt's secretary, Angela Stringer, appeared bearing coffee in cups as elegant and fragile as herself.

'Hallo, Angela . . . thanks. Richard's just gone out.'

'Oh, don't let me interrupt you. Is there anything for me?' Coulman never used a secretary since one that he had been fond of was kidnapped and tortured in the Argentine. Angela did their bits and pieces, kept the office tidy.

'I don't think so. How are things down below?'

'Mr Durandt's just slipped down to the Hayward to look at some Anthony Caro.'

'I wish I could join him.'

'He always says you're his best student.' She said this in all sincerity. Angela affected never to know that she lived and worked at the heart of an intelligence unit. Eckstein watched her with a smile as she tidied a few papers, then moved quietly away.

He resumed Greb.

'At the outbreak of war Reisener was given a senior post with the airline, Lufthansa, in Berlin. He was obviously in favour with the top echelons and earmarked for higher things. In fact the job may have been partly a cover. He spent a good deal of time on diplomatic missions to neutral countries, Spain and Turkey in particular. But early in 1944 he was in a house in Mannheim which was hit during an air raid. His wife was killed and Reisener was dug out of the rubble with spinal injuries. He spent the next eighteen months in hospital, paralysed from the waist down.

'When he finally recovered a lot of other things had happened. For instance there was the assassination attempt on his beloved Führer.

'One of the conspirators was Otto John, a fellow-executive of Reisener's at Lufthansa. John was one of the few to escape. He managed to get on a plane to Madrid.

'This must have been particularly unpleasant for Reisener to swallow. No doubt he thought that if he hadn't been injured he could have got wind of what was going on. After the war John became chief of security in the new Federal German Republic. He was subsequently kidnapped, smuggled over the border into East Berlin, and handed over to the Commies. He returned about a year later and was tried as a defector.

'There's strong evidence to suggest that Reisener and his friends organised the snatch as an act of revenge for his treachery during the last days of the Third Reich.

'In one way I suppose Reisener was lucky to get put out of action when he did. If he hadn't been underneath that bomb he could easily have got much deeper in with the Nazis, and maybe finished up with a rope around his neck. But it's also possible he doesn't see it that way. The fact that it all happened without him could have left him with a feeling of serious frustration, as if he had somehow been prevented from making his contribution through no fault of his own. In other words maybe he feels he still has it to make.'

41

Eckstein wondered about the quality of hate. He had some-times felt a strong detestation of certain ideas but never a personal hatred of another human being; if it came to the point of having to destroy one it would need to be motivated by a dispassionate conviction that a diseased ideology, or rather its representative, had to be eliminated for the greater good.

So far it had never got to that point. He hoped it never would.

'Apart from the Otto John episode,' the voice of Greb con-tinued, 'nothing much was heard of Reisener for about fifteen years after the war, for the simple reason he was making his pile out of the wreckage. He's certainly no slouch in the busi-ness world. By 1960 he had large interests in property and construction companies involved in the rebuilding of Stuttgart and Karlsruhe and had also acquired about eight thousand acres of forest and farmland in Upper Bavaria.

'It wasn't until '65 that he started to show in politics, as one of the leaders of the right wing National Democratic Party under Fritz Thielen, a cement manufacturer. He was one of twenty ex-Nazis out of thirty on the management committee. The party was well funded by Reisener and other industrial barons. There's a story they managed to get their hands on a lot of the loot which was stashed away in the mountains by the Nazis in the later stages of the war.

'The party policy was what they called a "Europe of the Fatherlands". In other words one of autocratic states of which Germany would become the dominating partner. There were about twenty-thousand members, mostly young bully-boys of the extreme right.

'They were surprisingly well-supported considering recent events. In the provincial elections of '68 they won sixty seats in the state parliaments. Reisener stood for a seat in the province of Hesse and won it with a big majority . . .'

Eckstein liked Victor Greb because the man had a genuine sense of humour behind his exaggerated laugh, and, unlike Coulman, whose middle-age he was approaching, he didn't seem to want to be anyone's uncle or pass on anything he knew. He had come from being the son of a back-street tailor in Seattle to a languages graduate at Harvard and Eckstein had vaguely sniffed the whiff of a frustrated talent similar to his own. What was it with Greb? Possibly an actor, or a politician? There was a restraint in his voice, a deliberate boredom, the imprisoned drone of an imagination in hock.

'But then the party started to have problems internally. Thielen lost the leadership to Adolf von Thadden and left to form a splinter group in opposition. Reisener went along with von Thadden for a while but he wasn't too happy with the new policy which was known as *salon-fahig*—dressing up dangerous policies to make them fit for the drawing-room . . .

'I guess Reisener thought that this was the beginning of a soft approach, especially . . .'

At this point Eckstein turned down the volume to nothing. The monotonous voice began to bother him. He relit his pipe, watched the rotating tape in peace for a while before he felt the worm of guilt. He was sure to be missing the vital piece of information.

'Strong links,' said the renewed voice of Greb. 'I talked to a guy who was a senior party member and knew Reisener well at this time. He reckons that Reisener was the fiercest Nazi of the whole bunch. He was always trying to reinstate the Hitler image, the soul-of-Germany stuff.

'He was working a sixteen-hour day at this period, running his business empire as well as being deeply involved in politics. He didn't smoke and drank very little and was quite a fireball by any standards.

'When Thielen left the party Reisener made a strong bid to take it over. This guy says the reason he didn't make it was that most of the other executive members were so scared of him they ganged up against him and gave the job to von Thadden.

'In 1969 the magazine *Der Spiegel* did a piece about Reisener under the title, "The most dangerous man in Germany".

'When Willie Brandt became chancellor in '69 and started

the policy of Ostpolitik the National Democratic Party began to lose a whole lot of ground. Within two years they lost most of their seats in parliament—including Reisener's—and the membership fell away badly. In 1970 one of their front groups called Action Resistance organised a rally in Bonn to protest about Brandt's goodwill treaty with Russia. But only about a thousand turned out and they were given a bad time by students and organised labour groups.

'That was about the end of the N.D.P. as a political force and the leadership started to break up and move off in various directions. Reisener resigned in May '70 and hasn't been involved in politics since. He obviously decided he was going to get nowhere by normal political methods, and elected to go underground. It would seem that the Olympic Games massacre was the first big operation he was involved in on his own.

'I'm still working on that. It's not quite clear whether it was Reisener's idea in the first place, or whether he was approached by the Palestinians.

'But he was obviously into it from some time back. One of Reisener's construction companies had a big slice of the contract for building the Olympic village. They employed a fair amount of foreign labour, mostly Turks. I got talking to a guy in a beer hall who worked on the project for Reisener's company. He said there were four Arabs working on the site for around six months before the completion, and they didn't know their ass from their elbow on the building side. He was sure they were involved in the business. Also Reisener made at least one visit to the Lebanon in early '72. I checked out on the passenger lists.

'Just a couple more items. Reisener just is not fond of us Hebrews. He won't have any working for him, and he won't trade with any company with a kike on the board of directors.

'That's about all, I guess. Love to Judy.'

Greb always signed off in this way. Eckstein switched off.

Coulman had suggested taking the rest of the day off. The idea was appealing.

A long, restful lunch down in Chelsea somewhere, perhaps. Or an unexpected call on a girl friend. And during the evening Pinchas Zukerman was playing Mozart with the English Chamber Orchestra at the Queen Elizabeth Hall.

He thought also of Reisener, then discovered that Reisener was paramount in his thoughts. A few minutes later he made a booking for that night at a hotel near Ipswich.

6

It hadn't been one of Nick's better days. He was stuck in the middle of the piece about Richard Nixon and, worse still, his play had come back in the morning post together with a curt rejection note.

He sat moodily watching the television set with which he had a continuous love-hate relationship. It was showing, intermittently, a production of Brecht's *Mother Courage* but every few minutes the picture would burst into dazzling harlequin fragments and the sound would become a harsh and menacing drone. All through the opening scenes Nick had fiddled with the knobs. Now he stood over it and dealt it a hard thwack with the flat of his hand. Immediately the actors returned to the screen.

From outside he heard the sound of Marianne's car. She'd been working late and he hadn't seen her all day. Now she came bursting into the room, flushed with excitement.

'Nick, I've found someone at last.'

'Found who?'

'A gynaecologist. You know I was telling you that none of them were interested because we're not married? Well, this one doesn't mind. I rang him up from work and we had a long chat over the phone. He said he's interested in people, not bits of paper. As long as he knows we both want one he's willing to treat us.'

'I'm trying to watch the god-damned play.'

But her enthusiasm was irrepressible. 'I've arranged to go and see him next Wednesday. He said he'd like you to come along as well.'

46

'Next Wednesday I can't manage. I've got an appointment with Ursula Andress.'

'Oh, and he wants you to bring a sample.'

The screen fragmented again. Nick said, 'Fuck.' He got up and switched off the set. 'Sample of what?'

'Well, you know, a sample of your whatsername.'

'Jissom?'

'They have to test it.'

'Jesus. How did I ever get myself into this situation?'

'Oh, Nick, you don't really mind, do you?' She gave him a hug. 'Come on, smile, say you don't mind. Please.'

The small, wry smile began to materialise. 'Okay okay, relax. For you I would jerk off in a bottle fifty times a day. Who is this father figure, anyway?'

'His name's Dr Stephen. He's got a private clinic down in Suffolk. It's only about thirty miles from here. He sounded so nice on the phone.'

Nick was a congenital fiddler when he was idle. He could never keep his fingers still. In the car going to the clinic, with Marianne driving, he fiddled with the radio knobs, alternating the exuberant tones of a disc jockey extolling the art of Elton John with a Scarlatti sonata and a panel game. Eventually a tense Marianne begged, 'Nick, could we have some peace for a few minutes?'

'Sure. Why not?' Nick seemed surprised by the plea. He turned off the radio, found an abandoned fountain pen in the map pocket, and began to dismantle it. She reached out with a hand and squeezed his knee.

'I know you hate all this,' she said. 'I know you're just doing it for me. I do appreciate it.'

'I could definitely think of more agreeable ways of passing the time,' he argued. 'How did you manage to find this Dr Stephen in the first place?'

'From one of my clients. Her husband left her when she was six months pregnant and she became an alcoholic. Her doctor thought it might harm the baby so he sent her to Dr

47

Stephen's clinic for the last month. She said he was marvellous. Apparently he could make a fortune out of abortions alone, but he never does one unless he thinks the mother's life is in danger.'

'Does it make any difference to the baby if the father is an alcoholic?'

'I shouldn't think so. Anyway, you're nowhere near it.'

'I'm a late developer.'

Nothing could dent her enthusiasm. 'Nick, I just know Dr Stephen's going to make it happen. He'll soon find out what's wrong.'

'That's for sure. As soon as he inspects my gunge.'

'Oh, come on, love. Cheer up.'

Marianne parked her Viva next to the Rolls. As they got out Nick flung a cursory glance at it.

'Wombs are booming,' he commented.

Inside the entrance hall they were confronted by a broad carpeted central stairway in the manner of Inigo Jones, flanked by columns in polished Portland stone, a high carved italianate ceiling, a showcase of Wedgwood china, family portraits in oils. Arrowed signs indicated the whereabouts of Reception, Billiard Room, Sauna, Surgery, Massage, Residents' Lounge, Dining Room. The reception nurse who took their particulars and confirmed their appointment was cheerful and trying to seem busy.

There were two other occupants of the waiting-room, a middle-aged West Indian woman with thick legs and a maternity smock fashioned from some sort of blanket material. The bulge beneath it seemed to Nick to be about to burst. Her three-year-old son clambered all over the furniture, then ran up to Nick and peered into his face.

'Now don't you worry that nice man,' scolded the mother. Marianne glanced at Nick, knowing his fear of domesticity. She squeezed his hand.

'Nick, don't look so doomed,' she whispered. 'It'll soon be over.'

'I'll be with you in a couple of seconds. Please sit down.'

Dr Stephen scrawled a few notes, looked across and frowned at the far wall, then wrote what appeared to be a final assessment on the previous case and slipped it into a file cover.

Marianne watched him with interest. She was used to working with doctors and found many of them—even the younger ones—rather stiff and formal and unforthcoming, as if they were the sole custodians of the secrets of the human body, and these must on no account be passed on to the layman.

But there seemed no sign of a proprietorial attitude in this one, although he was a man of about sixty. His casual garb—tweed hacking jacket, maroon turtleneck sweater—seemed to testify to this. There was a warmth behind the grey eyes which he now fixed on Marianne and also, she thought, a hint of world-weariness.

'Now you're, let's see—Miss Marianne Seal?'

'That's right.'

'And you're Mr Kirkham?' Nick grunted agreement.

'How long have you been living together?'

Marianne glanced at Nick. 'Oh about three years.'

'Well, I think that can be regarded as a permanent relationship these days . . .' he smiled '. . . for better or worse. You won't mind if I ask you a few rather personal questions?'

'Of course not.'

He settled back in his chair behind the desk and tucked a stray hank of grey hair behind his ear.

'How long have you been trying to conceive?'

'For about six months now.'

'Well, that's a bit on the short side. What did you use before that, the pill?'

'No, I used a diaphragm.' She glanced at Nick. 'I've never liked the idea of the pill, somehow.'

'Why not?'

She considered this. 'It's a . . . sort of interference with nature.'

49

'Yes I quite agree. As a matter of fact I believe that it sometimes causes infertility. I never prescribe it myself for that reason. Are your menstruations regular?'

Marianne smiled. 'Yes, like clockwork, every twenty-eight days.'

The doctor shifted his gaze to Nick. 'Why do you want to be a father, Mr Kirkham?'

Nick looked distinctly uncomfortable. 'I don't know. Because Marianne wants to become a mother, I suppose.'

'That would seem to be a perfectly adequate reason.' The eyes travelled back. 'And what's yours, my dear?

'I don't think I'd be happy if I never had a child.' This didn't seem adequate to her so she added, 'If I had one of my own I think I'd probably be able to understand other people a lot better. D'you understand what I mean?'

'Yes, I'm quite sure you're right.'

Marianne asked earnestly, 'Is it important—I mean, the reason?'

Stephen plucked at his lip. 'I've always thought so. Some couples want a child because they've never been able to, so they feel inadequate. They just want to repair their egos. The child isn't important to them for its own sake.' He leaned back, thrusting his hands into his jacket pockets. 'A woman came to see me a couple of weeks ago. She wanted me to make her fertile because she was afraid of losing her husband, and she thought she'd have a better chance of keeping him if she had a baby. Of course I'd never treat anyone in those circumstances.'

He made a brief note, then glanced keenly at them both. 'However—in your case, I think perhaps we ought to have a go.'

Marianne's eyes sparkled with gratitude. 'Thank you.'

The doctor glanced at Nick. 'Did you bring the sample along?'

Marianne said quickly, 'It's here, in my bag.' She produced it and handed it over, a small jar. The label read, 'Heinz Garlic Salt'.

50

Nick said, 'There's not much of it, but it's fresh this morning.'

Dr Stephen smiled. He fixed a gummed label on the bottle, wrote 'Mr Kirkham' on it, and put it in a refrigeration cabinet.

In the reception office the nurse picked up the ringing telephone and found herself talking to Eckstein.

'Grasspool Clinic.'

'Hallo. Do you have facilities for sauna and massage there?'

'Yes, we do.'

'I'm staying in this area for a couple of weeks. Maybe I could drop in occasionally. I like to keep in shape.'

'Well, we're open for sauna, massage, and heat treatment for non-residents at the week-ends. Would you like to make a booking?'

'How about next Saturday?'

'Yes, I think I can fit you in for Saturday. Morning or afternoon?'

'Afternoon.'

'Right . . . Saturday afternoon . . . three o'clock?'

'Fine.'

'Could I have your name, please?'

'You can indeed. It's Joe . . . Joe Clark. Hey listen, will you be around on Saturday?'

'I won't actually. It's my week-end off.'

'Well, I had to be unlucky some time.'

'Let's get down to business.' The doctor pulled a pad towards him and picked up a ballpoint. 'First of all, let me put you in the picture. Infertility is due to the man in about forty per cent of cases. In the other sixty per cent, the woman is responsible. And the causes can be either physical or emotional. Let's concentrate on the emotional ones first.'

'Mind if I smoke?' said Nick.

'No, not at all. Go ahead.' Nick lit a small black Ritmeester and drew on it furiously.

'Would you say your sexual relations are satisfactory?'

'Oh yes, very,' vouchsafed Marianne.

'How often do you have intercourse?'

'It varies. About three or four times a week on average.'

'Good.' Stephen made a note, then looked up sharply at Marianne. 'Do you usually have an orgasm?'

'Oh yes, nearly every time.' She gazed fondly at her frowning consort. 'Nick's very good at timing.'

Nick said, 'That's right. When I was at school I used to practise for hours. For Christ's sake, do we have to go into all this?'

'I'm sorry,' said the doctor, 'I'm afraid we do. But don't worry, there's not much of it.'

Marianne implored, 'Nick, please.'

'Just one last question Mr Kirkham. When you have intercourse . . . is there usually a strong emission of semen when you ejaculate?'

'Yeah. I'm like the god-damned fire brigade.' Nick rose, stuck his hands in his pockets and turned away with an expression of huge disgust. Marianne said urgently, 'Yes there is. I can vouch for that.'

Dr Stephen scrawled a few more lines on the pad. 'Good, well the emotional side seems pretty well in order.'

He scratched an ear with the blunt end of the ballpoint. 'I shall get the result of the sperm test tomorrow and if it's positive I think we can leave Mr Kirkham out of the equation and concentrate on you.' He accompanied this statement with a quizzical smile.

'I always thought it was my fault,' Marianne said.

'These things are nobody's fault, just their misfortune.' He folded his hands. 'Now just supposing,' he said, 'that we find Mr Kirkham's sperm count is too low for conception to take place. Would you both be prepared to consider artificial insemination by a donor?'

Marianne glanced apprehensively at Nick. 'I'm not sure that . . .'

He interrupted her fiercely. 'If the doctor is suggesting that I play the proud father to a brat sired by some shithead

52

squash professional, the answer is very definitely no!'

Stephen said equably, 'All my donors are medical students, Mr Kirkham.' He gestured with his hands. 'Still, I take your point.'

He wrote it down.

'Aaah, Jesus!' Nick turned to Marianne, his features haggard with misery. 'I'll see you in the car park when you're through.' He went out abruptly.

Marianne said, 'I'm sorry. Nick gets a bit uptight sometimes.'

'Don't worry, Miss Seal. I always find that husbands are much more emotional than wives on these occasions—or perhaps we should say lovers on this one.' His smile was more sympathetic, he seemed more at ease in Nick's absence, she thought. 'If it so happened that you presented him with a bouncing boy, you would find that he'd be as pleased as a . . . what do you say . . . the dog with the nine tails?'

Marianne felt a twinge of surprise. This apparently urbane English doctor had suddenly revealed to her, in a single phrase, a continental origin.

'Yes,' she said. 'I know he would.'

'Well, I won't keep you much longer . . . just a couple of routine questions. How old are you?'

'Twenty-nine in August.'

'Yes, well it's about time, isn't it?' He wrote it down. 'What is your occupation?'

'I'm a social worker. I work mainly with children.'

'How fortunate for them. Can you get leave of absence at short notice?'

'Oh yes, that's no problem.'

He looked up. 'Now when is your next ovulation due? The middle time between menstruation.'

'I'll have to think . . . Mm, let's see . . . six days from now.'

'You're sure about that?'

'Yes.'

He wrote this down then tucked the ballpoint in his pocket. 'Right, I'll tell you what we'll do. Some time tomorrow I'll telephone you and give you the result of the sperm test. If it's negative then I'm afraid that's the end of the story.'

'Yes.'

'If it's positive, then I would suggest you come in fairly soon for examination.'

'All right. What time will you ring me?'

'Let's say five in the evening. Is that convenient?'

'I'll make sure I'm sitting by the phone.'

Dr Stephen rose, came round the desk and grasped her hand warmly as she stood up. 'Well, goodbye for the moment Miss Seal. Perhaps you'd better go and find Mr Kirkham and reassure him that we're not going to eat you alive.'

The tall Englishman Coulman had identified as Fox-Hillyer came down the central staircase as Marianne walked through the entrance hall. He stopped and gave her a long, searching glance as she went out, then made as if to follow her through the main entrance, but checked, and strolled to the reception office.

'That young lady who's just gone out,' he said pleasantly to the nurse. 'May I have a glance at her treatment card when it comes through?'

She glanced at him nervously. 'All treatment details are confidential, sir.'

'Then perhaps you wouldn't mind asking Dr Stephen.'

She spoke into the intercom: 'Dr Stephen . . . Mr Harrington wants to know if he can see Miss Seal's treatment details.'

After a brief pause, the doctor's voice came through: 'Yes, of course. Please give him any information you can which will assist his research.'

When Marianne reached the car Nick was sitting in the driving seat with the engine running. She hugged him, and peered anxiously into his impassive face.

'Darling, are you all right?'

'Sure.' He reversed out. 'Where's the nearest bar?'

'Nick, he's a very nice man.'

'I know, but I'm hooked on bastards.' He let in the clutch.

The little Viva got to seventy before it reached the end of the drive.

The telephone call was seven minutes late. The secretary said, 'Hallo, is that Miss Seal?'

'Yes, speaking.'

'I have Dr Stephen for you.'

She heard him talking to someone in the background and then he came on. His voice sounded weary.

'Ah, Miss Seal. You can tell Mr Kirkham he's a very potent young man.'

'Oh, marvellous. That's really great.'

'I suppose figures are of no importance but technically he's capable of producing about a hundred and fifty offspring at a time, which is rather above normal.'

'But I only want one.'

'Yes, I know. Well, we'd better have a look at you. When can you come in?'

'When do you want to see me?'

'Next week perhaps? I'd rather like to examine you during the ovulation period. Could you manage, say, Tuesday?'

'Yes, I think I could arrange that.'

'Good. Look, you'd better make arrangements to stay for a day or two. We may need to keep you in for up to a week, according to the treatment you require.'

'All right. Look, could you possibly hang on for a second, I want to tell Nick.

'Nii . . . ick. . . . Nick!'

She returned to the telephone. 'He doesn't seem to be around.'

'Right then, we'll expect to see you on Tuesday morning. Perhaps you would bring your personal documents . . . birth certificate, medical records, educational qualifications, that sort of thing. . . .'

7

The masseur's name was Leonard, but professional nicety had shortened this to Leon. Short and stubby, with a sympathetic beard, he kept up a constant barrage of chitchat as he pummelled away at Eckstein.

'Not much spare flesh on you, mate. I reckon you're wasting my time, you are.'

'Do they keep you busy?' Eckstein asked.

'I'll say they do. Hardly got time to turn round sometimes. It's mostly women o' course.'

'You prefer working on women?'

'So-so . . . you hardly notice the difference when you've been at it a few years, 'cept they got boobs o' course, but you're not supposed to touch those, unless they ask you specially.'

'Do they?'

'You'd be surprised how many. Specially the older ones funnily enough. I'll say one thing about this job, there's never any shortage of crumpet. You don't have to chase it either, it comes lookin' for you.

'Oh yes, I'll be sitting in my room about ten o'clock at night and there'll be a little tap on the door. "I was feeling a bit lonely," she'll say, "and I saw the light coming from your window, so I thought I'd drop in for a chat." I've 'ad to turn 'em away before now.'

'You stay here all the time?'

'That's right. I've got a flat on the top floor. Mind you it gets a bit tedious sometimes, stuck out 'ere in the middle of nowhere. I'm a Londoner myself. There ain't a lot to do around 'ere in the evenings except watch the telly. I usually wander down the local pub for a game o' dominoes.'

'What sort of a guy is this Dr Stephen?'

'Oh, he's a very decent bloke. If you've got any problems he'll always listen and try to do something about it. Supposed to be one of the best gynaecologists in the country. Would you like to turn over and rest your head in your hands . . . that's the idea.'

'You've known him for a long time?'

'Ever since he took over the lease, about five years ago. Oh, he's a very clever bloke. Speaks fluent German.'

'He does?'

'There's three people staying here at the moment, friends of his, one o' them is a German. I heard Dr Stephen talking to 'im the other day, rattling along with the old *sprechen sie Deutsch* just as if it was 'is mother tongue.'

Leon delivered a series of crisp, stinging slaps to Eckstein's buttocks. 'Right, that's you finished for today.'

Eckstein slid off the massage table and reached for his towel. 'Where's the pub you go to?'

'Dog and Badger. Turn left as you go out, it's about half a mile down the road.'

'I'll be staying around here for a while. I may drop in one evening and try this game of dominoes.'

'Sure. Any time.'

Marianne rose at a quarter to seven on the morning of her appointment, having already been awake for two hours. She brewed a cup of tea and while the kettle boiled the radio informed her that President Nixon had agreed to pay back the sum of $432,787 owed in income tax, but that the Internal Revenue Service of the United States had declared there was no suggestion of attempted fraud in this transaction. She took a cup to Nick, wanting to apprise him of this, but he was still a slumbering hulk.

There was still a long time to go so she took a fork into the

57

garden and planted four rows of broad beans but this took only an hour. Then she checked the car for oil and water, put half a tin of Kit-E-Kat in the bowl for their neutered tom, Bullnose, posted a cheque for the telephone bill, threw a couple of empty wine bottles into the dustbin and ironed fourteen handkerchiefs. She was a satisfactory two minutes late as she rushed upstairs to plant a kiss on the brow of the stirring Nick.

'I've got to go now. I've left some things for lunch under the grill. Don't forget the man's coming to sweep the chimney at half-eleven.'

Nick struggled to a sitting position as the sound of the car receded. He picked up the cup of tea which was now cold and had a thin scum on the surface, took a sip and washed it around his mouth. He felt distinctly uneasy about the whole business and wanted to push it back into the recesses of his brain, but it wouldn't go. He hated the idea of having to share the intimacies of that tender body with anyone, least of all have it treated like a piece of meat by an impersonal stranger. Still, maybe in another couple of days it would all be over. He knew that he was going to grope his way through that interim in a haze of booze.

Why did women have to get broody, for Christ's sake?

The reception nurse stopped typing and came across to the window. 'Good morning, Miss Seal. Dr Stephen is ready to see you. Would you like to go straight through.'

There was no one in the waiting-room. As Marianne turned to walk across it the nurse said, 'Oh, by the way . . . I'll be keeping my fingers crossed for you.' Her features resolved into an intimate woman-to-woman smile. Marianne said, 'Thanks a lot . . . I might need it.' She smiled back.

She was surprised to find, when she knocked on the door of the consulting room and entered, that the doctor was in the company of two other men.

'Come in, Miss Seal. I'd like you to meet two colleagues of mine—Mr Harrington, Doctor Schultz.'

Both men rose courteously to their feet, putting down brandy glasses, giving her a slight bow and a smile.

'Very happy to meet you,' said Fox-Hillyer. 'Doctor Stephen has just been telling us something about you, and I must say I admire your courage, wanting to raise a child in this troubled world of ours.'

'I hadn't really thought about it like that,' she said. She sat down, allowing them to resume their seats. The doctor said, 'These two gentlemen are thinking of opening a clinic in Germany.' He looked rather ill at ease.

Marianne felt slightly bewildered. She said, 'I don't want to interrupt your conversation—I can easily wait outside.'

'No no, please,' said Fox-Hillyer hurriedly. 'We wanted to have the pleasure of talking to one of Dr Stephen's patients . . . assuming you don't mind, of course.'

There was a slight hiatus. Marianne was accustomed to men of Fox-Hillyer's type—she had often come across them during her father's career as a bank manager—but the German made her feel extremely uncomfortable. He sat leaning forward, not much bigger than a dwarf, with blue eyes gazing at her appraisingly from beneath jutting eyebrows which looked as if they'd been cultivated. The whole room seemed charged with his personality. He breathed heavily and rhythmically, the breath ending now and again with a little rasping grunt as if he was about to speak. Suddenly he asked, 'How many children are you wanting altogether, Miss Seal?'

'I think one will be enough.'

'Ah,' he said, wagging a finger. 'Perhaps you will change your mind. You may finish up with quite a big family.'

Stephen said, 'Did you bring the documents?'

'Yes.' She handed them over.

'Just one or two things I wanted to check. You don't have any hereditary diseases in your family, I hope.' He smiled. 'Epilepsy, that sort of thing?'

'No, nothing like that.'

'Good.' He glanced at her birth certificate. 'I see your antecedents are British.'

Reisener said, 'You don't have any grandparents of foreign nationality . . . Polish . . . Russian . . . Jewish perhaps?'

'No,' she said, surprised. 'Does it make any difference?'

Stephen said hurriedly, 'Sometimes if there's an ethnic mixture it can produce a condition which affects the ability to conceive.'

Reisener leaned forward again. 'Miss Seal . . . you have graduated at a university . . . yar?'

'Yes, I have.'

'Did you get a good degree?'

She felt a sudden surge of anger. What right had this unpleasant little man to sit there and cross-question her.

She said, 'Dr Stephen, I'm sorry but I'd much rather talk to you alone. I'll wait in the waiting-room.'

As she rose, Fox-Hillyer stood up simultaneously. 'Miss Seal, please stay where you are . . . we won't intrude on you any further. Thank you so much for talking to us.' He moved towards the door, and added with a smile, 'I do hope you achieve your ambition. You're certainly in very good hands.'

He went out. As Reisener followed, he gave Marianne a slight nod and a small grunt of approval.

Stephen looked rather abashed. He said gruffly, 'I'm sorry about that. It was unavoidable.'

Marianne said, 'It's all right. I was just feeling a bit nervous.' But she felt very relieved that Reisener was no longer in the room.

'That's very understandable.' He spoke into the intercom: 'Ask Sister Ferry to come in.' He returned his attention to Marianne. 'Right, I've arranged to examine you in the surgery at two o'clock. If you'd like to get settled in . . . find your bearings . . . lunch is in the dining-room at one o'clock. There's plenty of grounds and gardens to wander about in if you feel inclined.

'Ah, here we have Sister Ferry. She'll be looking after you while you're here.'

'Hallo, Marianne, is that right? I'll show you where your room is. Have you got your things in the car?'

The round, slightly owly features of the woman in nursing uniform who had just entered beamed at her cheerfully from metal-rimmed glasses. She wasn't as neat as most nurses in Marianne's experience, looking a bit hammered by fate, with strands of loose hair straying wilfully around the starched collar. Her north country inflection seemed spiked with warmth and honesty. Marianne took an immediate liking to her.

Eckstein picked up the telephone in the blue-distempered bedroom of the Five Bells Hotel in Ipswich. Coulman was on the other end.

'Barry?—Richard. I've been checking on Dr Stephen with the British Medical Association. He was originally Johannes Steffen, a native of Germany. He got his medical degree at Leipzig in 1936, changed his name, was naturalised British in 1953.

'I've got Greb working on it over in Munich. I'm pretty tied up now . . . will talk to you later.'

'Right, if you'd like to take your clothes off, we'll get down to business.'

Dr Stephen, white coated in his surgery, exuded a brisker, more professional air. Sister Ferry took Marianne's clothes as she removed them, folding them neatly on to a chair.

'Would you get on to the table?' The nursing sister made an adjustment to the examination table as Marianne climbed on to it. 'Just put your feet in the rests, love . . . that's the idea.' She proceeded to record Marianne's temperature, pulse rate and blood pressure with deft efficiency and passed these details to the gynaecologist, who was studying a set of X-ray plates. Eventually he came across and listened to Marianne's heart with a stethoscope, began to explore her body with probing fingers. Then he changed the position of a lamp and readjusted the footrests, easing her legs apart.

'I'm afraid this is the part where modesty flies out of the window,' he said. With what seemed to Marianne surprising ease, he squeezed his hand inside her.

She almost had to suppress a giggle at the indignity of it. At the same time she was aware of a strange lack of feeling as if her body, even in its most sensitive region, was made of plasticine.

The game of dominoes has this in common with back-gammon—a modest player believes he has an occasional chance of beating an outstanding one by virtue of the superiority of luck over expertise. Eckstein was aware of this but nevertheless he had lost four games of dominoes in succession, and although these were the first games of dominoes he had played he was not a man who enjoyed losing at anything.

As he returned from the bar counter with Leon's fourth pint of bitter he wasn't unhappy to see the masseur stacking the evil-looking black rectangles in the box.

'You're coming on,' said Leon. 'You're improving. Another couple of dozen games and I shall have to start trying.'

Eckstein simulated a rueful grin. 'How's the sex life?' he inquired.

'I can't complain. There's this actress came in yesterday, she's got some part in a TV series and she's got to lose five pounds in a week. Uncle Leon will see she does it—I should be all right there. Then there's a Swede and a Dutch chick and this gorgeous blonde piece that wants to 'ave a baby. I reckon I could solve her problem in no time at all.'

Eckstein guessed that the actress would be in her forties and the others for various reasons unavailable as far as Leon was concerned. If loneliness had a smell the man would reek of it. Yet he would remain fixed in his world of sexual fantasy for as long as the occasional woman, out of frustration, nibbled at the fringe.

'Everybody keeps askin' me when I'm going to get married,' Leon was saying. 'The answer to that one's obvious. Why pick a chocolate when you can help yourself to the whole bloody box? Cheers!' He lifted his pint.

'That German guy you were talking about,' asked Eckstein, 'Is he still around?'

'Schultz? Yeah, 'e's still hanging about . . . and the other pair. Christ knows what for. There's a rumour going around that they're going to buy the place. It's that other feller that gets up my snout.'

'Which other feller?'

'The one with the big gob and the little piggy eyes. He's a right nosey bastard . . . wanders around all day asking questions about the clients. Who are they, where do they come from, 'ow long 'ave they been coming for treatment.'

'Did he ask about me?'

'Oh sure, 'e wanted to know all about the Yank. I told 'im to mind 'is own fucking business. I don't know why Stephen puts up with that bunch. Still, I suppose money talks.'

'It has been known to,' said Eckstein.

She looked out of a window at a bank of daffodils and narcissi bending their blooms to the fading light, then closed the curtains. They had given her one of the chalets about a hundred yards from the house and she felt pleased to be so detached.

The room was agreeable even if it lacked spontaneity and could cheerfully be lived in for a reasonable while—there was even a colour TV. She was pink and fresh from a recent shower, and had begun to wonder hungrily what might be for supper in the restaurant. If there were potatoes, she might even allow herself a couple. After all it was an occasion of sorts. There would be others there, some losing weight and eating only yoghourt, others having problems with their babies, oddments of staff, perhaps the fierce-looking German stuffing himself with steak and sauerkraut. It was funny being a patient, she'd never been one before and felt rather guilty about it as if she'd shed her social responsibilities without an adequate excuse.

Sister Ferry knocked and entered. 'Are you all right, love?

I just thought I'd look in. I've brought you a flask of coffee. Or you can have hot chocolate if you like.'

'Coffee's fine. Thanks a lot.'

'Is it too warm for you?'

'No, it's just about right.'

'Aye, well, if you want to control the heating just push the switch on the thermostat. If you should happen to feel a bit queer during the night just ring the switchboard, there's always someone on duty . . . only you can't make personal calls after ten o'clock at night, only emergencies.'

'I'll remember that. Are you here all the time?'

'Oh aye, love. I'm a permanent fixture.'

'It's such a lovely place. Aren't you . . . you know . . . just grateful to be here?'

The sister looked at Marianne quizzically, then gave a wan smile. 'I'm just grateful to be wherever I am.'

Shortly afterwards Doctor Stephen entered the room and the sister immediately left. The gynaecologist, Marianne thought, looked a little strained. She caught the tang of whisky on his breath.

'I just wanted to put you in the picture,' he said.

'Have you found out what the trouble is?' Her voice was eager.

'No, not yet. It has to be a process of elimination.'

'Oh, I see.' She was disappointed.

'But we're on the way. First of all we can rule out any effect of general disease which might affect the endocrine glands. In other words, you're bursting with rude physical health, Miss Seal.

'So we can now concentrate on local disorders of the genital tract . . . that's the place where it all happens. Have you got a piece of paper?'

She gave him her writing pad. He sketched on it quickly and expertly.

'Look, here we have the uterus—the womb in other words. Here is the vagina, with the two ovaries . . . about the size of walnuts. These are the fallopian tubes . . .'

64

In the rear seat of the Rolls, parked two hundred yards away, Fox-Hillyer frowned in concentration as he listened through earphones to the crackling conversation, relayed through a microphone bug attached to a radiator in the chalet . . . 'now during the ovulation period one of the ovaries will shed an egg which will be squeezed through one of the tubes into the womb. Hopefully, if intercourse has recently taken place, the egg will meet a stream of sperm swimming from the other direction . . . like this . . . and one of those sperm will fertilise the egg inside the tube. After that happens the egg will pass on through to the womb and embed itself in the lining . . . somewhere around here. . . .'

The doctor gave her a rather wan smile. 'It will then proceed to grow into another suffering human being.'

Marianne, crouching beside him on the settee, said, 'It all sounds so easy.'

'Most women find it all too easy. Right, now what could be the problem with you. It could be a failure to ovulate—to shed an egg at the appropriate time—but the usual reason for this is emotional stress and you seem a very well-balanced young lady. I think it's more likely to be a blockage of the fallopian tube, which prevents the egg coming into contact with the sperm.'

'What's the cause of that?'

'Could be inflammation, or a small obstruction. I propose to find out tomorrow.'

He picked up the sketch again. 'I'm going to try what we call gas insufflation. I shall blow some gas through the fallopian tubes and I'll be able to discover, by watching the pressure, if there's a blockage. At the same time, if there is a minor obstruction, the gas itself may clear it.

'As you're coming up to the ovulation period I'm also going to implant some of Mr Kirkham's semen in the neck of the womb . . . here . . . ready to pounce on any egg which may emerge in the next few days. I think it's worth a try. Sometimes there's a better chance of impregnation under clinical conditions than by the more natural method.'

He leaned forward, rested his head in his hands for a few seconds, then stood up abruptly.

'Well, I'll see you at half-past ten tomorrow morning and we'll see what we can do.' He walked slowly towards the door, but paused in front of it.

'By the way, some women have been known to change their minds, so I always ask my patients at this stage if they're quite sure they still want a child. If you want to give up the treatment I won't be the slightest bit offended.'

The features of Fox-Hillyer, sitting in the darkened car, became tense and alert as he strained to catch the reply.

'Oh, but I wouldn't dream of giving up now. I just know it's going to be all right.'

He touched her on the shoulder. 'Thank you for your faith in me.' But his voice sounded strangely dispirited. He turned and went out.

A couple of miles away Eckstein was again talking to Coulman on the telephone.

'The security element,' said Coulman, 'would seem to be a guy called Paulson. There are seven in the London telephone directory and I've checked out five. Of the two who aren't at home one is a fishmonger and the other runs a private detective agency.'

8

Sister Ferry said, 'How are you feeling, love, all right?'

'I'm a little bit nervous.'

'I'll just give you something to help you relax.'

She swabbed Marianne's arm and gave her an injection. After a few minutes she felt considerably more confident, the doubts and fears draining out of her consciousness. When she was stretched out on the table she thought of herself as a human sacrifice, and smiled inwardly.

Dr Stephen connected a gas bottle to the insufflation equipment and tested the meter reading, as the nurse fitted a felt pad over her eyes and drew the band over her head. 'This will stop you from being dazzled by the lights.'

Marianne felt almost light-hearted as the gas nozzle was inserted. The flow of gas into her body gave her a not unpleasant tingling feeling while the murmuring voices of the gynaecologist and Sister Ferry seemed remote but comforting. She drowsily surrendered to their skills.

Then she felt the gas nozzle withdrawn and after a few moments replaced by another instrument, heavier and colder to the touch. It was at this precise moment that she heard someone breathing quite close to her, and a little wheezing grunt.

Nick had intended to drop into the village pub for an hour, but somehow it had got extended to two and a half. Perhaps it was because he had somehow got involved with a student who said he was working part-time at the local sugar-

67

beet factory in order to save up for a trip to Mexico. Nick had at one time spent a fortnight in that country and had found it incumbent upon himself to dispel the young man's gaucho fantasies.

The whole place was swarming with flies, he explained, and lousy with American tourists who looked like Nelson Rockefeller or Shirley Temple Black. The women were admittedly beautiful but eighty per cent of them had got religion and the remainder had got the clap. The place did have certain possibilities, Nick admitted, but the only way to develop these was to start by getting rid of the priesthood.

Nick maintained that he had no personal bias against religion, most of the religious prophets had got the right idea, but the priests had subsequently screwed it all up for motives of personal power. 'Could you imagine J. Christ,' asked Nick, 'walking around in a dog collar, for Christ's sake?'

At this point Nick's intellect had somehow got fuzzed and he had taken refuge in silence while the student earnestly propounded his own specific line of bullshit.

Afterwards, in the car park, Nick's car had declined to start, and it had taken him half an hour to realise that he was trying to turn on the ignition with the key that unlocked the boot.

He stumbled into the cottage just before eleven, and once safely inside the kitchen door he noticed things like pots and saucepans and Kenwood mixers and it occurred to him that he ought for the first time that day, to have something to eat.

He decided to cook himself an omelette with onions but he couldn't find the onions and when the second egg broke on the floor he considered it was hardly worth the effort, and settled for a couple of cream-crackers and half a tin of stale salted peanuts, washed down by a glass of Marianne's cooking burgundy, the only booze left in the house.

While consuming this meal he tried to reflect upon his intake for the evening, starting with a large Scotch and ginger, proceeding to three pints of lager and lime—or was it four—

followed by a couple of pernods recommended by some amiable character who had just returned from a holiday in France. Nick tried hard to remember his face but his memory refused to throw it to the surface, insisting instead in throwing up the image of the total stranger who had sat in a corner of the bar for half an hour and talked to no one. Those features were unpleasant, tanned and wrinkled with the wrong sort of experience, the eyes slotted back in dark sockets, mean and little. Nick had felt them boring into the back of his neck while he was talking to the student. But there was something rather more urgent than unsalubrious characters in bars knocking around in Nick's memory and he suddenly realised what it was.

He found the number and dialled the Grasspool Clinic. The secretary answered after a dozen rings. 'Is this an emergency call?' she asked.

'It sure is. I've got to talk to Marianne Seal.'

'I'm afraid we don't allow personal calls to patients after ten p.m. Who is it speaking?'

'The name is Kirkham. Nick Kirkham. Will you put me through, please.'

'Oh yes, I remember . . . you came in the other day. Miss Seal is asleep now. Why don't you call her first thing in the morning?'

'Never mind the morning. I am calling now and I want to talk to Marianne.'

There was an appreciable pause at the other end of the line, then the secretary said, 'I've just been having a look at Miss Seal's treatment notes. She had a minor operation this morning and it's left her rather exhausted. I'm afraid we can't possibly allow her to be disturbed at this time of night. I'm awfully sorry.'

She hung up. Nick put the phone down carefully, groped his way across the room, and picked up the burgundy bottle. It was empty. He hurled it at the fireplace.

Sister Ferry brought her breakfast in bed and she was just

c*

finishing this when Dr Stephen came in. 'I'm glad to see you've still got a good appetite,' he observed.

'It's too good. I never eat breakfast as a rule,' she told him with a rueful smile. He sat on the bottom of the bed. 'Well,' he said, 'by and large I think you have a reasonable chance of being a mum in the not too distant future.'

'Oh really?' Her eyes widened. 'Did everything go all right?'

'There was a slight obstruction in one of the tubes but this seemed to be removed during the insufflation test; otherwise the tubes seemed to be working perfectly. Now what I would normally do next would be to take an X-ray and see if there's something else wrong, but on this occasion I have a pretty strong, well, call it a hunch if you like, that the insemination might take.'

'You mean I might be pregnant already?'

'Let's say it could happen in the next day or two. That's why I'd like you to stay in bed and relax for the time being, so as to give it every chance of success.'

As he was leaving she asked, 'Why was Mr Schultz there?'

He looked startled. 'Where?'

'In the surgery. Just after you finished the gas treatment. I'm sure I heard him cough.'

The gynaecologist laughed. 'That was the effect of the gas,' he said. 'It does tend to stimulate the imagination. I can assure you that I don't allow visitors in my surgery when I'm treating a patient.'

She had just the tiniest suspicion, from an inflection in his voice, that he was lying.

'Right, I'll look in again tomorrow.'

Nick arrived an hour later. He wandered in looking harassed, fighting off a king-sized hangover. She hugged and kissed him gratefully. 'Nick, I've been longing to see you. Why didn't you say you were coming? I've been trying to ring you this morning.'

'I tried to ring you last night, but the cow on the switchboard wouldn't put me through.'

70

'Nick, are you all right?' She surveyed him seriously. There was a graze on his cheekbone. 'What have you done to yourself?'

'The cat fell on top of me. Hey, I'm supposed to be asking the questions. What have they done to you?'

'Oh nothing very much. I feel fine, but I've got to stay in bed for a few days. 'Nick,' . . . her eyes shone . . . 'Dr Stephen thinks I might be pregnant by the time I leave here.' Nick frowned. 'How come? I thought you were just being tested.'

'Yes, I know, but he also inseminated me with some of your you-know-what.'

'He did what?'

She was startled by the strength of his reaction. 'It's all right, Nick. He said it's sometimes easier to do it in hospital, and that was the whole idea, anyway, wasn't it?'

'Who gave the bastard permission to do that?'

'Nick, what's the matter?' She was suddenly anxious, seeing he was so deeply disturbed.

'Listen, don't you get the message? The good doctor finds my gunge is no good, right? But he doesn't want to miss out on another score, so he tells us the opposite. Then he brings you in here, pretends to mess around with you for a while, then gives you a dose of some other bastard's jissom. So you have a baby, nobody knows the difference, and the good doctor is even more of a fucking genius.'

'He wouldn't do a thing like that, Nick.'

'In a pig's ass. I don't trust him. I want you out of this place now.' He really meant it.

'But I can't leave now. It would ruin everything.'

'It's going to ruin a hell of a lot more if you stay here.'

'Nick, please don't say things like that.' She was becoming distraught. She had never seen him like this before, so tense with anger.

He crouched beside the bed, rubbed his knuckles into his forehead, striving to control his emotions. Eventually he said, quietly and deliberately, 'Listen baby . . . okay we want to have a kid but we can't, so there's something wrong either with you or with me, so we ask this Dr Stephen to find out which. Okay, so he inspects us both, and he says you are the one . . . he says you can't conceive so he gives you the treatment so you can conceive, okay. So then you come back home and we make a child like it has to happen, just like between you and me in the sack, okay? Wasn't that the idea?'

Marianne's eyes filled with tears. 'Nick, Doctor Stephen wouldn't cheat us, I just know he wouldn't.'

Nick reached out and squeezed her hand fiercely. Then he said, 'Aaah, Christ!' He turned and walked quickly out of the room.

At the same moment Fox-Hillyer removed the headphones, emerged from the Rolls, and walked quickly into the main building.

Nick walked to the reception window and told the nurse, 'I'd like to see Dr Stephen.'

She gave him a bright smile. 'Oh yes, it's Mr Kirkham isn't it?' She picked up the appointments book. 'Now, let's see when we can fit you in.'

'I mean I want to see him right now.'

'I'm afraid that's impossible. He's seeing patients until one o'clock and he's operating this afternoon. Could you manage tomorrow morning . . . say about . . . half-eleven?'

Nick glanced at the three or four women in the waiting room and past them at the door beyond. He thought of charging through it. But the thought of finding the gynaecologist plying his trade on the other side suddenly filled him with disgust, tinged with despair. He said brusquely, 'Tell him I'll be back,' and walked away.

As he reached the car the man whom Coulman had identified as Paulson emerged from the house and, for the second time in two days, regarded him with keen interest.

When Sister Ferry came in a few minutes later, Marianne was sobbing. The nurse sat beside her on the bed and put a comforting arm round her shoulders.

'What's the trouble, love? Did you have a row?'

'He doesn't . . . want me to have a baby . . . by insemination . . .'

'Don't worry about it. He'll soon come round. Dr Stephen'll sort 'im out. It's a funny thing about men y'know, they get more worked up about babies than women.'

After his visit to the clinic Nick hung around the cottage trying to work, but after a couple of days he found he couldn't stand the place any longer. He had always claimed to Marianne that he suffered from both claustrophobia and agrophobia, that he could only be lonely in a crowd, that his ideal situation was about the size of a saloon bar. This was true in essence—he never, if he could avoid it, travelled in lifts or walked across mountains. But this was not the only current problem—he felt, as of the moment, impotent both in mind and body, combined with a taut feeling in the guts. He felt he had to get away.

He decided to go to London for a while and lose himself in the place, disappear into its belly. Maybe it would help him get things together. He recalled an acquaintance, Steve, an American scriptwriter working in London. The last time they had met, at somebody's party, Steve was about to leave on a six-weeks trip back to the States, and invited Nick to use his pad if he needed to stay in town during that period. He had scrawled the address somewhere on the back of an envelope.

He spent an hour searching every pocket for Steve's London address, eventually finding it under a soup plate in the kitchen. Marianne had on some forgotten occasion scrawled another note under his own: *Don't forget to switch the oven off at seven, oh, and I think there's a tin of pears around somewhere.*

'Alison,'—they were on Christian name terms now—'you don't need to do everything for me. I can easily hop out of bed and get things.'

73

'Aye, I know, love, but I don't want you to take any risks.'

After five days in bed Marianne was feeling bored and restive and worry about Nick gnawed at her frequently. He hadn't been in touch. She had rung him five times but there was nobody at the other end. She was also concerned about a certain lassitude which was taking control of her. For the last three days she had slept throughout the afternoon. She considered this disgusting.

She watched the nurse bustling about the room, tucking in the blankets, picking up a magazine, small round head on plumpish, rather featureless body, now and then the little tizzicking cough, and wondered vaguely about her sex life. There was a hint of unspent passion about her prowling walk, she couldn't yet be forty—yet Marianne couldn't quite imagine her quenching it with any man she knew. She searched her imagination—rather fatuously she felt, but there was nothing else to do—looking for a man who might fit Alison in bed.

She asked, 'Alison, have you ever had any children?'

The sister glanced at her in surprise. 'Who, me? No, love.' The question seemed to embarrass her.

'Have you ever wanted one?'

'I've never thought about it.'

At this moment Dr Stephen came in quietly. Alison Ferry remained unobtrusively at the other end of the room. He seemed rather preoccupied as he sat beside her, checked her pulse rate.

'Well, how do we feel today?'

'I'm fine. Just a bit drowsy and lazy.'

'I know. Staying in bed when you're not really ill can be rather a tedious business. I think we can let you get up for a couple of hours tomorrow.'

She said quickly, 'Oh, but I thought I was going home tomorrow.'

'Well of course you can if you wish, but I'd rather you didn't.' He gave her wrist a quick squeeze of encouragement

74

as he withdrew his hand, and smiled. 'You see, this is only my personal opinion, but I think you have a better chance of conceiving now than you ever may have again.'

He picked up her temperature chart from the bedside table. 'There's something I want to show you. You see this slight dip in your chart—on the fourteenth day of the cycle—and then a rise of about one degree in your body temperature. This means that you are ovulating normally . . . all right? And we've now reached the twentieth day and the temperature is still at the higher level. In another ten or eleven days we ought to know for sure. Now I think, if you want to give yourself every chance, you should stay here until we know if you are pregnant or otherwise. While you're here I can keep an eye on you, and, what's more important, you'll be able to relax. If you return to your normal life, any slight emotional strain could upset the whole of the applecart.'

'Another ten days?' She tried to digest this prospect. 'I don't think I could afford it.'

'My dear Miss Seal, don't worry about the economic situation. What we lose on the swings of fertility we can make up on the other roundabouts. It won't cost you any more.'

She felt bewildered, trying to shrug off her semi-comatose state. 'But . . . I've only got a week's leave from work.'

'If you'd like to give Sister Ferry your employer's name and telephone number, I'll explain the situation.'

'But what about Nick?'

'Oh, Mr Kirkham. I'll have a word with him also. I'm sure he'll understand.'

He went out. Alison moved quickly across and sat beside her. 'Don't worry love, he's one of the best, he'll see you all right.' Marianne was close to tears, thinking of Nick. The nurse reached out to re-arrange a straying lock of her hair. 'I'll go and get you some breakfast. The hairdresser's coming this afternoon, I'll get her to pop across.' As she withdrew she said, 'You know what? I'm sure you're going to click. I feel it in my bones, and I've never been wrong yet.'

After she had gone, something hung in Marianne's mind.

75

Alison's hand had remained for an appreciable time, re-arranging her hair, caressing her forehead—until she had begun to feel a twinge of revulsion.

Eckstein had taken to nocturnal prowling again. One of his favourite haunts was a clump of trees—chestnuts, Scots pines, a few cedars, situated about a hundred yards from the main building. From here he was able to monitor most of the movements during the hours of darkness and he accumulated some useful information. He knew for instance that Reisener and Fox-Hillyer were quartered inside the house, that Fox-Hillyer came and went frequently but the German hardly appeared outside the doors. That Paulson and the chauffeur lived in the chalet next to the girl who, according to Leon, was having fertility treatment. He had become aware that every time Dr Stephen visited this patient, either Fox-Hillyer or Paulson listened in to the ensuing conversation through headphones in the back of the Rolls. He knew—also confirmed by Leon—that business had fallen off sharply during the last ten days. There were now only half a dozen patients staying in the place.

Watching from the security of the trees, he saw a rather bulky nurse scurry across to the girl's chalet with a tray. Paulson emerged, clearing his throat raucously, from the hut next door.

Eckstein began to take a particular interest in the girl inside the chalet. Everything seemed to revolve around her. He was also conscious of a growing sense of impotent frustration. But it wouldn't be long now, he assured himself. Coulman had told him on the phone that morning that it would soon be time to move.

9

Steve's flat was high in a crumbling block in a narrow street leading off St Martin's Lane. Nick had to wait in the rain for half an hour before one of the other residents, a screwed-up little woman, hobbled up with a street door key. She stared at him with grave suspicion as he squeezed in behind her and loped up the narrow stairs.

The key to Steve's flat was not, as he had promised, behind the electricity meter. Instead, the door was wide open and emitting a solid blast from The Who. He went in tentatively, peering around.

Shortly a tall, ginger-bearded figure wearing only a striped pair of Marks and Spencer's underpants emerged from the bathroom. 'Hallo blue . . . you looking for someone?'

'Is this Steve's place?'

'Yeh, that's right.'

'He's a friend of mine. He said I could stay here for a while.'

The Australian grinned. 'Snap, baby. Come and join the happy throng.'

He gestured in the direction of the sole bedroom. Through the half-open door Nick glimpsed a large Ghanaian girl hurriedly dressing.

'No thanks. Is there some place I could make a cup of coffee?'

'Try the kitchen, blue.'

For the next three days Nick lurked around the East End pubs, keeping away from the places where he might be recognised and heartily greeted, returning late at night to curl up on the sofa in a sleeping bag loaned to him by the Australian, lulled to sleep by the moans and grunts of the sexual congress from the other side of the wall.

He had an unpleasant feeling that what was growing inside Marianne had transferred itself to his own body. It lay there like a stone in his gut, getting bigger all the time. On the fourth day he had an irresistible desire to talk to Marianne, but found that Steve har prudently disconnected the telephone before leaving. Nick roamed the streets for over an hour searching for a phone box which hadn't been vandalised, but when he eventually found one he realised he didn't have the number of the clinic . . . and by this time the urge had evaporated.

It was now April 13th—a Friday—but Nick was conscious neither of passing time nor the state of his luck. He spent the morning at a succession of pubs in Hackney, feeding the one-armed bandits, stumbling out at closing time and wandering through the streets in an alcoholic miasma. He stopped for half an hour in a betting shop and lost a fiver, and was about to risk another when he realised that he was breaking his neck for a piss.

He walked with much greater urgency now, eyes searching despairingly for the comforting words, ladies, gentlemen. By the time he found a public toilet the pressure was causing acute physical pain. As he ripped open his zip and exploded against the porcelain, Nick remembered to check his watch. He ticked off the seconds, hoping to beat his all-time record for one continuous slash . . . forty-four . . . forty-five . . . forty-six . . . that was it. But what was the previous record? Nick knew he had it written down somewhere. He groped for his pocket diary. At this moment he saw the notice on the wall above his head.

Confidential Pregnancy Tests
can be obtained from
The Lambert Laboratories Ltd.

Christ, why hadn't he thought of it before. He wrote down the address.

There were five women in front of Nick in the queue and it didn't help that three of them were attractive. It helped even less that the one in front of him asked all sorts of questions which took up five minutes which seemed like fifty. The girl behind the 'Enquiries' window was dark with huge eyes and Nick found himself almost speechless in her presence. 'Listen, ahm . . . do you carry out, ahm . . . you know, sperm tests?'

'Yes, I think we could do that for you.'

'How long does it take?'

'About three to four days. Could I have your name and address?'

Nick gave his name and said, 'Never mind the address. I'll call in.'

The girl said, 'All right, I'll give you a sterilised container, and if you'd like to bring in a sample some time . . .' She lowered her voice, confidentially. 'By the way, it needs to be within four hours of . . . you know.'

Nick leaned forward, conscious of the woman behind him straining her ears. He said, almost in a whisper, 'Hey listen, I'm a bit short of time. Is there some place I could . . .' She put a plastic bottle in front of him. 'Yes,' she whispered, 'of course. If you go out into the corridor and turn right it's the second door on the left.' She said this without a flicker of a smile and Nick loved her for it.

He closed the door of the cubicle behind him, sat on the edge of the pedestal, and began to concentrate all his thoughts on Marianne.

Behind the house lay a flight of wide curved steps approached through an ornate arch and guarded by stone lions. These steps led to the gardens below, laid out in the form of a gigantic clock face, blazing with spring flowers, brooms of various hues, yellow splashes of forsythia. In the centre a circular pool fed by a fountain swarmed with gold-fish. Marianne leaned over the parapet and watched the fish gliding between the fronds of weed. She looked round curiously as footsteps crunched behind her on the gravelled path. It was a man she hadn't seen before.

'Hi there,' called Eckstein as he approached. He came and crouched beside her.

'It must be great to be a goldfish,' he said. He reached a hand into the water and gave a flick to the tail of a large shubunken, which wriggled lazily into the nearest cover.

She said, 'It must get a bit cold for them in the winter.'

'That could create problems,' he agreed, 'such as getting trapped under the ice.' She gave a wan smile at his. He turned to look into her face. 'Are you staying here?'

'Yes, for a while.'

'Looks a marvellous place to relax.' He gazed around. 'It seems incredible that one person used to own all this.'

'Yes, I'm glad those days are all over.'

'Mind if I ask your name? Mine's Joe Clark.'

'Marianne,' she said. 'Seal.'

Eckstein was suddenly aware of a third presence. He looked round and saw Paulson standing, arms folded, some fifteen yards away.

He moved forward slowly. 'Who might you be?' he asked.

Eckstein said, 'Why do you want to know?'

'Are you a patient?'

'I just dropped in for the sauna . . . thought I'd take a look around the garden.'

'This garden is out of bounds to non-residents,' said Paulson tersely. 'In any case the sauna's closed today—or didn't you know?'

'I guess I must have got the dates mixed up.'

'Right, away you go.'

'Okay, if I bother you.' He gave a farewell nod and a smile to Marianne. 'Maybe we can finish the conversation another time.' He walked slowly away towards the steps.

After a few moments Paulson hurried after him. They walked side by side for a few yards.

Paulson spoke almost in tones of weary resignation. 'Just a friendly word of advice. Don't let me catch you hangin' around here any more. Otherwise somebody might get hurt.'

Eckstein stopped and glanced appraisingly at the other man. He smiled, as if mildly amused. 'Could be,' he said. Then he walked up the steps.

Paulson turned back and walked towards Marianne. She watched him with rising apprehension. His lips, as he approached, twisted into a self-satisfied smirk. 'Sorry about that . . . hope he didn't bother you too much. I shouldn't stay here too long, you don't want to catch your death of cold.'

Nick drove through the gates of the clinic just as dusk was falling. It had been a blustery day and as he got out of the car he was met by a flurry of rain. He could hear the surrounding trees creaking in the wind. There were now only three or four cars parked outside the house, including the Rolls.

The outer office was deserted and Nick went through it and opened the door of the consulting room without knocking. Dr Stephen was sitting at his desk writing in a large red notebook. He glanced up as Nick entered, almost as if he was expecting him.

'Ah, Mr Kirkham, I was hoping you'd drop in for a chat.' He closed the notebook and switched off the desk lamp. 'I'm sometimes asked to contribute to one of these medical journals,' he said. 'I can't think why I bother, they never pay me anything. Take a seat.'

Nick remained standing. The gynaecologist rose rather wearily, pushed his reading glasses to the top of his head and walked stiffly across to the drinks cabinet, pausing to clutch at the small of his back. 'Touch of arthritis. Take my advice, never grow old.' He picked up a bottle and glasses. 'Care for a drop of Scotch?'

Nick said, 'No thanks.'

'How very abstemious of you. I should be on the wagon myself, to tell you the truth.'

He poured one for himself, came back and leaned against his desk.

'You have something on your mind, so they tell me.'

'I sure as hell have something on my mind.'

'Well, before you unload it, let me give you the good news. I can't be absolutely sure at the moment, but you're almost certainly going to become a father.'

'I have news for you,' said Nick. 'Whatever you've done to Marianne doesn't have anything to do with me.'

Stephen frowned, jutting out his lower lip. He took a sip of the neat Scotch and nodded slowly.

'In as much as every human being is a totally different individual, I suppose you could be right.'

Nick wished he had taken the drink. He said, 'I mean I am not the god-damned father, and you know it, you devious bastard.'

The doctor looked genuinely puzzled. Then it was as if he had seen the light. 'Ah, you think I've got your semen mixed up with someone else's? It's a very natural fear. But it doesn't happen in my clinic, there are far too many checks.'

'You still say my stuff was fertile?'

'Certainly. I tested it myself.'

'In that case how do you explain this?' Nick took a printed form from his pocket and handed it across. Stephen took it, readjusted his spectacles, and read it.

The result of your sperm test is as follows:
The sperm count is twenty four and a half
millions per millilitre.
This is ~~well-above~~ / ~~above~~ / below / ~~well-below~~
the normal fertility level.
No evidence of general disease was discovered
during this testing procedure.

Nick watched the doctor's features as he read the document. He raised his eyebrows, then clamped his lips together and wagged his head slowly from side to side. He handed the piece of paper back with a wry smile.

'Ah, so you've found me out,' he said. 'All right, I'll grant you that your sperm count is rather below average, but it also depends upon the fertility of the woman. I have also developed a method of making sperm cells much more active, where the count is on the low side, so I am able to make it much easier for a woman to conceive in these circumstances, under clinical conditions, than in the usual way. I have quite a number of satisfied customers, I can assure you, who will never produce a child by sexual intercourse.'

'I don't believe you.'

Stephen took another drink, appeared to deliberate on the situation. 'Tell me, as a matter of interest, why you think I would impregnate your lady love with another man's seed?'

'Just so you can notch up another score, I guess.'

Nick's mouth was dry with tension. He had imagined the conversation on his way down in the car. It hadn't gone at all like this.

The gynaecologist gave a brief burst of laughter. It sounded to Nick uncomfortably genuine.

'You seriously believe we keep some sort of a league table, like racing tipsters?'

He became serious again. 'Mr Kirkham, I'm afraid you are indulging in fantasies. Mind you, it's not so unusual. Parenthood, particularly in these sort of circumstances, is a very emotive business, all the more so according to the sensitivity of the people involved. And I'd say that both you and Miss Seal are very sensitive people.' His smile was conspiratorial. 'It wouldn't surprise me if in a few months you were getting labour pains.'

The telephone rang. Stephen picked it up and said, 'No, not just now. I'll talk to her in the morning.' He eased himself further on to the desk and swung a leg.

'No, my dear fellow, you've got nothing to worry about.

In a day or two you'll have the splendid Miss Seal back with you, and you can start planning your family.' He picked up the bottle. 'Sure you won't change your mind? About the drink I mean?'

Nick had the disastrous feeling of his resolve beginning to melt, of a natural urge for compromise permeating his will. It was the doctor who was giving it all, trying to find a solution, himself who hadn't budged an inch. A small, cowardly Nick inside him wanted to say, 'Okay, I'm not trying to be unreasonable, I appreciate all you've done. But you must understand my position, I'm not just blowing my top for nothing. Look . . . if you're prepared to give me a written undertaking . . .'

But the real Nick managed to assert himself.

'Miss Seal is coming with me right now,' he said. 'And I'll tell you something else. If she so happens to be pregnant she is going to have an abortion.' As he moved to the door he said, 'I suppose you couldn't recommend a good gynaecologist?'

'Just a moment,' Dr Stephen spoke more briskly.

'Mr Kirkham, I'm sorry I haven't been able to set your fears at rest. But I'm afraid that as Miss Seal's physician I can't allow you to see her while you're in your present frame of mind.'

'You mean you're going to stop me?'

The light had almost completely faded now, and when Nick emerged from the front entrance he had to stand in the drive for a full minute before his eyes became accustomed to the darkness.

A hundred yards away, against a dark smudge of trees, he could see the lights of the chalet where Marianne was, and began to walk in that direction. He had got about half-way when a silhouette appeared from nowhere.

'Where d'you think you're going?'

Paulson stood in front of him, blocking his path.

'Is it any concern of yours?' asked Nick.

'I suppose you know this is private property.'

'I'm visiting a patient,' said Nick. The words sounded hugely incongruous in the circumstances. Paulson's lips crinkled into a grin, as if in recognition of this.

'Did Dr Stephen give you permission?' he inquired.

Nick suddenly ducked and ran, skidding and sliding across the slippery turf of the lawn, making for the lighted windows. He got to within twelve yards when someone else came at him from an angle.

Nick went down, and the other two were on him immediately. He heard Paulson say thickly, 'Keep him quiet,' then an arm locked itself round his throat. He kicked out wildly and heard a grunt of pain. But his legs were quickly held and he was pinned down on the wet grass. He stopped struggling. Paulson said, 'Right, lift!' They carried him back to the drive and stood him up against the door of his car. 'Now we don't want any more trouble from you,' Paulson said.

Something seemed to explode in Nick's stomach and he sprawled on the gravel, doubled up in pain, gasping for breath.

The chauffeur said, 'That's just for starters, mate. Just give me a shout when you want the second course.'

It took Nick several minutes to recover. The other two men stood silently watching him as he eventually climbed unsteadily into his car and drove away.

He had to wait for twenty minutes in the interview room at the police headquarters while the inspector finished his evening meal in the staff canteen. When this officer finally appeared, brushing crumbs from his tunic, he proved to be a younger man than Nick, with chubby, almost cherubic features radiating an essential optimism.

'Now then, squire . . . sorry to keep you hanging about. Could I just have your details first of all?' He wrote these down at Nick's dictation. 'Right, what seems to be the trouble?'

'I wish to report an assault,' Nick said. 'Also I have a

friend at the Grasspool Clinic who is being kept there under false pretences.'

'I see. Would you like to tell me all about it?'

Nick gave his version of the events. Even as he related them he felt that they became less and less plausible. But the inspector listened with keen attention. He said nothing until Nick had finished speaking, then he asked, 'This patient you mentioned . . . Miss Seal, wasn't it. Is she your fiancée?'

'We live together.'

'Ah, so she's your wife in all but name.' He paused, clicking his fingers, then reached for the telephone and riffled through a local directory. 'Why don't we find out what Dr Stephen's got to say about it?'

The inspector got through almost immediately.

'Am I talking to Dr Stephen?' he asked briskly. 'Good. Inspector Charlesworth here, Suffolk Police. I've got a Mr Kirkham with me. He says he went to your clinic this evening to visit a Miss Seal, and he complains that when he tried to see her he was assaulted by two members of your staff.'

Nick could hear the buzzing tones in the receiver as the doctor replied but he couldn't decipher them. He seemed to be doing most of the talking. Now and then the inspector would slip in a question . . . 'What time would this be? . . .' '. . . and you informed him of this? . . .' '. . . is this the normal procedure? . . .' 'yes, I see. Right, I'll tell him.' Finally he said, 'Yes, I'd be glad if you would . . . yes, I'll do that certainly . . . sorry to have troubled you.'

He put the phone down and clasped his hands.

'Well, the doctor says he told you Miss Seal wasn't in a condition to receive visitors. He says that you got very excited and tried to break into her room . . . he also says that you were escorted to your car and that was all . . . he says that none of his staff laid a finger on you.'

'How would you describe a knee in the guts?' asked Nick. The inspector shrugged. 'Do you have any witnesses? Any cuts or bruises? Any other evidence?'

'No, I don't. So what are you going to do about Marianne. Are you just going to leave her there?'

The inspector spread his hands. 'Look, what can I do? It's not as if this lady was your wife. If Dr Stephen says you can't see her he's well within his rights. As it's a private clinic he could even say you were trespassing. He's got a very good reputation y'know. I can't go up there without a warrant and start kicking up a fuss on the evidence you've given me.'

Nick shouted, 'For Christ's sake! How d'you know what those bastards might be doing to her?'

'I'm sorry, squire,' the inspector said in tones of regret. 'Look, why don't you sleep on it, then you can go down there again tomorrow . . . and if you still have any trouble, let me know and I'll see what I can do.'

Nick said, 'Aah, shit!' He got up quickly and almost ran from the building.

The security of the closed car, the view of the glistening road in the swath of headlights, the comforting *burr burr* of the windscreen wipers, helped to assuage his raging desperation.

All the same, he could hardly believe it. How could he possibly be totally cut off, so entirely divorced from his Marianne, and in what he had come to regard as the world's most civilised country. His mind rotated rapidly through the personal, the social and political, Christ, how could this be happening to himself, Nick Kirkham, in a place like England?

He passed a number of pubs with glowing signs, with fairy lights strung across their façades and large inviting car parks, and the urge to stop at one of these and get stone blind pissed was only marginally overcome by his determination to stay stone cold sober.

It was just after nine when he reached the cottage. Putting the key in the door had once been habitual. Now he had to use his lighter to find the slot.

A dark shape darted towards him from the corner of the garage. As he flinched away, it bulged against his ankles.

'Oh my God,' said Nick. 'Bullnose.'

He picked up the tomcat, which vibrated like a dynamo, and held it against his cheek, realising with a surge of guilt that he had left the animal to fend for itself for the last ten days. Marianne would never forgive him. But when he entered the living-room and switched on the lights Bullnose, far from showing resentment, ran round him in small circles uttering deep-throated cries of pleasure.

'I'm sorry, Bullnose.' Nick patted the cat's emaciating flank. 'I am truly sorry.' He searched in the food cupboard, ignoring the conventional cat food, and emerged with a can of salmon and three of anchovies. He placed the contents of these on a plate in front of the ravening animal.

It was almost freezing in the living-room. Nick scraped away the dead embers in the hearth, replaced them with half a dozen logs, poured a couple of pints of kerosene on these, and threw a match on them. A sheet of flame roared up the chimney.

He sat down in front of the blaze, warming his hands and trying to think logically. How was he going to expose Dr Stephen? Perhaps he should complain to the British Medical Association . . . but he quickly rejected this idea. Dog does not eat dog. And he'd already discounted the idea of consulting a solicitor—he had a deep and instinctive distrust of lawyers and never went near one.

The newspapers seemed a better bet. As a magazine journalist Nick didn't come across too many newspaper men, but there was one he knew who worked for one of the lurid Sunday papers. He found his number and called him. His wife said, 'Sorry, Tim's in Brussels at the moment. He should be back tomorrow sometime. Can I take a message?'

'No, don't bother. I'll call again.'

He suddenly felt very tired and rather hungry. He realised he hadn't eaten all day, but didn't feel like cooking anything. He prowled into the kitchen to see if there was anything edible left in the fridge. At this moment the front doorbell shrilled.

Nick checked, then went back through the living-room and

opened the door. A man and woman stood there, hunched against the rain. The man, who had spiky blackish-grey hair, wore a tweed suit, and was somehow redolent of race-courses, spoke with a quietly pleasant Irish intonation.

'I'm sorry to bother youse at this time of night sorr, but the car's broken down and I wondered if you could lend us such a thing as a torch.'

The woman, who looked younger, with auburn hair emerging from a headscarf, gave a somewhat tired smile. 'We've got to get back to London tonight,' she said.

'I think I have one somewhere.' Nick went inside and fetched one from a drawer, tried it.

'Seems to work okay,' he said.

The Irishman said, 'I suppose you wouldn't know anything about cars? I'm no mechanic myself.'

'Where are you?'

'We're stuck right outside the gate. I can't get the thing started.'

'I know a little,' Nick said. In fact he probably knew less about cars, as he had often freely admitted, than almost anyone living. He followed them on to the grass verge outside where the car, a Volkswagon estate, had pulled off the road.

The Irishman raised the bonnet. 'Sure, I think the carburettor's flooded,' he said. 'Would ye give us a bit o' light on the subject.' Nick shone the torch on the engine, having no idea where the carburettor was.

'A bit further to the left.'

Something very hard smacked into Nick's temple, just above the eyes, and he blacked out instantly. As he fell against the radiator the Irishman grabbed him by the arms. The woman came round quickly from the passenger seat and together they lifted Nick on to a heap of blankets in the back of the vehicle.

The Irishman drew a six-inch bayonet from a scabbard inside his jacket, and forced it into Nick's body half a dozen times at carefully selected points. While he was doing this the woman ran quickly into the house, switched off the lights,

89

put the cat out, and locked the door. By the time she returned her companion had extracted everything from Nick's pockets and wrapped his body in half a dozen blankets. He gave her the keys of Nick's car. They drove off, the woman driving Nick's Cortina, following the Volkswagon. It had all happened in five minutes. Two hours later Nick's body, still wrapped in blankets, was buried under four feet of gravel at an abandoned sand works near Berkhamsted, seventy miles away.

About a fortnight after this event Nick's ageing Cortina, with a new coat of paint, a new log book, and a different number plate, appeared for sale on the forecourt of a garage in Golders Green at a saleable price. On the same day the Irishman, who was known in his profession as the Badger, picked up a suitcase from the Left Luggage office at Euston Station which contained £6,000 in five- and ten-pound notes.

This money had been drafted from a Munich bank to the account of Fox-Hillyer at Coutts in Fleet Street. The Badger neither knew, nor cared about this. On this occasion he had worked through an agent and had no idea who his real employers were.

He gave £1,500 of this money to his partner, known professionally as Mrs McCombe, who had now returned to her normal trade, high in a tower block in Whitechapel, where she rented a council flat. Her customers were a few selected gentlemen of means, all of them over fifty, who were looking for something a little different. She worked only during the hours of darkness, made a good living, paid no income tax, and drew unemployment benefit every Thursday.

Marianne knew now that she was pregnant. There was a slight but perceptible change in her body chemistry which suffused it with a new energy. She could feel it glowing in her veins, her whole body seemed to be stirring, readjusting itself in preparation for the challenge. Her principal reaction was not joy so much as relief; from the first day of her arrival at the clinic she was sure that she would conceive.

'Doctor Stephen is going to give you a couple of tests tomorrow,' said Alison cheerfully, 'and then we should know for sure.' She was filling a syringe at the table. 'What would you prefer, a boy or a girl?'

'I don't mind which.'

The nurse dabbed her wrist with a swab. 'My parents always wanted a boy. They were right disgusted when I turned up. I'm just going to give you a little jab so as you'll get a good night's sleep before the big day.'

'Alison, it's all right. I've been sleeping like a log.'

'Aye, I know, love, but we want to make sure.' She picked up the syringe and held Marianne's wrist, but the girl pulled it away. 'I'm sorry, but I'd rather not have an injection, thank you.'

The nurse looked uneasy. 'Dr Stephen said it's very import-ant to have a good rest, tonight of all nights. Come on, love, it won't hurt.'

Marianne was suddenly aware that her nerves were on edge. The other woman was beginning to frighten her.

'I don't want an injection, Alison, and I'm not going to have an injection.'

Alison sounded hurt. 'We're only trying to look after you, love. You do want a baby?'

'Yes,' said Marianne more calmly, 'but I don't want to be filled with drugs.'

'Aye well, I'd best go and see what the doctor's got to say.'

She went out, and seemed gone for a long time. Eventually, she returned with Dr Stephen, who was accompanied by Fox-Hillyer.

The gynaecologist looked drawn and haggard, his hair awry. 'Sister tells me you're refusing your injection.'

'Yes, I am.'

'It's just a mild sedative. I think it's advisable that you should have it.'

Paulson entered quietly, followed by the fierce-looking German. Marianne felt her skin prickle with fear.

'We've come rather a long way together,' said Stephen. 'Surely we're not going to spoil the ship for a ha'porth of tar?'

She tried to smile. 'Please. I'm perfectly all right.'

Fox-Hillyer said suavely, 'Don't you think Dr Stephen is the best judge of that?'

She gazed around her in a panic. 'I don't want an injection.'

Stephen said briskly, 'Well, all right. I shall respect your wishes. Gentlemen, I suggest we leave Miss Seal in peace.'

Fox-Hillyer came across and loomed over the bed, 'Miss Seal, I really think you ought to accept the doctor's advice. Please carry on Sister Ferry.'

Marianne cowered away, gazing imploringly at the nurse. Alison made no move. She glanced at the doctor. He shook his head. The German, standing just inside the door, watched the situation with keen interest.

Fox-Hillyer said, 'Are you defying my instructions?'

Stephen bowed his head. 'I have never given a patient treatment that she doesn't want and I am not going to start now.'

'Really?' Fox-Hillyer smiled. 'Are you sure about that? I must say it's rather a curious statement, coming from you. But of course I understand your reticence.' He nodded to Paulson. 'Right, carry on.'

Paulson picked up the syringe and held it up to the light. Marianne watched him, with rising horror.

Fox-Hillyer said, 'Or would you prefer Sister Ferry to administer the treatment? I'm sure she's much better at it.'

The doctor glanced at the nurse, signifying his agreement. He was pale and shaking with distress.

Sister Ferry took the syringe from Paulson and moved towards the terrified girl. 'Now come on, love,' she pleaded. 'Don't make such a fuss.'

Marianne slipped under the sheets and tugged them over her head. But within a few seconds her fingers were prised open by larger, more powerful hands, which ripped the sheets away, grasped her arms, and forced them back on the pillow.

92

'Are we going to be sensible, or not?' said the voice of Paulson, close to her ear.

She struggled and fought and bit, but in five minutes she was exhausted.

She gazed despairingly into the eyes of the doctor.

'Are you going to let them do it?' She was gasping and sobbing. Stephen turned away and said, almost inaudibly, 'I'm sorry, I have no choice.'

Alison inserted the needle into the wrist held firm by Paulson. She slipped almost instantly into unconsciousness.

IO

When she came to, Marianne was in a state of shock for some time, her mind refusing to acknowledge its recent experience.

She was drowsily aware of being in bed, in a confined space, of people appearing and disappearing, vague shapes in an indistinct landscape, a blur of voices.

Eventually, after a sustained period of sleep, she awoke in broad daylight and slowly and painfully began to return to a condition of full awareness.

She was lying in a steel-framed truckle bed, surrounded by the drab green walls of a tent. She looked around her, taking in the delineaments of the sparse furniture; a bare, scrubbed table mounted on trestles, a couple of tubular-steel canvas chairs, one or two packing cases from which clothing spilled, a metal wash-bowl, and, rather incongruously, a couple of car batteries wired to a small light bulb suspended from one of the tent poles. In the centre was a drip-feed stove fed by a four-gallon can of petrol.

Sounds began to infiltrate her consciousness—the plucking and tearing of the wind against the walls of the tent, the crying of sea birds, the distant roar of surf. The tent poles creaked. The interior was crossed with keen and biting draughts. She tucked her head inside the sheets away from the cold and the unfamiliar noises, and in the dark and comforting womb she found there, she at last compelled herself to think about the events of the recent past, and tried to come to terms with her situation.

She stayed in this position for well over an hour, repairing the last dregs of the trauma, rebuilding the confidence she required to cope with the future.

Finally she climbed out of bed, found her clothes, and dressed. She paused for a moment in front of the tent entrance, then pulled aside the flap and squeezed through. She stood outside, gazing round her in bewilderment.

She was standing in a broad, rock-strewn pasture, littered with the ruined blackhouse dwellings of former inhabitants. Beyond the glen the land flowed into a broadening saddle, rising at each end to a high summit wreathed in low cloud.

The sea stretched in every direction. Half a mile away a stac of rock rose 500 feet through boiling surf like a dirty wedding cake, encrusted with centuries of guano and serrated with the nesting ledges of the gannets which swarmed around it. Beyond this a distant, loaf-shaped land mass appeared through the haze.

It was the bleakest, most hostile landscape she had seen. The wind tore at her in savage gusts. She braced herself against it and began to walk across the glen. As she surmounted a small rise she noticed two more tents, but of a smaller, ridge type, pitched close to the crumbling ruin of a drystone barn. As she got closer Marianne saw a bulky figure moving behind the shelter of the walls, and with a sick jolt of recognition she recognised Alison Ferry.

Marianne walked up unseen behind the nursing sister, who was busily working on field kitchen equipment in a corner of the building, sheltered from the prevailing wind. She stopped a yard behind her. 'Alison, why have I been brought here?'

The sister looked round quickly, but showed no surprise.

'Don't ask me, love, I'm not the oracle.' She continued with the cooking, breaking eggs into a sizzling pan.

Marianne moved behind her, and swung her round by the shoulders.

'Don't tell me it's nothing to do with you. Why did you give me that injection?'

The other woman tried to look unconcerned. 'I thought it were the best thing . . .' She moved away and began to carve slices from a loaf of bread.

95

Marianne followed her. She confronted her once more and gave her a stinging slap across the cheek.

Alison winced. Her features coloured. A hand strayed to the place where the blow had landed. Then she said, 'Aye well, if that's the way you feel, best to get rid of it.'

Marianne heard a noise behind her and turned to see Dr Stephen emerging from one of the nearby tents. He looked incongruous, wearing tight blue jeans and a fisherman's sweater. He started to say, 'Miss Seal, I think perhaps I ought to say, on Sister Ferry's behalf . . .' But he was cut off in mid-sentence from thirty yards away, by a louder and much more authoritative voice.

'Ah, so we're up and about and taking notice, are we?'

Marianne saw Paulson walking briskly towards them. He was wearing a military combat jacket with a green beret perched at a rakish angle on his head. A .300 Garrand carbine was slung across his shoulders. He was followed at a few yards distance by the grinning chauffeur.

Paulson came to a crisp halt a few feet in front of Marianne. The chauffeur tried to emulate him, but slithered on a wet rock and nearly went over.

'Right!' The small mouth wrinkled into a smirk as Paulson relaxed his body. 'Now we're all here together we might as well have a few words. I don't think we need to stand on ceremony—you have my permission to smoke if you like.' He produced a small black cigar from his pocket and lit it, wagged it up and down in his mouth. He clasped his hands behind him and began to prowl up and down in front of them, drawing occasionally on the cigar.

'First of all, let me put you in the picture. You are now on the island of Ahd Skeir, somewhere in the Outer Hebrides. The island covers some two hundred acres and is dominated by two heights. . . .' He gestured. . . . 'On your left, Muttach Rial . . . and on your right, Sennay. Oh, by the way, the piece in the middle is known as Gleann Chillidh. The island is entirely cliffbound, and can only be approached from the sea from one small inlet . . . down there . . . which I regret to say is out of bounds. If there are any strong swimmers amongst us, I would like to point out that the nearest land is over a mile away'—he pointed to the loaf-shaped peninsula—'and the sea around here has a very strong tidal race, just in case anyone starts getting fancy ideas.

'Right, now we're all going to have to stay here for quite a while, so let's get one or two things straight. I am in charge of the island, and I expect my instructions to be strictly obeyed. I've marked out two compounds, one for Miss Seal here, and the other for the doctor and Sister Ferry. None of these personnel will move outside these compounds, which you will find clearly marked with white-painted bands on the rocks. Miss Seal will not be allowed to talk to Dr Stephen or Sister Ferry, except in the line of duty. Dr Stephen will act as medical officer, and Sister Ferry will be chief cook and bottle-washer. My assistant here, name of Nelson, will assist me in the running of the camp.

'The day will start at eight o'clock each morning, and three days a week I will organise an exercise period just to keep us on our toes. Miss Seal will be excused from all exercise periods. I'll expect everyone to be in bed by ten-thirty. Any questions?'

He glanced around. There was no response.

The leathery face relaxed a little. 'Right then. There's no reason why we shouldn't enjoy ourselves . . . there's no reason why it shouldn't be like one long holiday. You play the game with me, and I'll play the game with you. If you try to step out of line, you'll find I'm a very bad enemy . . . I'd much rather be a very good friend.'

He turned abruptly and strode away. The chauffeur fell in behind. Paulson stopped when he had gone fifty yards and called out, 'Right, come on Miss Seal, get back to your area.'

She glanced to Stephen for support. He said quietly, 'All right, my dear, I think you'd better go. Try not to worry too much.'

She walked back towards her tent. As she reached Paulson she said, 'Why have you brought me here?'

He grinned down at her. 'Ask no questions and you'll hear no lies. There's nothing for you to worry about, you're a very special guest. Oh yes, you're the queen bee, you are. You're going to be looked after like a piece of porcelain china, believe you me . . . long as you behave yourself.'

'You've got no authority over me.' Her voice trembled.

'We shall 'ave to see about that, won't we.'

She spent the rest of that day, and the two or three which followed, exploring her situation.

She found that a compound had been marked out with white dabs of paint on the rocks, surrounding her tent and covering some five acres of the glen. A similar locality had been allocated to Dr Stephen and Alison, but the two areas were separated by some fifty yards of no-man's-land. At a further hundred yards distance a tent occupied by Paulson and the chauffeur was strategically placed to afford a view across the whole of the glen.

Events quickly fell into a familiar routine. At eight o'clock she was woken by Paulson banging an iron bucket with a ladle outside the tent. Half an hour later the chauffeur would come into the tent and light the stove, bringing a can of hot water. At nine—by which time she was expected to be up and dressed—he would return with breakfast on tin plates and a flask of coffee. Other meals, cooked by Alison, were served at one o'clock, and seven in the evening.

The chauffeur, Nelson Burr, had obviously been delegated to watch her constantly. He was not much more than a youth, short and squat, with a fuzz of black hair wisping around his ears. He was never more than twenty yards from the tent when she was inside, and when she walked around the compound he always followed her at a respectful distance.

On the second day she watched him as he placed the supper meal on the table, and picked up the plates she had used for lunch. She asked, 'Nelson, how long do you think we're going to be here?'

He seemed embarrassed by her scrutiny. The thick lips parted in a sheepish, lopsided grin.

98

'Don't ask me,' he said. 'They don't tell me nuffink. I just do as I'm told.'

Gradually a chilling certainty lodged itself in her mind—that somehow her pregnancy was directly linked to her incarceration on this island.

The only crumb of comfort was that Dr Stephen and Alison Ferry were also prisoners. Although she was unable to communicate with them, they were allies. Yet she knew she would never forgive the nursing sister for her part in the kidnapping. The treachery seemed so much worse through being enacted by another woman.

Most agonisingly of all, she thought almost constantly about Nick, who now seemed a world apart, wondering what he would do when he found she was no longer at the clinic. She could hardly believe that he would abandon her, simply because she was carrying his child. Yet during the last week at the clinic he hadn't been in touch. . . .

The tall Englishman checked in at the best hotel in Tarbert on the island of Harris at 11.35 on the morning of 21 April, and asked for a room to be placed at his disposal for the next eight months.

He was, as he explained to the manager, writing a book on the Outer Hebrides, and he wanted to establish the hotel as a headquarters for his field research.

It was not particularly convenient, particularly as the visitor selected the best room in the hotel, which was already fully booked until the autumn. Yet the manager readily acquiesced, not simply because Fox-Hillyer was a man whose easy assumption of authority made him difficult to refuse, but also because he proffered a letter of introduction from an old friend, Major-General Sir Colin McGregor. The general was a major landowner in the area, and the hotel was among his many properties.

Fox-Hillyer took a light lunch in the restaurant, washed it down with a glass of Glenfiddich whisky, then climbed into his Range Rover and drove along the coast road to the south.

A mile past the tiny hamlet of Bovermore he pulled off the road, and followed a steep, narrow track down to a small disused quarry.

There was a short-wave radio under the passenger seat. Fox-Hillyer connected the aerial, switched on the microphone, and spoke into it.

'Sunray to Pima. Are you receiving me?'

He repeated the question three times before Paulson, sitting in his tent on Ahd Skeir two miles away, replied.

'Pima to Sunray. I am receiving you.'

'What's your situation? Settling in all right?'

'We're not complaining, sir. No serious problems so far.'

'How is your niece, Susan. Is she enjoying herself?'

'Yes, sir, she's fine. Having the time of her life.'

'Right. This time next week I'll bring down some fresh food supplies for you to collect, and some more petrol. Anything else you need?'

'We could do with another bottle of calor gas, sir. Oh, and there's just one other thing. It tends to get pretty cold at night time. I thought perhaps the occasional tot of rum might cheer us up a bit.'

'No, I'm afraid not,' he said brusquely. 'I will not permit alcohol on the island under any circumstances. You'll just have to get used to the idea—it won't do you any harm.'

'Very good, sir.'

'Right, anything else?'

'Not that I can think of for the moment.'

'Good. I'll see you next week. Over and out.'

In the summer the rats thrived on the rocky outcrops of Ahd Skeir among the burrows of the puffins and shearwaters, feeding on the eggs and young of the nesting birds. Over the course of the seven-month winter, when the birds were absent, the rats came near to starvation, surviving only on guano, the small amount of carrion available, and by cannibalising their own young.

Now, for the first time in years, the skeletal hordes slinking among the rocks of Muttach Rial caught the whiff of cooking smells drifting up from Gleann Chillidh.

All through the day they gathered, rival colonies running and nuzzling together.

It was Marianne's third night on the island. As she drifted uneasily in and out of sleep, she became aware of the squeaking and rustling. She turned on the small light fed by the car batteries, and sat upright in the bed. There were at least a dozen rats in the tent, gaunt, reddish brown, moving across the floor in quick darting runs.

She tried to remain calm, struggling out of her sleeping bag, pulling an anorak over her pyjamas, rapidly putting on her boots, but she was compelled to cry out when a furry body brushed against her ankle. She heard Alison shrieking hysterically from a distance.

As she stumbled out into the open the dawn was breaking. Paulson came out of the half-light rubbing his eyes. 'What's going on?'

He moved on quickly towards the barn. Nelson Burr ran over and followed him. Marianne could see rats running about all over the uneven ground. They seemed to grow in numbers as she picked her way fearfully across to where the others were gathered.

Hundreds of rats were running around the tented area. Most of them had found the food store, just inside the shelter of the barn. A heaving torrent of emaciated rat bodies, some of them half bald, or with patches of mange, were tearing at the sacks of potatoes, bags of rice, packets of lard. They seemed totally impervious to the human presence.

Marianne joined Dr Stephen and Alison, standing beside the tents, as Paulson appeared from behind the barn with a sharp-pronged gardening fork. Nelson Burr followed, brandishing a spade. They quickly began their task.

Paulson jabbed savagely at the squealing horde, spearing two or three at a time, and pushing the bodies from the prongs with his boot. The chauffeur stood beside him, whacking down on the animals which were still arriving for the feast;

sometimes he would jab down with the sharp edge of the spade, severing heads from bodies.

After some fifteen minutes of this the two men were nearly exhausted, but still the rats swarmed through the barn. Paulson stopped and stepped back. There were three rats clinging to his flak jacket. He knocked them off and crushed them with his boot. 'Hang on a minute,' he said. He laid down the fork, and grabbed a half-hundredweight sack of potatoes. 'Grab another of these,' he shouted to Burr, as he knocked away half a dozen rats from the sack—the inside was bulging with them.

Paulson ran with the sack and put it down in the open some fifteen yards away. Burr placed another beside it.

They stood watching as most of the rats in the area converged on the potatoes and tore the sacks to pieces. After some five minutes Paulson said, 'Right, you've had your fun!' He went and fetched two or three gallon cans of petrol. Together they began to spray the petrol over the rats which swarmed over the potato sacks.

'Stand clear!' Paulson, from a few yards distance, lit a match and tossed it. The petrol ignited at once with an echoing *flaammp*. More than a score of blazing rats leaped from the sacks, jumping in the air, squealing with frenzy. Marianne turned away, distraught. She saw Dr Stephen pick up a rock and attempt to put some of the animals out of their misery as they hopped and skipped around him.

Paulson and Burr returned to the barn and began hacking and stabbing at the survivors. In another ten minutes it was nearly all over. The area surrounding the shelter was littered with scores of dead and twitching rodents.

The occasion had generated a great excitement in Paulson and the chauffeur. They moved quickly around the camp, lifting slabs of rock to seek out refugees. For some time after Marianne returned to bed she could hear them moving around, clubbing and chopping and yelling with laughter.

I I

'They've certainly tightened up security at the airport,' said Victor Greb, who had arrived twenty minutes earlier from Munich for a conference at Parlane Close. 'Some guy in front of me had an orange in his overnight bag. They stuck something like a tuning fork in it, wired to a box of electronics the officer was wearing on his shoulder. The thing gave out a kind of high-pitched whine. I was just about to dive for cover, but they let him through . . . negative, I guess.'

Coulman walked about fretfully, wanting to get on with it. 'Barry should be here any second,' he said. 'It's murder trying to find somewhere to park around here.'

Greb sat down at Coulman's desk and spread *The Times* across it. There were reports of bombings in Birmingham and Manchester. 'It could be Reisener has gone over to the IRA,' he wryly observed.

'I have a theory,' said Coulman, 'that if there isn't a regular war in progress, some people have to exercise their natural talents in other directions.'

'That's right,' said Greb. 'Maybe we should have kept Vietnam going, but thrown it open to the general public.'

'That's a great idea,' Coulman agreed. 'There must be at least a million psychotics dying of sheer frustration.'

Eckstein came in, sucking at his pipe. 'Sorry, I had a puncture. Vic, nice to see you again.'

Greb, a stocky, hirsute man, who looked more like a trawler skipper than an intelligence agent, wagged a hand. Coulman perched on the arm of a setttee and squashed his butt in a rose bowl adapted for that purpose. He switched on the tape.

'We may as well get started. Barry, I haven't told Vic about the latest developments over here, so you may as well run through them again. By the way I'll be flying to Tel Aviv tomorrow for a security conference. I'll give them all the dope we've got so far, and ask for further instructions, okay?'

Eckstein said, 'Right.' He glanced across at Greb. 'Last Tuesday, the good Dr Stephen called all his staff together and told them his lease for the clinic was up for renewal at a highly increased rent, so he was obliged to close down and he was giving them all a month's notice. He hinted that the place had been losing money for some time, which was something of a surprise, because everybody thought it was making a bomb.

'The next morning Dr Stephen left the place and nobody seems to know where to find him. At the same time Reisener and Fox-Hillyer also disappeared, with the security guy, Paulson, and a nursing sister called Ferry who is Stephen's right-hand woman.'

Eckstein fiddled with his pipe. He looked like an earnest, overgrown student. 'There's a guy on the staff I know—he works in the massage parlour. I had a beer with him Wednesday evening. He was still trying to believe it. He said they were all paid off inside an hour and told to leave the premises within a week. There aren't any patients left, and the property is now in the hands of a firm of London solicitors acting on behalf of the owners.

'I gave them a call pretending I was interested and asked where I could contact Stephen, but they said as far as they knew he'd taken a long holiday abroad—but they didn't know where. They also said they were as surprised as anyone when the clinic closed down. The lease still had another two years to run and the next term hadn't been negotiated.'

Greb stretched a hand under his jacket to scratch an armpit, without relaxing his frown of concentration.

'I wouldn't know how material this is but the last patient to leave was a woman called Marianne Seal. She was having treatment for infertility. I happened to come across her once, while strolling in the grounds.'

'Good looker?' asked Greb.

'She wasn't exactly ugly. I had a few words with her, then Paulson appeared from somewhere and broke it up—that guy is exceptionally ugly.

'I had an idea the girl was on dope.'

'That's not unusual,' said Coulman, 'in a clinic.'

'Sure. But the interesting thing is, she disappeared from the place at roughly the same time as the others. Also I managed to get her address. I told the masseur I fancied her and he kindly copied it for me from the office records. She lives at a place called Broxfield—a small village in Essex. I've just come from there and she's not at home—the place is locked up.'

Greb said, 'Maybe they transferred her to another clinic.'

'Could be. Also she was living with a boy friend—an American apparently. He hasn't been seen around for a while, either.'

'We could try the embassy,' said Greb 'Did you get his name?'

'He was known as Nick. Nobody knew his other name. I asked around the village long and loud, even in the post office.'

'You mean nobody ever wrote to this Nick?'

'Could be. Or maybe they were clamming up on me in case I was from some debt collection agency.

'Another thing—while I was in the village I found out that this Marianne was a social worker for the county council, so I called her department and asked to speak to her. They told me she was having a baby and had been given indefinite leave of absence.'

'Which tells us what?' asked Coulman.

'Not much, except that she was in the clinic having fertility treatment. So it must have worked.'

'Anything else?'

'Just the obvious one—that whatever was going on down there, somebody blew it, so they had to get out fast.'

'Okay, let's keep that on ice for the time being.'

Greb had walked across to study a portrait in oils by Soutine, one of Durandt's more recent purchases. The features were those of a diseased potato, the limbs grotesquely twisted. Greb seemed to be trying hard to assimilate the quality of the work. A hand fondled the bald patch on his skull, the size of a saucer.

Eckstein asked, 'Does that grab you?'

Greb said, 'I'm not quite sure. I used to think a perverse nature was a handicap.'

'About Fox-Hillyer,' said Coulman, anxious to return to more important matters. 'I have a contact in the British Secret Intelligence Service, Peter Kerridge. We swap information occasionally. He knows quite a lot about the guy already. He reckons that any time there is an attempt at a right-wing takeover, Fox-Hillyer is going to be found somewhere in the middle.

'Until about eight years ago, he was a Brigadier in the British Army with the appointment of director of tactical studies at the Staff College, Camberley. He had a reputation as a whizz kid and an advanced military thinker, particularly with regard to urban warfare.'

'A man before his time?' asked Greb.

'Could be. Anyway, around this time he wrote a pamphlet which advocated the use of the military to oppose industrial action—how to keep the docks and railways going on an emergency basis. He suggested that chief constables of police should be given the rank of temporary colonel in a national emergency, and empowered to call up reservists on the spot to break up picket lines and control civil disturbances.

'This document was circulated among senior officers but somebody leaked it to the trade unions. There was a Labour government in power and it didn't go down too well with the politicians when they got to hear about it from the wrong end. Fox-Hillyer maintained that it was simply an academic study—a basis for discussion. But he was shifted to another post and advised to keep his mouth shut in future. He left the army in the following year.

'Since then we don't know a lot about him except he's written a couple of books including the whitewash job on the Nazis I've just read it, and it's a lot more persuasive than you'd imagine. He saw Hitler as a political genius who made the mistake of interfering with his generals—he claims the same could be said of Churchill.'

Greb considered the point seriously. 'I don't think I'd dispute that.'

Eckstein pointed out, 'Right, but Churchill had allies, and Hitler had no opposition.'

'I wouldn't dispute that either,' said Greb.

'Apart from that,' Coulman continued, 'Fox-Hillyer was called in as military adviser to the Biafrans during the Nigerian Civil War.'

'He picked the loser that time,' said Greb.

'Sure, but he wrote a book about that as well and made a couple of interesting points. For instance he says that Biafra was all about possession of oil, and that the future control of diminishing mineral resources is about to succeed religion and political ideology as the major catalyst for armed conflict.'

'Which means it could happen just about everywhere?' Greb said.

'You name it.' Coulman flicked through his notebook. 'He's still highly regarded in military circles, and his lectures at Camberley are still legendary. There's no evidence he's ever been involved in extreme right-wing politics, but he once wrote a newspaper article in which he said there was a case for a strong political party to the right of the Conservatives—but nobody was going to have faith in political leaders who scrawled rude words on synagogues and lifted ladies' underwear from department stores.'

'That sounds like the National Front,' said Eckstein.

Angela Stringer had provided a vase full of fresh Scilly Island narcissi for Coulman's desk and Eckstein lifted one out, sniffed at it, and put it back. Its orange centre made a sharp contrast against the white petals. He was disappointed that the flower had no perceptible scent. It had been bred purely for the visual effect. In twenty years' time, he thought, the only smells would be bad ones.

He watched Coulman reverse the tape. Now here was a man who was properly organised. At the end of the conference he would carefully annotate the spool and lock it in the wall safe—his only filing cabinet. And no doubt he would play it again to himself, perhaps in the small hours when he couldn't sleep, along with the others in the series, trying to complete another small section of the picture. Coulman would have made quite a powerful civil servant, if only he could have got rid of his romanticism.

However—Eckstein's thoughts ran on—screw the personalities—in what direction do the established facts tend to lean.

But there was one personality he couldn't tuck into the recesses of his mind, the girl Marianne. He was stuck with the image of that wan face looking up at him from the goldfish pool. She had looked lonely and vulnerable. Somehow he was convinced that she had got herself innocently involved in whatever particular brand of unpleasantness had been going on down there.

But Coulman was clearly not diverted by such irrelevancies. 'I've been doing some digging on the Paulson character,' he continued crisply. 'He runs a private detective agency called Apex Inquiry Services which is located in the Islington area. He's got about four detectives working for him. They do a bit of the usual stuff, divorce, missing people—and also, it would seem, a bit of the strong-arm stuff. There used to be another detective on the staff, but he's serving a couple of years for grievous bodily harm. They're also involved in politics. They were prosecuted a year ago for trying to bug a trade union executive meeting, and refused to name the client. They got away with a fine.

'It's a registered company, so I checked the register. The share capital is owned fifty-fifty by Paulson and Fox-Hillyer. The only other connection I can find between these two is that Paulson was in the army at the same time, as a regimental sergeant-major in the military police.

'He was in some trouble in Cyprus during the EOKA campaign. He was accused of torturing suspects but he was cleared by an inquiry. It made the newspapers at the time.'

'Who was on the board of inquiry?' asked Eckstein.

'Army officers, I guess.' Eckstein smiled at this.

'Fox-Hillyer was also serving in Cyprus at around that period but that's about as near as I can get to a tie-up.'

Greb said, 'You're suggesting that Fox-Hillyer got to know Paulson while they were in the army together, and liked his style, so he staked him when he came out. Is that it?'

'Well, that did occur to me, Vic, so if it also occurs to you, it must be a reasonable supposition.'

There was a small hiatus, then Coulman spoke into the intercom. 'Angela, my angel, if you could rustle up some coffee for us philistines up here . . . and hey, thanks for the flowers.' He stood up, stretching himself, and nodded to Greb. 'Can we have your stuff now?'

'Sure.' Greb came across and sat beside the desk. He took a small notebook from his pocket and riffled through it, as if uncertain where to begin.

'We may as well start with Johannes Ludwig Steffen, alias Dr Stephen,' he said eventually.

'While on the subject of personal backgrounds, you may believe that Big Brother is not too far away from New Jersey these days. Well, you can take it from me that the krauts can leave us cold in the computer research stakes.

'There's a firm called Kredit Vermögen with branches all over Germany. All you need is an address or a car registration number—they don't even ask for the name. Within five days they will send you a copy of the subject's latest bank statement and his stockholdings, the date of his birth, marriages, divorces, trade or profession, education qualifications, military record if any, and convictions down to the last driving offence. They are not cheap, but they are undeniably efficient. So,' he glanced again at his notebook, 'Steffen was born at Osnabruck on June 5 1910. He studied medicine at Leipzig and qualified in 1936, but stayed on for another three years studying endocrinology. One of his tutors was a Professor Heinrich Buechner who was a well-known medical scientist of the time—he had his own research unit attached to the medical school.

'Steffen must have been pretty useful because he was appointed the professor's principal research assistant when Buechner established a new research centre at Magdeburg.

'I haven't been able to establish exactly what Buechner was working on during this particular period, but he was principally known for his work on infertility in women and he had an international reputation in that field. But the Nazis must have thought that what he was doing was important because he was allowed to carry on all through the war and Steffen was never drafted.'

'He could have been unfit for military service,' Eckstein suggested.

'Right. But by the end of the war the Nazis needed so many doctors at the front, they were calling up the over-seventies with wooden legs.'

'Point taken.'

Greb gave a slight nod and a grin. 'However. A year after the war, in '46, Steffen was back in Osnabruck working as a gynaecologist in a military hospital there. But in '48, he turns up in England, and five years later becomes a British subject.'

Eckstein's mind was ticking over furiously. 'You said this professor specialised in fertility techniques—and Steffen was his assistant?'

'That's right. I thought you'd pick that up. I did, too. So I spent some time working on his background. I asked a couple of contacts in Frankfurt if they could turn up anything there, and one of them recalled that just after the end of the war Buechner was accused of being involved with the Nazis in some kind of genetic engineering.'

Coulman began to prowl around the room. He was listening intently.

'So I turned up the records of the Allied War Crimes Commission on the Nuremberg trials—the CIA have them on file over there and they were happy for me to take a look. Buechner didn't appear at Nuremberg, but he was listed as a defendant at the preliminary hearings at Bad Mondorf in Luxemburg. I found a verbatim record of his investigation over there and I have it on microfilm if you want to look at it in detail.

'It seems that Buechner was charged with collaborating with the S.S. in experiments on the inmates of Ravensbruck. In particular he was accused of taking part in sterility experiments on twenty-four Jewish women who were sent from Ravensbruck to Magdeburg.

'Buechner strongly denied this. He claimed that he had accepted the women, and pretended to co-operate, in order to try to save their lives. I have the judgement of the tribunal here. I'll read it.'

Greb produced a roll of microfilm from his pocket. He put on a pair of steel-rimmed spectacles in order to read it. With a skull cap, Eckstein thought, he would have passed easily for a rabbinical lawyer.

'This is what it says. "In the opinion of the tribunal the defendant's avowal—that he merely pretended to collaborate with Clauberg in order to preserve the lives of the women who were placed in his custody—is not convincing. The supporting evidence of his junior colleague, Dr Steffen, is invalid, since Dr Steffen would himself have been a party to any criminal act practised by his chief in this respect. We consider that Professor Buechner's response to Clauberg's suggestion that he should participate in these appalling and inhuman experiments should have been an absolute negative.

' "While there is no direct evidence that the defendant did in fact experiment on these women, there is also no evidence to the contrary, since those who might have shed more light on the situation are dead.

' "The verdict of this tribunal is accordingly that Professor Buechner has been proved guilty, at least of serious professional misconduct.

' "We have taken into account the defendant's distinguished career and past achievements, and we recognise the intense pressure he must have been subjected to by the Nazi regime.

' "We therefore recommend that the defendant shall be discharged by this tribunal with the following proviso : that he has shown himself under pressure of being incapable of sustaining the highest standards of integrity necessary for the pursuit of medical research, standards which are more important than the life of the individual. We direct that this conclusion of the tribunal shall be circulated to all universities and medical foundations in Germany and to the German medical authorities when these bodies are reconstituted under the Allied Control Commission." '

Greb said, 'It's signed, R.K.W. Harley, Wing Commander, Royal Air Force, Chairman.' He carefully tucked the document back in his pocket.

Eckstein inquired, 'This professor. Is he still around?'

'I'll give you the rest of the stuff,' said Greb, 'then you can come back.' There was a perceptible note of triumph in his voice.

'First of all, as you guys may have noticed, I've been keeping an eye on Reisener's place for quite some time. I've checked on all his visitors and I've established the identities of most of them. They're mostly either industrial barons, or right-wing politicians. Then there were a few other casual visitors who seemed to have no real connection, but I checked on them just the same. When I came across this stuff about the professor I recalled that one of these casual visitors to Reisener's place was called Rudolf Buechner. It's a fairly common name in Germany, but I checked anyway, and sure enough it turns out that Rudolf is the professor's son. So I back-tracked on Rudolf—he's an industrial chemist by the way, nowhere in the Reisener class. Well, it seems that Rudolf moved his family into a house in Munich three weeks ago and is working at Reisener's plant, *Münchener Elektronishe Montage.*'

He checked his notebook again.

'Right, let me answer Barry's question. After the war Professor Buechner was forced to give up his scientific research because of the tribunal's report. He went back to private practice in Frankfurt until he retired in 1969. He died about six months ago.

'So if we check through the dates, it goes something like this.

'On November 7 of '73 the professor dies, okay? Then on November 25 his son Rudolf makes his first visit to Reisener. He makes two other visits during the next month, and three more in January.

'On March 3 Reisener flies to London, and meets up with Fox-Hillyer, a known British right-winger. They pay a visit to Dr Stephen, the professor's late assistant, taking a mobile deep-freeze cabinet with them, and stay around for a while. We all know what's happened since then.

'Hey, something I almost forgot to mention. Reisener's back in Munich. I passed him in the airport lounge on the way over.'

12

'You wouldn't believe it,' said Nelson Burr, 'but me and my old man used to be quids in . . . used to go to football matches, fishin' down the canal, always 'avin' a laugh and a joke . . . that was until I was fourteen.'

'What happened then?' asked Marianne.

They were sprawling, a yard apart, in the lee of a rocky slope. Not far above them wisps of greyish cloud drifted across a mackerel sky.

'Well, I just couldn't stand school, I suppose, and the old man was dead keen on it. He always used to say that I was clever enough, but I was too bloody lazy to put my mind to it. He told me once that if I passed for university 'e'd give me ten gold sovereigns that 'is grandfather 'ad left 'im.'

'That would have been worth quite a lot.'

'Yeh, but I wasn't interested. I just wanted to leave school and get a job in a garage. I was dead keen on motors . . . always 'ave been. I used to stay away from school for days on end. The teachers never used to bother, they were only too glad I wasn't there makin' their lives a misery.

'Anyway, when I was fourteen I nicked a motor-bike and rode it all the way to Brighton. They stuck me on probation for two years. The old man did 'is tank over that.'

'Why did you take it?'

'What, the motor-bike? I just wanted to see if I could 'andle it. I could an' all. I was doin' eighty down the dual carriageway when they picked me up.'

'What did your mother think about it?'

'She kicked up a bit of a fuss, but she was always on my

side against the old man, funnily enough. Every time 'e used to start carryin' on, she used to say, "You're always gettin' on to 'im. Why don't you leave 'im alone?" '

'What did your father do for a living?'

'Used to work in a factory that made pork pies and sausage rolls and stuff. Supervisor, 'e was. Anyway, I left school when I was fifteen, and after that I was on the dole for a bit. Then I started workin' in a sugar ware'ouse, but there was a charge hand there who was always breathin' down my neck . . . why didn't you do this, why didn't you do that . . . so eventually I thumped 'im and broke 'is jaw. I got a suspended sentence for that.'

Marianne had now been a month on the island and was getting accustomed to her situation.

Her strongest urge was to escape, but she knew that until she saw an opportunity her best chance lay in pretending to acquiesce, as if she had become resigned to her plight.

Once she had heard Paulson talking to someone over a short wave radio, and she strongly suspected that the operation on the island was being organised from the mainland.

Each week he went across to the mainland in the Gemini—the big rubber dinghy with an outboard motor which was their only means of contact with the world outside—and collected fresh supplies. On one of these trips he had brought her back half a dozen paperbacks to read. From the choice of authors—Jane Austen, Graham Greene, James Baldwin—she guessed that the selection had been made by a more refined intellect than Paulson's.

She had no hope of winning over Paulson, and felt afraid of him. She saw very little of Dr Stephen and Alison, who kept strictly to their compound. The chauffeur, Nelson Burr, seemed a more promising prospect. He treated his assignment seriously, and followed her around everywhere, almost like a faithful dog.

She had begun to communicate with him, a little at a time, not pushing it, trying to gain his confidence, whittle away at the tensions of their forced relationship.

Now, for the first time, he had begun to talk freely about his background. She recalled a precept from her early training as a social worker: *Try to get them talking about themselves, and never make a moral judgement.*

He stretched himself in a brief shaft of sunlight, cupped his chin in his hands.

'After that I 'ad two or three other jobs, then I saved enough to buy myself a Triumph Bonneville, and joined the Hell's Angels.' He grinned to himself at the recollection.

'Really? Did you enjoy that?'

'Yeh, it was really great. It was only a small chapter, about sixteen of us, but some of the lads could really motor.

'Some o' the things we used to get up to . . . whippin' up the drive o' some big palatial country place at two o'clock in the morning, beltin' up and down outside. . . .

'I remember once we went to one of these village fêtes. There was this brass band comin' straight down the high street, blarin' away, and we went straight through the middle of 'em. They scattered in all directions . . . you should've seen 'em.'

'That must have been a bit dangerous.'

'Yeh, it was for them. We was doin' about seventy.'

He paused, reflecting.

'Oh yeh, they were all dead scared of us. Even the fuzz wouldn't take us on.

'Another time we went down to Tottenham. There was a bunch o' lads there reckoned they was lookin' for us. They found us all right, round the back o' the Odeon car park. We dusted 'em off good and proper, stuck four of 'em in the casualty ward. The only trouble was, one of 'em caught me across the 'ead with a razor. I still got the scar.'

He traced it, a long, thin crack just below the hairline, with a rueful finger.

'Course, when I got 'ome I was covered in blood. The old lady was waitin' up for me, about four in the mornin' this was. Well, she started to bathe my 'ead, and then the old man came down from the bedroom, shoutin' and 'ollerin', tryin' to lay down the law. He reckoned if I didn't leave the Angels 'e was going to kick me out.'

'What did you say?'

'I told 'im to get stuffed.'

Marianne was becoming aware of the remote and savage beauty of her surroundings. And she had never before been so strongly aware of the birds.

It was now the height of the nesting season. On the ledges of the stac the gannets flapped and fluttered restlessly among the serried ranks of nests. Overhead the gulls and kittiwakes cried perpetually, wheeling in the air currents. Sometimes a great black-backed gull would swoop low over the camp with a harsh cackle of protest.

The gannets moved purposefully through the swirling gulls, often in geese formation, on their way to more distant fishing grounds. Frequently, a lone gannet would plunge vertically, from a hundred feet, into the water.

The sea around the island bobbled with puffins, razorbills, guillemots. At dusk the shearwaters returned, scudding low across the wave crests.

The whole place belonged to the birds. Marianne felt herself an intruder.

Except in one small, but important respect. Like the birds, she was also deeply involved in the process of reproduction.

'Anyway,' said Nelson Burr, 'about a week after that the old man upped and offed without a word to anyone—just disappeared. 'E didn't send any money either, so I had to support the old lady.'

'What happened to your father? Did you find him?'

'Yeh. About six months afterwards I saw him on a traffic island down Shepherd's Bush way. So I follered 'im back to where he was livin', and found 'e'd taken up with another woman. I never thought 'e'd got it in 'im. I'd left the Angels by this time, but it didn't make any difference. 'E still wouldn't come back.'

'Why did you leave the Hell's Angels?' asked Marianne.

Nelson lit a cigarette and drew hard on it as he pondered this question.

'I got cheesed off with it in the finish. It was all over a chick. In the Angels there's two sorts of chicks, those that belong to everybody, and the ones that belong to one special bloke. If you belong to one special bloke you're not allowed to go with anyone else in the chapter. Well, one of 'em did . . . Sandie, they called 'er.'

'What happened to her?'

'Well, they knew she couldn't swim, see, so they took her down to the Grand Union Canal one night, tied a rope under 'er armpits, and chucked 'er in. Every time she went under they pulled 'er out, then slung 'er back in again. Five times they did that, then she passed out and they left 'er on the bank. Well, she 'appened to be my special chick—but I don't think they should 'ave done that to 'er. She's been on drugs ever since.'

Marianne shuddered inwardly at the mindless cruelty of this. Yet beneath the bland account of the episode she sensed an undertone of guilt, as if Nelson wanted to alleviate his conscience by describing it.

'Didn't you try to help her?'

'No-o.' He smiled at the naïvety of the question. 'They'd 'ave carved me up, wouldn't they?'

Then he said, 'I did go back about 'alf an hour later but somebody else 'ad found 'er and taken 'er 'ome.'

Being listened to with sympathetic interest by a woman was something new in the experience of Nelson Burr; and even more so when the woman was someone like Marianne.

He recognised that she functioned in a realm above his head. Yet he knew that the reactions from her voice and eyes were genuine. She was really interested in what he had to say, even though she was his prisoner, which ought to make her despise him. He had never really talked to a woman before, not even his mother.

His former experiences with women had been almost exclusively with sharp-eyed teenagers out for kicks, his sex life fragmentary and without affection, confined to hedges and the back seats of cars.

Except the occasion he had once screwed a woman of fifty in a Reading hotel for a fiver and his booze for the evening. That was in a bed, and he had reflected at the time that there was one thing women of all generations had in common—between their legs.

Once or twice he had aspired to something else and been rejected. But he had so far managed to convince himself that on these occasions the rejection had been his own decision, the women concerned mere prick-teasers.

'After I left the Angels,' he said, 'I sold the bike and got a job driving a minicab.'

'Did you enjoy doing that?'

'It was all right in a way, except that I had to work all hours. I used to like drivin' through London about four in the mornin' when there was nothin' else on the road and you could zip straight through the traffic lights without waiting for 'em to change, and take short cuts up the backs of one-way streets.

'Mind you, they were just about all villains in that trade. The bloke I used to work for, in Hammersmith, he used to run one of these escort agencies for foreign businessmen, only the escorts was all on the game.

'I used to drive 'em down the West End, and pick' em up again next mornin'. 'Undred quid a night they used to get, and most of 'em used to slip me a fiver on the way 'ome.

'The Special Branch caught up with 'im in the end, and 'e copped five years. Still doin' 'em now.

'It's a funny old thing, justice, when you weigh it up. 'E wasn't doin' no 'arm to anybody. There's another firm that specialises in running drugs up from the docks . . . been doin' it for years and nobody wants to know.'

On the far side of the ridge Marianne saw Paulson, the

gun slung from his shoulders, move past and disappear below a ridge.

'When did you first get a job as a chauffeur?' she said.

Nelson dapped his cigarette. The ash vanished in the breeze. 'Funny you should ask that. About a couple of years ago I was talking to a bloke who was a chauffeur with one of those foreign embassies . . . only a young bloke like me. 'E reckoned it was a really cushy number. Good pay, plenty o' time off, free food and accommodation . . . so I thought I'd give it a try.

'Well, about a couple o' weeks after that I saw this advert for a chauffeur in *The Times*, so I thought, well, cheek of the devil, I'll see what 'appens. So I got myself an interview, went round to this big place in Russell Square, some maid let me in, and there's this big tall feller sittin' in the lounge.

'Have a seat, Mr Burr,' he said in one o' these posh drawly voices, and he gives me a glass and a bottle o' brown ale. Then 'e starts askin' questions, 'ow old am I, 'ow long 'ave I been drivin', 'ave I ever 'ad any convictions, did I 'ave a regular girl friend, all that sort o' thing. So I told 'im straight. "I don't pretend to be a saint, if that's what you're after." Then 'e laughed and said, "I've never yet met one who could drive and maintain a Rolls."

'Then 'e says, "Let me tell you what I'm looking for. First of all I want a good driver who knows about engines, but there's no shortage of those. In the second place I need a man who has no family ties and complete freedom of action. And in the third place I want someone who keeps his mouth shut and his eyes open. Do you think you qualify?"

'So I said, "I don't see why not."

'Anyway, 'e took me on for three months' trial, and I've been with 'im ever since.'

Marianne said, 'Are you talking about the tall man who was staying at the clinic?'

His eyes widened. ' 'Ow did you know that?'

'I met him once. He just seemed to fit your description.'

'You're not supposed to know that.' Nelson Burr glanced

across the glen. 'Don't you ever let Paulson know I told you.'

'You didn't tell me. I guessed.'

From this moment Marianne realised that the man she knew as Harrington was in charge of the operation. But she decided not to press the point.

'I think I'll go and wash my hair,' she said. 'It's been nice talking to you.' As she stood up the staccato sound of repeated shots came from below the ridge.

'What's that?'

Nelson grinned. 'Nothing much. Just Paulson 'avin' a bit o' target practice.'

Marianne felt uneasy as the firing continued. As she walked back towards her tent she looked across at the stac. The continuous pattern of birds flying to and from the nests was disturbed. Scores of gannets were now rising high above the rock, circling and calling.

After a few moments she noticed a break in this pattern. One of the birds appeared to flutter from the top of the stac straight down into the sea.

Paulson's .300 Garrand carbine had always been his favourite weapon since he had exchanged it with an American Air Force sergeant, late at night, for a couple of bottles of whisky.

Its effective accurate range, in terms of a moving man, of about 250 yards, was quite sufficient for his purposes.

At 800 yards, the distance from the rock on which he was sitting to the stac at which he was aiming, a good marksman would have been hard pressed to hit a cathedral door. But Paulson was aiming at a colony of nesting gannets occupying a rock face the size of the whole cathedral, with a population of something like three sitting birds to a square yard. It was just a question of how many shots it would take to hit one.

As he now replaced the empty magazine with a full one he was suddenly confronted with a woman, raging with anger.

'Leave them alone!' Marianne tried to wrench the gun from his hands, but he easily wrestled it free.

'Hey, careful . . .' he raised the gun above his head, smirking. 'You're going to cause an accident one of these days.'

'What have they ever done to you?'

The leathery lips formed a small and cynical hole. 'They make such a terrible noise . . . keeps me awake all night.'

She tried to strike him across the face, but he caught her hand as if it was a passing butterfly. He looked astonished for a moment or two. Then the grin came back.

'Well, if it worries you that much . . . by the way, I suppose you know you're out of bounds. . . .' He released her wrist, and shouldered the carbine. 'Right, tell you what I'll do, I'll make a bargain. The guard commander will cease target practice . . . provided the queen returns to her compound. Is that agreed?'

He turned and walked languidly back along the ridge.

Marianne returned to a white-flashed rock which marked her boundary and sat on it. She glanced towards the stac again.

The gannet which had fallen was now quite close, riding on the water, being drawn along by the tide. It seemed to be grinning.

She watched the big bird rise in the water, unfold its wings, and try desperately to take off. But it merely lurched forward a yard or two. One of its wings remained half-extended, trailing in the water. The bird began to swing round in slow circles in the conflicting currents, as it drifted out to sea.

For the first time since her arrival on the island, Marianne wept uncontrollably.

Nelson Burr approached her but stopped a few yards away. He looked awkward, diffident.

'There's nuffink to get upset about,' he said. 'There's plenty more of 'em . . thousands.'

13

Coulman arrived in Tel Aviv on 2 May 1974, but was then obliged to loiter about in his hotel for the next forty-eight hours.

Henry Kissinger happened to be on one of his peripatetic tours of Egypt, Israel, and Syria, and most of the people that Coulman had come to see were involved in the security operation in Jerusalem.

Eventually, at eleven in the evening, he sat around a table in a conference room in the Defence Ministry with Shahan, now a major-general and Director of External Security, Colonel Moshe Zuleiman, his deputy, and two other men whom Coulman had not met before.

Shahan introduced them: 'Sholem Kahn, who is the head of the forensic department and David Nir, our director of aerial reconnaissance. There are two other members of my small committee but they are presently unavailable I'm sorry to say.' He glanced around the table as he sat down. 'I believe you've all read Mr Coulman's very interesting report.'

They nodded acquiescence.

'Is there any part of it which is not fully understood?'

'I thought it was very lucid,' Zuleiman murmured.

'Good. In that case let us go on to discuss it. First of all, it is my personal opinion that something rather unpleasant is being organised in England with serious implications for our security.'

'I'm not completely convinced of that,' said Nir. 'It's certainly true that Reisener is no friend of Israel, but isn't it possible that he's involved in something which doesn't concern us this time? There's no evidence of Palestinian involvement.'

'There's plenty of time,' observed Zuleiman.

Shahan had a habit of cocking his ear towards each successive speaker. He returned his attention to Nir. 'I think I might be more inclined to agree with you,' said Shahan, 'if it wasn't for the involvement of Professor Buechner.'

Zuleiman said, 'Yes, one of the things which interests me most is the direct link through Reisener to Steffen, then through Steffen to Buechner and his son, and back to Reisener again.'

Kahn asked, smiling, 'May I ask Mr Coulman's opinion?'

Coulman said, 'I would agree that something pretty big is brewing up over there. Whether it concerns us directly I wouldn't like to say for sure but at least it's a very strong possibility.'

'Strong enough, certainly, not to be ignored,' said Shahan briskly. 'I think we must all agree on that.'

He glanced, rather fiercely, around the table, but no one came back.

'Now,' he continued, 'from the evidence which Mr Coulman has presented, we must try to work out what sort of operation has been organised. I would like to mention one factor here. Reisener has now returned to Germany and from this we must assume that the control of the operation has passed into other hands.'

'Or otherwise it has failed,' suggested Nir.

Coulman said rather brusquely, 'That isn't my impression or I would have said so in the report. If it has failed already why should Steffen and several other people involved suddenly disappear? Apart from that I have suggested on page seven that Fox-Hillyer may have taken over.'

Nir replied, 'All right, I don't disagree with you. I was just flying a balloon for the opposition.'

'With regard to the nature of the operation,' said Zuleiman, 'I would have preferred a little more time to consider the possibilities.'

The colonel had been a member of the party which had seen the U.S. Foreign Secretary off to Damascus that same morning. Shortly afterwards, a staff car had transported him to Tel Aviv. It had been a hot day and the creases of his uniform showed traces of the white dust which had blown in through the open windows. He had read Coulman's report, for the first time, during the journey.

Into the pause for reflection which followed, Nir interpolated, 'As far as Reisener is concerned, the Olympic Games business must have bolstered his confidence. It's only a matter of time before he tries something else.'

'I believe you're preaching to the converted,' Zuleiman said.

Shahan said, with a note of impatience, 'Does anyone have any logical theories about the nature of the operation?'

There was an appreciable pause. Then Kahn said, 'Can I ask—this woman you mention in your report. Is she a Jewess?'

'We looked into that,' Coulman replied. 'With a name like Seal I suppose she could be, but maybe a long time ago. I don't think there's anything there, quite frankly.'

'It's just that I did have a thought. Shoot it down if you like, I'll be quite happy. But just suppose that . . . well I haven't had time to do any homework on this so far but supposing the operation was concerned with some form of germ warfare concerned with sterilisation techniques . . .'

Kahn paused, as if expecting a rebuttal, but none was forthcoming.

'Let us suppose that some new strain of bacteria had been developed for this purpose,' he continued, 'and that Reisener had asked Dr Steffen to try it out on a pregnant woman. Maybe it would be a culture that lived in the womb and attacked the foetus.'

'Then maybe if they find it works they grow it in some laboratory and scatter it around this land of ours . . . so they kill a thousand babies for the price of a kilo of gelignite.'

Nir looked sceptical. 'You have some support for this theory?'

Kahn replied, with a rueful smile, 'Before I came here I rang my doctor and put it to him as a hypothetical situation.'

E   125

'What did he say?'

'He told me it was very much like a bad dream he had when he was a student.'

Shahan said, 'All right. David, you have a more practical suggestion?'

Nir shook his head.

Coulman said, 'I certainly would say it's worth thinking about.'

The man who boarded the British Airways VC 10 for Munich at Heathrow Airport on 7 May 1974 had shortish fair hair, a trim moustache, and wore a beige lightweight suit with matching polo neck sweater—a suitable garb for one of the younger breed of business executives in the commercial world of art. He travelled on an American passport which bore the name of Harry Vincent Murdoch.

There was little, if any aspect of Jewishness about the appearance of Eckstein on this occasion, and there wasn't much more on those when he projected his normal identity.

Neither he nor his parents had practised the orthodox religion. Eckstein knew only a few fragments of Hebrew and sometimes wondered why he still felt committed to his genesis.

The answer, he supposed, was in the empathy he always felt with others of the ilk, and an instinctive sympathy with the survival problems of a small beleaguered country at the wrong end of the Mediterranean.

It was rather like belonging to a club with an exclusive membership, as a fellow member had once pointed out, and the accuracy of this analogy had made Eckstein feel uncomfortable at the time.

He was met at the airport by Greb, driving a somewhat mud-stained BMW.

Within half an hour of Eckstein's arrival the two men were lunching on kalbshaxe at a discreet table in a restaurant off the Sendlingerstrasse.

Eckstein briefed his colleague on Coulman's discussions in

Israel. Greb listened with the occasional grimace.

'So what's the action?' he finally asked.

'Two courses of action were proposed,' Eckstein said. 'One was that we stay back in England and carry on looking for Steffen and Fox-Hillyer and the girl until we find them. The objection to that was it could take too long.

'The other idea was that I come over here and we work on Buechner's son.'

'That figures,' said Greb. 'At least we know where to find the guy. So what do we do with him?'

'We snatch him and find out what he knows.'

'I had the idea we didn't get involved in the rough stuff.'

'That's right, Vic. All we do is set up the situation, then when we say we're ready they send us a specialist.'

Greb looked faintly disappointed.

'You don't like it?'

'Sure. Sure I like it. Only it's like you make this big birth-day cake and some other bastard puts the icing on.'

Eckstein smiled. 'Maybe you'll get the chance to blow the candles out.'

They went back to Greb's flat inside a squat building, a green door in a long grey corridor, and Eckstein parked his bag while Greb poured a drink.

'This place has one advantage.' Greb wandered across to a window. 'That heap across the street'—he pointed to a rococo mansion opposite—' is Reisener's headquarters. He lives in a penthouse on the top two floors.'

He swung a pair of binoculars.

'One can sometimes see things of interest.'

Greb seemed curiously nervous, Eckstein thought. He had been watching Reisener for over a year now. Perhaps the prospect of approaching the end of the tunnel unnerved him, upset his routine. He drank up abruptly and said, 'I'll take you for a drive round—you'll need some idea of the geography of the place.'

He drove through the central areas of Munich pointing

out landmarks—Marienplatz, Frauenkirche and Rathaus, the Schiller Monument, while frequently swearing at the peccadilloes of other drivers.

'I've never yet met a kraut who could drive a god-damned automobile.'

He turned north-west through the suburb of Nymphenburg, skirted the park, and stopped outside the gates of a large detached house fronted by expansive lawns. A line of flowering cherry-trees were in full blossom.

'This is the residence of Herr Rudolf Buechner,' Greb said.

Two small children, both boys, came yelling and scrambling across the lawn.

'He seems to be doing very nicely.'

'This property is worth all of a hundred thousand dollars, and Rudolf gets a salary to match. Reisener has made him director of chemical processes at his plant.'

'What was his job before?'

'I gather he was just a laboratory technician.'

Greb re-started the car and drove on.

He struck north-west again, and turned on to the autobahn towards Stuttgart.

Eckstein asked, 'Where are we going now?'

'There's a place not far from here which I thought you might like to see—at least, what's left of it.'

'What might that be?'

'Dachau.'

Eckstein said, 'Forget it.'

Greb looked surprised.

'You mean you don't want to go there?'

'I was never stuck on archeology,' Eckstein said.

During the next seven days Eckstein and Greb studied Rudolf Buechner assiduously.

They observed that he left punctually for work in his grey Mercedes at 8.15 a.m. and arrived at the engineering works at 8.40, give or take a couple of minutes according to the density of the traffic.

He drove slowly, rather casually, often smoking a cigarette with his elbow resting on the car window.

He wore bifocal spectacles, and was rather on the portly side, say in the region of two hundred pounds, height about five-feet-nine, fair thinning hair, clean shaven, age about forty.

He left the works for home at any time between 6.05 p.m. and 7.20 p.m. and always alone.

His wife Heidi was younger, around the mid-thirties, but looked rather careworn, nerves easily frayed. A sloppy dresser, always fiddling about in the garden, planting things. A shrill voice, often exercised by yelling at the children.

Their social life was negligible but this was probably due to the fact they had not been in Munich very long.

There were two children, twin boys aged about sevenish. These were picked up at nine each morning by an education authority truck and despatched to a local primary school, returning at 4.05 p.m. Household pets comprised some cats and a boisterous red setter.

The two agents also knew that Buechner's wife had brown eyes, that the couple spent most evenings watching television and went to bed around 11.15, that they ate a lot of pork and drank a little wine, and sundry other things.

On 15 May Eckstein telephoned Coulman in London and asked for the specialist to be sent.

That same evening Greb suggested that it was time for a little social relaxation.

He took Eckstein to a wine cellar not half a mile from his flat, and they ate a three-course meal during which not one word of the impending exercise was mentioned.

At one point Greb told him, 'You can get the best Bavarian wines in here, but the stuff is cheaper in London.'

There were hostesses in the place. Greb said, 'We're going to entertain a couple of ladies. Take no notice of the virginal appearance and the bit on the menu about saying goodbye at the door. They all screw for a price.'

'Which one?'

'Just take a look around.'

'I mean which price?'

'Eighty-five bucks.'

They were joined by a blonde German lady and a dark, small-boned Yugoslav who stirred Eckstein appreciably. He was beginning to feel deprived. He envied the facility with which Greb communicated with the German blonde, and also had time to translate between him and the little dark girl.

After an hour four bottles of Reisling had been drunk and the empties smartly removed.

'More of the same?' asked Eckstein, whose turn it was to order.

Greb leaned towards him, cupping a hand over his mouth.

'Not for me, but you go ahead if you want. When I was your age I could drink a bottle of scotch in any evening and hit the bell tower three times before midnight. But not any more. Listen, why don't we take the ladies back to the flat in a couple of minutes—okay?'

Eckstein said, 'Not for me. I never pay for it on principle.'

'Aaah, for Chrissakes! What are you trying to do, complicate the issue?'

'Don't bother about me—go ahead.'

Greb had an urgent conversation with the women in both their languages. During the course of this Eckstein was the recipient of a number of fiercely disapproving glances. Finally the Yugoslav girl departed, giving Eckstein a last look of reproach.

Greb said, 'Irma's coming back with me, okay? Sure you won't change your mind?'

'About paying for it? No thanks.'

All three of them returned to the flat. Greb attacked a full half-bottle of Scotch while the woman made the coffee. During this exercise Eckstein suddenly found himself looking into her eyes. The second or third time he held it for about five minutes while Greb was talking volubly about the necessity of the Western countries to give economic aid to the Third World.

Eventually Greb finished the bottle and went to sleep on the settee. Eckstein and the German girl undressed him and put him to bed.

The German girl was very thin, almost scrawny, with small, but very soft breasts. Eckstein, on the whole, preferred slim women, believing they were more passionate by virtue of their nerve centres being closer to the surface. Irma seemed to confirm this theory, and also she showed considerable expertise, coaxing him through four separate orgasms in the course of the night, with perfect timing. Just as daylight began filtering through the curtains, she slipped into Greb's bed.

It was nearing midday when Irma served them with a late breakfast. Greb ate very little and was unusually quiet. At the end of the meal he stripped a number of banknotes from his roll, and gave them to the girl. 'You were really great, baby. I'll remember you some other time.'

She left smiling, gazing into Eckstein's eyes as he let her out. Greb said, 'Well, she certainly took all I had to offer.'

14

As the rubber dinghy approached the shoreline of the little shingle bay where the Range Rover was parked, Fox-Hillyer came forward to meet it, his soles crunching on the loose stones. He helped Paulson drag the dinghy up on to the foreshore.

'How's the lady?'

'Oh, she's fine, sir. Just like a happy laughing sandboy.'

'What about yourself. How are you surviving? Got any problems?'

'Nothing that a few days in town wouldn't fix.'

Fox-Hillyer looked at him appraisingly, a commander shrewdly appraising the condition, mental and physical, of his flesh and blood material.

'I'm afraid there's no question of that.'

'Not even a long week-end?'

'Not even a short one. I couldn't possibly leave young Burr in charge. In any case I certainly don't want you to be seen around London until all this is over.'

They walked round to the back of the vehicle and began to transfer the stores.

'I appreciate it can't be much fun for you, but I'm afraid you'll just have to stick it out.'

'Not to worry, sir. I'm not complaining.'

'I thought you were.'

'We shall survive, sir,' Paulson said.

Fox-Hillyer reflected for a few moments. Then he said, 'I'll tell you what I'll do. I'll make it another thousand. Call it hardship money if you like.'

'That's very generous of you, sir. I suppose you won't change your mind about the other business?'

'What other business?'

'Well, as you know, I've always been a man who enjoyed his tot. It's rather hard having to go without completely. I suppose you wouldn't agree to a small ration—a couple of bottles a week?'

'Paulson, I'm afraid I'm going to be very firm about this. The answer is no.'

'I thought you might say that.'

It was beginning to warm up on the island. Although the breeze was still fresh off the sea there were areas of the glen, sheltered by slabs of rock, which trapped the sun.

Marianne, lying in one of these, raised her head at the faint puttering noise of a marine diesel engine.

A small trawler was approaching Ahd Skeir, turning into the narrows under the lee of the island. A hundred yards away she saw Paulson studying the vessel through binoculars.

He made her increasingly uneasy. He prowled about the island in a fever of boredom and frustration, the epitome of a compulsive city-dweller trapped in the wilds.

Occasionally she would see him sitting on a rock, fishing for pollock, but he seldom caught one. Paulson was much too impatient. Half an hour without a catch was his limit. The only time he seemed in his element was when he was conducting his 'exercise periods'. These would consist, early in the morning, of bullying and cajoling Dr Stephen and Sister Ferry halfway up the slopes of Muttach Rial and down again, flicking a length of electric cable like a switch, shouting them on, while Nelson Burr went on ahead, swiftly and easily, setting the standard.

One afternoon, Dr Stephen appeared in her tent, just as she had finished the midday meal. He was wearing a sweat shirt and a pair of baggy khaki shorts, and she noticed that he had lost a good deal of weight. He carried a small black, rather battered-looking attaché-case.

E*

'Miss Seal,' he said, 'if you still have faith in me as your doctor, I think it might be useful if I examined you.'

Marianne said immediately, 'Yes, I think it might be a good idea.'

He spent the next hour testing her pulse rate, blood pressure, temperature, exploring her inside and out, scarcely uttering a word until finally he said, 'Well, there's not much the matter with either of you, so far as I can judge.' He added, in a low murmur, 'You can be sure, my dear, that we shall emerge from this nightmare. Do you have any stomach pains . . . any sickness?'

The voice of Paulson cut in brutally from outside the entrance to the tent.

'All right, that's enough. Cut out the talking!'

Although she tried to keep Paulson at a distance he had begun to talk to her in a sardonic, rather oleaginous fashion.

Once he said, 'We're going to have to make friends some time, so why don't we start now?' And he had taken her reluctant hand and squeezed it. She stared at the crinkled leathery features and tried to conceal her revulsion.

Her communication with the chauffeur, on the other hand, was growing steadily. He had begun to treat her with a rough and diffident sort of courtesy, fetching things for her, becoming almost protective. She knew instinctively that this factor was beginning to create tension between the two men.

Her recurring problem was a strong sense of guilt. There were times when she realised that for two or three days together she hadn't thought about Nick.

She still firmly believed that the embryo developing inside her was his. Except that during the last few days she had felt the first faint squirm of doubt.

The trawler dropped anchor in the channel between Ahd Skeir and the coastline of Harris. Marianne saw people moving about on board. She identified four men and two women, bustling about, storing equipment, briskly and cheerfully involved. A woman wearing a bright green headscarf emerged from the wheelhouse, handing round cups.

They seemed so naturally to belong to the atmosphere in which Marianne was accustomed to moving that she could hardly believe that she couldn't shout, wave, swim across, jump aboard and be one of them.

After about half an hour two of the men launched a dinghy and began to row across to the island.

Paulson who was watching the situation with Nelson Burr moving up beside him, walked quickly down to the landing bay. Nelson came over to Marianne. He grinned, almost apologetically.

'Seems we've got visitors. Terry wants you to go back to the tents until we get rid of 'em.'

She walked slowly back towards the camp. Nelson followed. The dinghy bobbed out of view behind the ridge.

She sat outside her tent, wondering if she should make a run for it, try to get down to the inlet as the boat came in and shout at the strangers, 'I am a prisoner'. Even the words seemed ridiculous, and anyway Nelson was squatting on a rock barring the route and she knew that he would stop her if he had to.

After a while she heard the faint sound of voices drifting up on the wind.

Of the two men in the boat one, middle-aged, with a rough and reddened complexion, was obviously the trawler's skipper. The other, a pale adolescent, could have been his son. Both wore maritime-blue sweaters and woollen bobble-hats.

Paulson stood waiting for them on the landing stage as they approached. They stood off ten yards offshore, back-paddling against the current.

The older man called, 'Halloa there. All right if we come ashore?'

Paulson shouted, 'No, you can't. This is private property.'

The dinghy swivelled round, and drifted past. They drove it back again. 'We're doing a bit of diving around here. I just wondered if we could put a tent up for a couple of nights. The girls would like to have a look at the birds.'

'I can't help you I'm afraid. I've got strict instructions from the owner. Nobody lands.'

They held course with some difficulty.

'All right. Could you let us have some water. We're a bit short.'

'So are we. You can get plenty over the other side.'

'Thanks for the hospitality.'

'It's no trouble.'

They began to pull away.

Paulson shouted after them. 'I'll make a deal with you. You can have ten cans of water for a bottle of Scotch.'

The two men in the boat stopped rowing, exchanged a few words, and laughed.

Then the higher-pitched voice of the younger one floated across the water.

'Aye, and you can kiss my fuckin' arse.'

For the next few days the trawler moved around the island and Marianne spent much of her time watching the divers slip, frog-suited and gas-bottled, from the comparative security of the boat to the unknown depths below. After intervals of about twenty minutes they would reappear, the black goggled heads popping above the surface, to be picked up by the cruising dinghy.

In the evenings when the lights on the boat came on, there were distant sounds of music, sudden shouts and snatches of laughter, which deepened her sense of isolation, and brought her sometimes to despair.

She felt almost like a leper in relation to the members of the diving club. Most of her time was occupied in thinking up ways and means of getting in touch with them.

It wasn't until the third day of their visit that she sensed the first glimmer of an opportunity.

On this day, a Wednesday, the good weather had broken. For most of the morning flurries of rain swept across the island. Not that it was cold—there was more of a steaminess in the atmosphere than a chill.

By lunch time—Alison had roasted a chicken—the rain had cleared, leaving an overcast sky and a mist which encompassed the higher ground.

Shortly before two o'clock Paulson announced that he had to make an emergency trip to the mainland of Harris to pick up a spare part for the generator.

He left within ten minutes. Alison sat down outside the tents and worked on her embroidery—her favourite pastime. Marianne began washing out some of her clothing outside her tent.

She could see the trawler anchored a quarter of a mile offshore on the north-eastern side of the island. The divers were operating under the cliffs of Sennay.

Marianne looked up at the lower slopes of that feature, and saw the mist rolling further down towards her.

She had never been allowed to explore that part of the island and knew nothing of its topography. She assumed that the further side was cliffbound, but perhaps this wasn't so. Suppose there was a way down to the shore. If she found one, she ought to get to within shouting distance of the divers. She might even be able to swim out to them. They would pick her up if she got into difficulties.

She glanced rather furtively across the glen, looking for Nelson. He was some distance away, wandering about with a spade, looking for peat.

Suddenly very tense, she walked quickly inside the tent and put on the climbing boots which had been supplied for her use. Then she went back outside, wrung out the clothing, bundled it together and walked—not too fast—across to a dry-stone wall which ran across one end of her compound. Here she hung the items of clothing over the stones, looking round meanwhile and assessing the situation.

Nelson was about two hundred yards away. On her near side—the lower slopes of Sennay—the edge of the mist was perhaps a little further off, three hundred yards perhaps.

Now!

Marianne turned and went towards the slope at a fast walk. She had gone perhaps thirty yards before she dared to glance back.

Nelson was trying to force the spade free from a crevice in the rocks.

She increased her walking pace to the maximum, the layers of mist ahead appearing to billow invitingly towards her, then recede. She reached the edge of the glen and began to half-climb, half-scramble up the now much steeper and rockier terrain of Sennay before a thin, distant yell drifted across to her.

'Hey, where the bloody hell d'you think you're going?'

She looked back, saw the chauffeur throw down his spade and begin to run across the glen towards her.

Marianne already had some experience of rock-climbing in Wales, and this proved invaluable now as she moved up the rough terrain, through patches of sphagnum and purple moor grass, inclining her posture towards the rising slope, making towards a stream which veined down from the mountains into the marshy places of the glen.

She was into the mist a good hundred yards ahead of Nelson Burr who was beginning to blow, pausing occasionally to plead with her to return.

Once surrounded by the mist Marianne felt more secure. It was patchy and drifting, the visibility varying at times from fifty yards to thirty. She followed the course of the stream, now little more than a trickle, pressing herself upwards by the scattered boulders. It was steep now and she was forced to rest every fifty yards. She could hear the chauffeur gasping and wheezing as he fell further behind.

She guessed that Nelson would also be following the watercourse, and moved away from it through an area of coarse and tussocky moorgrass and clumps of creeping willow. After a few more minutes, the ground began to level off.

Marianne sprawled on the grass and rested, feeling safe

138

from pursuit. But she realised that the mist was no longer her ally. It would be difficult to get her bearings.

A cloud of midges had begun to swarm around her head. She moved on, more cautiously.

Nelson was now reduced to climbing in ten-yard spurts, between rests. His feet—he was wearing thin-soled plimsolls—were bruised and sore, and his calf muscles felt as if they were on fire. Sweat trickled freely from his scalp across his forehead. His own personal halo of midges followed wherever he led. It bothered him that he had now lost track of Marianne completely. He yelled out, 'Where are you?'

Marianne heard the forlorn shout from a long distance away as she moved on. It was at this moment that she saw, some fifty yards ahead, two large brown birds watching her from the vantage point of a rock.

The Great Skua, a sea-bird of about the size and bulk of a white-front goose, has a capacity for soaring flight exceeded, among birds of its size, only by the eagles.

It is a pirate and a scavenger, finding most of its food by harassing and threatening less aggressive sea birds in mid-air and forcing them to disgorge.

As Marianne approached, the two skuas took off, rising almost vertically until they disappeared into the mist.

A few seconds later the first one reappeared, hurtling straight towards her. Marianne ducked instinctively as the bird swerved, missing her head by a foot. Almost simultaneously its mate came at her from behind.

The first she knew of this was when the trailing claw of the bird struck the top of her head, gashing it, and ripping out a hank of hair.

The skuas circled above, uttering their menacing little cries of alarm . . . eck eck . . . eck . . . eck eck . . . They came at her again, swooping from all angles.

Marianne was now emerging on to a moorland plateau near the summit of Sennay. Almost petrified by the sudden onset of the attack on her, she turned and ran.

The birds continued to buzz her for a hundred yards or more until she found refuge in a cluster of huge fragmented rocks. Then they vanished abruptly into the mist.

It took her some time to gather her senses, feeling the blood trickle from her scalp. She felt no hostility towards the birds who were simply defending their nesting territory. But the incident had shaken her confidence, made her feel like a blundering invader.

The rocks—some of them rising to twenty feet—afforded a welcome refuge.

She explored them a little further and found a large cavern formed by the fortuitous tumbling together of several large slabs of granite. It seemed ideal as a temporary refuge. But first she climbed to the top of the tallest rock and looked round.

The mist seemed to be thickening, although it was still drifting. She could hear the distant sound of surf, gulls calling, and knew that she was close to the cliff tops. She looked at her watch—4.20 in the afternoon. Already she had been on Sennay for more than two hours.

There seemed no hope of finding a way down to the fore-shore while the mist persisted. She decided to wait until it cleared, even if she had to stay there all night.

She returned to the cavern.

It was quite roomy—about the same size as her tent in the glen—but the only light came through chinks in the rocks and the atmosphere was dank and musty. Underfoot the ground was covered with a soft carpet of bird and rat droppings.

She waited until her eyes had got accustomed to the poor light, and began to explore her surroundings. She noticed a seabird—a fulmar—sitting in a crevice between the rocks a couple of yards away. The bird watched her as she approached it. It seemed so unafraid that she was sure it must be wounded. She stretched out a tentative hand towards it. The bird opened its beak wide, drew back its head, and hissed with anger.

Then the head jerked forward and a jet of oily, rank-smelling fluid struck Marianne on the cheek.

Nelson reached the top of the stream bed and stumbled cursing through a wide patch of spongy marshland into which he sank to the ankles at every stride.

But at least the ground had levelled off.

He sat down and rested for some fifteen minutes, aching and sweating, the midges feeding greedily on the sweat. He had lost his bearings completely by now, had no idea in which direction the camp lay, or where to look for Marianne.

He got up and trudged on, snatching at insects, peering around him through the mist. Soon afterwards he blundered into the nesting area of the skuas.

The effect of the birds' attack on Nelson was to stimulate his own aggression. As they swooped at him he threw wild punches in their direction.

'Piss off!' he yelled.

He sat down on a rock, sweat beading his cheeks. The birds came at him frantically, veering past his outstretched arms.

A few yards away, in a scooped-out hollow, he noticed two large eggs, olive-coloured and splashed with brown.

He walked across, picked one up, and hurled it at the hen as she came at him like a shell from near ground level. The bird swerved past the missile which smashed against a boulder.

Nelson crushed the other egg with his foot. He gazed up at the skuas as they circled above him.

'Now lay some more bastards!' he yelled in triumph.

He walked on. The birds did not bother him again. The ground began to firm up underfoot. Ahead of him lay a long grassy mound, pimpled with the spikelets of red fescue.

He reached the top of the mound and stopped. There was something wrong with the landscape. He could no longer see anything ahead of him. He crouched on hands and knees and considered the situation. The vague shape of a seabird rose and fell across his line of vision. Ahead of him and above, an infinity of white, misty nothingness.

He looked down. The ground disappeared a foot in front of him. He could hear the distant sound of the surf. After a

while he saw through a hole in the mist what looked like a
swirl of grey porridge.

He realised that he was staring down seven hundred feet
of perpendicular rock face.

During the days of the small community of crofters and
cragsmen on Ahd Skeir, wrongdoers were sent up to the
cavern on the clifftops of Sennay by the visiting minister, to
live alone for days and nights on end without food, dwelling
on their misdemeanours—normally sexual ones—and seeking
the forgiveness of their harsh Calvinistic God.

The place reeked of loneliness. Marianne, pressed against
the rock wall, watched the rat as it scurried back and forth
across the floor of the cavern, pausing occasionally to lick its
paws. Unlike the scavenging horde which had raided the
glen, this one was sleek and glossy. It gave a faint squeak of
alarm as it caught the human scent—probably for the first
time—and ran backwards and forwards in front of Marianne
sniffing the air. Then, quite suddenly, the rat seemed to lose
interest in the subject, and went off across the cavern floor
in a leaping run, squeezing through a small aperture between
the rocks.

By this time she was becoming increasingly frightened and
desolate. There were at least another five nesting fulmars sitting among the rock crevices around her, all of them staring
at her with resentment and hostility.

She remained in the cavern for several hours, hardly daring
to move from her lichen-covered rock seat, until eventually
twilight fell.

As it slowly approached pitch darkness she was aware of
a feathery swishing at momentary intervals as the Manx
shearwaters returned to their nests among the burrows in the
rocky crevices under the cavern.

The whole area became alive with the rustling and flutter-
ing of restless nesting birds. From somewhere below her feet
she heard the fowl-like Koo-ker-aa-kor cry of the shearwaters.
A fulmar spat, close by. Stormy petrels purred in the dark

interstices of the rocks, as they attended their young. She saw
the sharp glint of a rat's eyes as it pattered past. All around
her the world of the nesting birds and their predators came
to restless life and she felt totally divorced from it all, a resen-
ted and despised intruder.

Just after 9.30 she heard a sound outside, of someone
stumbling about among the rocks of the outcrop. She picked
her way outside the cave and saw the chauffeur loom up out
the misty darkness.

'Nelson! I thought you'd gone back.' She was delighted to
see him, her fears evaporating.

'Christ,' he said. 'Why did you have to drag me all the
way up to this bloody awful place?' He seemed close to
exhaustion and rather distraught. She took his hand and
guided him back to the cavern.

Inside, he lowered himself wearily to the ground. Marianne
watched him as he took a box of matches from his pocket and
lit one, staring around. He looked wild and dishevelled, plas-
tered with black mud.

'Are you all right?' she asked anxiously.

He fingered his wrist. 'I've only broke my bloody arm,
that's all.'

While she gently inspected the damage to his mud-caked
wrist, he said, 'I suppose you know there's bloody great cliffs
all around us?'

She was overwhelmed with relief at his presence. Marianne
was prepared to give up any immediate hope of escape, rather
than face the appalling prospect of a night alone in the
cavern.

The mist had now thickened appreciably as it merged with
the gathering darkness. There was no hope of finding their
way back to camp until morning.

Nelson, who was equally pleased to see Marianne, gradually
recovered his spirits, although his arm still pained him—he
had fallen on it heavily during his recent perambulations.
They talked for a long time. Marianne felt comforted by the
protective company of a man in this hostile place. They finally

drifted into a restless sleep, huddled against each other for warmth.

When Marianne woke, she walked outside the cavern and looked out across miles of sea, sparkling in the sun. In the far distance she saw several small ships, coasters and fishing boats, moving through the Sound of Harris. The trawler with the divers aboard was still anchored in the straits below.

Later, as they clambered down along the stream bed and entered the glen, they were met by Paulson, the carbine swinging from his shoulder.

He watched them approach, hands on hips. A supercilious grin wrinkled his lips.

'Well, well . . . the return of the happy wanderers! What have you two been up to? Don't tell me, let me guess.'

15

The specialist drove across the Austrian border in a hired Fiat. He was a broadly happy man whose smile flashed on customs officials and petrol pump attendants with equal compassion for the dullness of their lives.

Eliyahu Schen was a big man in almost every sense of the word. He enjoyed his way of life and did not regret that sometimes his profession made it necessary for him to hurt others. He never doubted that in such cases the pain, even the hurried departure from life itself, had been made inevitable by the shortcomings of those who suffered these indignities. He neither drank or smoked, but readily appreciated the necessity for others to do so.

In some ways it could be said that his outlook on life was similar to that of a successful heart surgeon.

He was a skilful professional who knew his limitations as well as those who employed him. Schen was never brought in at the planning stage. He was sent for when the start line was ready for crossing, after the spadework had been done by others with more patience and sophistication.

He had worked often in the Lebanon, being closely involved in the seaborne raid which had made inroads into the leadership of the P.L.O. at Beirut.

Damascus was another of his stamping grounds, and he had a good working knowledge of Baghdad. He had worked only twice before in Europe—an abortive mission in Italy, and an occasion in Paris a year earlier which had concerned the disappearance of a Libyan airline official.

The Sûreté was still looking into it.

Schen drove through the outer suburbs of Munich, but when he got as far as the Gartner Platz he parked, found a call box, and rang Greb's number, then waited patiently outside until Greb arrived in a taxi, and drove with him back to the flat in the Fiat.

It was an obvious precaution. Nobody thought it a good idea for Schen to be cruising around central Munich, stopping and asking, in fractured phrase-book German, how to get to Greb's place.

Schen parked the car neatly outside the block and took out his two items of luggage—an overnight bag and a heavy piece of electronic equipment which he smilingly referred to as his 'box of tricks'.

Eckstein was waiting for them. The three men ate a light meal brought in from a takeaway luncheon counter, fortified in Greb's case with a stiff gin and tonic. During this repast they indulged in some conversation of a social nature.

Immediately afterwards Eckstein spread a map on the table and they got down to business.

After that business had been checked and re-checked, Schen set up his equipment—a tape recorder with some refinements including a powerful built-in amplifier—and tested it. He found that the plug with which it was provided would not fit any of the sockets in the flat.

The plug from Greb's electric kettle was quickly substituted.

During the evening Eckstein and Greb removed all the documents in the flat as well as Greb's personal effects, and put them in the boot of the Fiat.

Eckstein noticed that among these items were a number of sketch books.

'I didn't realise you were a secret artist, Vic.'

'It's just another way of passing the time.'

Over a dinner of Eisbein and Sauerkraut, cooked by Greb in the flat's tiny kitchen, Schen was cheerfully expansive, dispensing his favourite stories of the October War with gusts of laughter.

The swarthy Israeli excused himself just after ten, explaining that he was tired after the long drive and wanted to be fresh for the following morning.

Eckstein and Greb played a few desultory games of backgammon before they also turned in.

Rudolf Buechner's house and garden were screened by tall hedges. A pair of impressive wrought-iron gates fed on to the road.

These gates were always kept locked. Buechner was a cautious and methodical man who locked everything—desk, car doors, brief case—instinctively. Like most people who are acquisitive, he was determined to hang on to what he had already. He carried a large key-ring in his pocket and this was produced at least twenty times a day, a fact already familiar to Eckstein.

At precisely 8.13 a.m. on May 21, a Tuesday, Buechner left his house and unlocked the door of his garage. He then unlocked the door on the driver's side of his Mercedes, climbed in, and backed out on to the driveway. He got out and re-locked the garage door; there were valuable tools inside.

He drove carefully to the gates, got out, unlocked and opened them and drove through. He stopped and got out again, closed the gates, got back in the car, fastened his safety belt, and turned out on to the road.

The road outside Buechner's property was a narrow, private lane which allowed access to half a dozen other, similar properties on either side.

Signs at either end read, *Kein Durchfahrt* (No Through Traffic).

As Buechner turned on to this thoroughfare he noticed, about a hundred yards ahead of him, two men pushing a BMW saloon which appeared to have got stuck somewhere in the middle of the road. Another man was steering.

They stopped as he approached.

One of them, a big fellow with sun glasses and a fedora hat, gave him a cheery wave.

Buechner pulled up about ten yards away and waited, a little impatiently, until there was room to pass.

Then the other man who was pushing turned and gave a shrug and a grimace of exasperation, and began to walk quickly towards the Mercedes.

He stopped beside the driver's door.

'You don't have such a thing as a jack we could borrow?' Buechner heard this distantly.

'I'm afraid I can't help you.'

Greb put an expressive hand to his ear. 'Sorry, can't hear what you say.'

Reluctantly Buechner wound down the window. 'I can't help you. I'm in a hurry.'

He found himself looking directly into the snout of a Walther automatic. At the same time Greb's hand snaked through the window and removed the ignition keys.

'Now do exactly as I tell you. Unlock all the doors.'

Buechner did so, hardly believing that this could be happening to him.

'Now get out and get in the back seat.'

Buechner complied. The big fellow got into the car through the other rear door and sat beside him.

By this time the BMW had started and was now receding into the distance.

Greb started the Mercedes and followed.

During this episode, two other vehicles had passed, a bread wagon and a Ford Dormobile. Neither driver noticed anything unusual.

Buechner was driven straight back to Greb's flat. He said nothing during the trip, his stomach turning with deep and unpleasant presentiments. As he was escorted into the block of flats, flanked by Greb and Schen, they were passed in the corridor by a couple of young women, probably secretaries hurrying to the underground station. Buechner moistened his dry lips as they approached but the moment came and went before he could respond to it.

Eckstein had reached the flat before them.

He said, 'Herr Buechner I believe,' and gestured towards a chair. 'Sit down. I'd like to ask you a few questions.'

Buechner looked puzzled until Greb translated. Then he asked, 'Who are you? I suppose you want money?'

Eckstein said quietly, 'No, we don't want money, you have some information that we need.'

He picked up the telephone and handed it to Greb, who dialled a number.

'*Münchener Elektronishe Montage*?' Greb spoke in German. 'Will you put me through to Herr Buechner's secretary, Fraulein Loeb . . . ?'

'Ah, Fraulein Loeb. This is Herr Buechner's brother-in-law. I'm staying with him at present. Rudolf asked me to ring you. He fell and hurt his ankle this morning. It's nothing very serious but his wife has just taken him down to the hospital for an X-ray. He probably won't be in today, but he said he'll give you a ring later on this afternoon . . .'

'Yes of course, I'll tell him.'

He put the telephone down.

Buechner had listened to this performance with deepening despondency. When the first shock of his kidnap had worn off he thought he had been picked up by a gang of local criminals; there had been a recent spate of muggings in Munich. Now he was becoming aware that this was something different. Two of his captors at least were foreigners, speaking in English. He felt a growing sense of bitter injustice. Whatever was coming, he had done nothing to deserve it. What could they want with him, a peaceful, ordinary citizen, devoted to his family, who had never wished to harm anyone?

Eckstein resumed questioning Buechner, with Greb acting as interpreter.

'Why did Herr Reisener give you a large house in Munich and an executive post at his factory?'

Buechner's voice trembled with fear and resentment.

'Reisener? He didn't give me the house. I bought it myself.'

'And the job?'

149

'I applied for the job in the usual manner and I was selected.'

'Why did Reisener go to London a couple of months ago?'

'How should I know that? Herr Reisener doesn't consult me about his movements.'

'What do you know about a man called Fox-Hillyer?'

'I don't understand what you are talking about. Are you sure you haven't mistaken me for someone else?'

'All right. Tell us what you know about Dr Steffen, who was once your father's assistant.'

'I have heard of him from my father, but that's all. I think he died some time ago.'

'Can you tell us anything about your father's research during the war?'

'Very little. I was a child at the time.'

'You know he was accused of experimenting on Jewish women?'

'That is all past history. The accusations were completely false.'

Eckstein paused for reflection. He studied the features in front of him, now pale with apprehension, the eyes restless and furtive. He drew a document from inside his jacket and passed it to Buechner.

'Do you recognise this?'

Buechner studied it with reluctance.

'It's a photostat of your bank statement for the last six months, isn't that so?'

The German was speechless with astonishment.

'Look at the item with a red ring round it—a payment of two hundred thousand marks on 16 January. The cheque was drawn on Reisener's account at the International Credit Bank of Zurich. How do you explain that?'

Buchner remained silent, glancing at each face in turn.

Eckstein added, 'What did you have to sell to Reisener . . . for which he was prepared to pay so much?'

From somewhere Buechner summoned an air of truculence.

'I have no intention of explaining anything to Jewish pigs.'

Schen smiled broadly at this, as Greb translated.

Eckstein added, almost with regret, 'Right, at least we all know here we stand. We are now going to persuade you to give us the information we require. How long it takes is entirely up to you.'

He gave the Israeli the nod. Schen picked up a handful of black, thong-like straps.

He sat Buechner, almost like a child, on a tall dining-chair and proceeded to strap his wrists behind him, his ankles to the chair legs, his chest to the spine.

When this had been accomplished he clamped a set of headphones on the German's ears, pulled a black canvas hood over his head, and tied it like a string-bag around his neck.

The headphones were already connected to Schen's box of tricks. He now switched on, and carefully, with his eye on the output indicator, turned up the volume control. A shrill whistling noise emerged.

Schen adjusted the volume carefully, then turned to the other agents with a wry grimace. 'I'm sorry about the inconvenience. I hope it won't be for very long.'

Schen's box of tricks had originally developed from experimental sound equipment especially constructed for a research laboratory at Princeton during the mid-sixties, for use in assessing the reactions of student volunteers to sounds of differing frequencies and volume.

One of the early models had fallen into the wrong hands, and later, more sophisticated variations had been assembled for commercial sale at a small factory not far from the European Economic Community complex in Brussels.

There was a steady demand for these machines, mostly for the export market, and particularly in the countries of South America. They were classified as tape recorders, and were nowhere illegal.

The model in Schen's possession was capable of producing ultra-sonic frequencies outside the range of human hearing which could burn a man's skin, and infra-sound which could disintegrate his skull.

But the cacophony which was currently pouring into the skull of Buechner was 'white noise'—a mixture of sounds extending over the whole range of audible frequencies, played at a volume of a hundred and thirty decibels—a level which has been described as the 'superpain threshold' by those who monitor the noise levels of certain aircraft at international airports.

Thus Buechner was listening to a fortissimo scream equivalent to that experienced by a man standing fifty yards from a Boeing 707 testing its engines at full throttle prior to take-off.

But the man in this situation has two alternatives. He can wait for the noise to go away, or he can go away from the noise.

Buechner had no such choice.

Schen had placed a switch control in the German's hands and had told him only to use it when he was ready to talk.

Eckstein asked, 'How long do you think it's going to take?'

The Israeli shrugged. 'With this one? Two hours . . . two and a half maybe.'

He stood beside the recorder, manipulating the controls. Sometimes he would decrease the sound level, then bring it slowly back to full volume. At others he would cut it off altogether for periods of a few seconds. All the time he kept a careful eye on the output indicators. When Buechner eventually unloaded, it would be inconvenient if he had become stone deaf in the process.

After an hour and ten minutes Buechner pressed the switch and a red light winked on the control panel.

Schen turned off the sound and nodded to Greb, who came across and spoke into a mike.

His voice was fed to Buechner through the headphones.

'Herr Buechner. What do you want to tell us?'

'I wish to go to the toilet.'

'I'm afraid that's not possible unless you wish to talk to us first.'

The voice coming through the hood quavered with emotion.

'I have already told you that I don't know anything.'

'In that case I think you ought to consult your memory. It could be lying.'

Schen switched on the sound again.

Twenty minutes later Buechner began to struggle fiercely, trying to free his hands. Schen moved quickly across and grabbed the chair as it was about to topple. He held it firmly until the struggles subsided.

Another fifty minutes passed before Buechner pressed the switch again. This time he was more forthcoming.

He repeated his assertion that he had no useful information to offer. He had heard of Reisener's reputation as a Nazi, but this was nothing to do with him.

In any case he had never been involved in politics himself, had always voted for the Christian Democrats. If they didn't believe him, all they had to do was to ask Reisener.

The payment from Reisener was quite a simple matter. When the professor had died, Buechner had inherited a number of pictures, including two by Dürer. It was these that he had sold to Reisener, who wanted them for his private collection.

He offered them thirty thousand marks for his freedom. He had only to collect the money from his bank.

After a brief discussion with his colleagues Greb said, 'I'm afraid that's not good enough. You'll have to try much harder. If you don't tell us all about it next time I am going to take the switch away for an hour.'

Schen resumed the white noise.

Eckstein prowled about the room smoking his third pipe in quick succession. It wouldn't draw properly and was beginning to scorch the membranes of his tongue.

He felt impatient and edgy and the continuous howl emerging from the monitor speaker had started to fret his nerves.

It was now 1.16 in the afternoon and Buechner had lasted just under four hours.

He looked at the victim and experienced the first faint nigglings of self-disgust.

Buechner was sitting quite still now, his head leaning back as far as the straps permitted. He clenched his fists occasionally. A pool of urine had formed beneath the chair.

The German had been right, of course, when he had suggested that Reisener should be sitting there instead of a podgy, domesticated chemist. But Buechner was the easier target and thus had been selected.

Reisener, sitting at his office desk no more than a hundred yards away, would have been so much harder to crack. He would probably have died in the chair.

Eckstein hoped that Schen would not have to hurt Buechner too much.

For the first time in his life he felt like a bully—and bullies, a schoolmaster had once told him, were by definition cowards.

On that occasion Eckstein had been on the receiving end.

He turned to Schen. 'How much longer?'

The specialist grinned cheerfully. 'Not very much. I'm surprised he's lasted so long already.'

'We're running short of time. Can't you move it along a bit?'

'Sure, I can give him the electricals.'

'Isn't there anything else?'

'There are other types of noise.'

'Okay, so let's try one.'

Schen stopped the machine and changed the tape. As he did so he chatted affably to Buechner through the microphone, rather in the manner of a dentist reassuring a patient during a difficult extraction:

'You are being very brave, Herr Buechner. I'm surprised at the strength of your resistance. Now I'm going to give you something else to listen to, for a change.

'This time I am going to play you something very beautiful. It is supposed to be the most beautiful sound known to the human ear. Many poems have been written about it.'

The recording that Schen next played was that of a nightingale in full song.

The cock nightingale sings for only six weeks in the year, prior to the breeding season. The song is delivered in a series of phrases lasting up to ten seconds, with intervals of about three seconds between each phrase. At a hundred yards distance each note can be heard with perfect clarity and lucidity.

It is very doubtful if Buechner was familiar with the nightingale's song or aware of its outstanding qualities; such things did not feature very prominently in his order of priorities.

Now, at a volume of a hundred and thirty decibels, every piercing cadence clamoured for recognition.

Krrrrrrrrrr . . . chuk chuk chuk chuk chuck kwi . . . Tsui tsui . . . ker ker ker ker . . . trrrrrrrrrr . . . wheee wheee wheee wheeee wheeeee . . . tutututututu . . . kerwhiddle kerwhiddle kerwhiddle kerwhiddle tsui . . .

One of the features of the nightingale's song is its infinite variety. No bird has ever been known to repeat the same phrase twice.

Ker ker tsui . . . kwip kwip kwip kwip krrrrrrr . . . tututu- tututututututu tsui . . . chirrr chirrr chirrr . . . chuk kwi . . .

Buechner had begun to struggle again as the nightingale began, but this time only apparently as a reflex action, an attempt to somehow get away from the ferocious din which Schen was hammering remorselessly into his brain. The struggles soon subsided. Ten minutes later he leaned forward and his whole body shook with convulsions.

Schen moved quickly to him as a thick dribble of vomit spread over his shirt front from beneath the hood.

He removed the hood, made a quick appraisal of Buechner's condition, then picked up a towel and wiped some of the vomit from the gaping mouth.

He didn't want his client to choke.

Wheee wheeee wheeeee wheeeeee wheeeeeee wheeeeeeee . . . ker ker ker tsui . . . chirrr chirrr tsui . . . krrrrrrrr . . . tututu . . .

chuk chuk kwi . . . chirrrrrrrrr . . . kerwhiddle tsui . . .

Buchner continued to vomit for the next twenty minutes— long after he had emptied his stomach.

Krrrrr . . . chu chu chu . . . tututu tsui . . . ker ker ker ker ker ker ker . . . chuk kwi . . .

He was still for a further ten minutes, then his shoulders heaved.

Schen stood beside him, bending down, listening.

He said, 'He is crying. It won't be long now.'

But it was another forty minutes—at precisely 2.44 p.m.— before Buechner was finally broken. And by that time Schen had been obliged to use the electricals.

Eckstein, watching Schen's performance with growing nausea, wondered how long in similar circumstances the Israeli would have lasted. Not nearly so long, probably. Schen would have realised, as a professional, that it was only a matter of time. So why suffer needlessly?

He was also wondering whether what they were about to hear would justify the indignity of forcing one surprisingly courageous little man to soil himself with his own shit and vomit—whether the information he was about to dispense would cause a government to fall, lead to the resignation of a senior civil servant, or simply justify the salaries of himself and his kind.

It was even possible that anything which was going to be achieved, had been achieved already.

16

She lay in the sun, under the lee of a lichen-covered rock, watching the gannets.

There were brief occasions such as these when she could forget the circumstances of her presence on the island, as if she enjoyed the same freedom of movement as the seabirds.

But the unpleasant actualities would soon come crowding back—especially when the figure of Paulson strode within her field of vision.

Since her escape attempt he had confined her to her tent for long periods, and she was allowed out only for 'exercise'. Dr Stephen, who had himself made an attempt to reach the divers while Marianne was on the slopes of Sennay, had been similarly confined, as well as being given periods of 'extra duty' which consisted of several hours a day spent uselessly rebuilding some of the drystone walls.

She had recently begun to experience the occasional bout of sickness, but had kept this to herself.

Nelson Burr, sitting on a flat rock some twenty yards away, appeared to be staring vacantly out to sea, yet he was very much aware of the presence of his hostage.

Alison Ferry had inspected his right hand on the return from Sennay, and declared that a small bone was broken. She insisted, much to his disgust, in putting the hand in plaster. Since then he had felt irritable and rather useless, only half a man.

He watched Paulson approach from the direction of the barn. The older man stopped beside him and placed a foot on the rock on which he was sitting.

'By the way, I forgot to ask you,' he said. 'What was she like?' He had a habit of speaking in a sly, confidential tone, with an air of nudging innuendo.

'How d'you mean, what was she like?'

Paulson jerked his head. 'Goldilocks. The other night, up the mountain. Did she give you a good time?'

Nelson gave a nervous grin. His first impulse was to uphold his reputation by lying. But something about Paulson's manner induced him to stick to the truth.

'I never touched her.'

Paulson's reaction was total incredulity.

'What? You were up there all night with her and you didn't poke 'er? A young bloke like you? I don't believe it.'

The chauffeur was on the defensive. 'You can't fuck a woman when she's in the family way.'

'That doesn't make any difference . . . she's only three months gone yet. It makes 'em all the more randy when they're up the stick . . . and you never touched 'er? Blind O'Riley, I reckon there must be something wrong with you.' He suddenly smirked widely, as if a waggish inspiration had arrived. 'Now don't tell me you've fallen in love.'

'Course I 'aven't. What makes you think that?'

'I thought I'd seen you lookin' a bit dewy-eyed lately.'

'Ah, don't talk bollocks, Terry. You don't know what you're talkin' about.'

'Don't I? You talk to 'er a lot, don't you?'

'What's wrong with that?'

Paulson put a hand on Nelson's shoulder. He became serious. 'Listen mate—this is for your own good. I wouldn't get too starry-eyed about that one if I was you. What do you think is going to happen to her after she's had what's inside her?'

'It's the kid they're after,' said Nelson. 'That's all they want. That's what the guv'nor told me.'

Paulson looked slightly alarmed. 'You haven't told her that?'

'I ain't told 'er nuffink.'

Paulson said briskly, 'Right, fair enough. Look—I'll tell you what's going to 'appen, shall I? In about four months' time we leave 'ere, all right? We take madam and the other two back to the guv'nor's place in London until she's delivered the goods. What'll 'appen to them after that is anyone's guess. But don't forget, we're all in this together, and after this lot's over nobody wants to be identified. I don't know about you, mate, but I don't propose to spend the rest of my life in the nick.'

Nelson deliberated on this. He said, 'Yeh, I see what you mean.'

'Anyway, while we're here we might just as well enjoy ourselves as much as possible.' The leathery grin reappeared. 'For instance, if I was to catch you creepin' out of Goldilock's tent at four in the morning I might even look the other way. In fact I don't see why she shouldn't give both of us fellow-campers a bit of joy.' He gave the chauffeur's shoulder a final pat and moved off with his usual stalking gait.

Nelson's thoughts churned disturbingly on what he had just heard. His instructions from Fox-Hillyer had not extended beyond keeping watch on Marianne while they were on the island. Was he getting sucked into something much deeper, that he didn't even know about?

Ten minutes later Nelson heard the Gemini's engine start as Paulson left to pick up the stores from the mainland.

He walked across to where Marianne was sitting and stood awkwardly beside her. He always felt inadequate in her presence.

She turned her eyes away from the stac and looked up at him excitedly. 'I think some of the chicks have hatched,' she said.

He crouched beside her. 'D'you ever have any trouble with Paulson?' he asked.

'What sort of trouble?'

'You know . . . any sort.'

'Not really. I hardly ever talk to him.'

'If ever 'e starts botherin' you,' said Nelson, 'just let me know.'

When Paulson picked up the stores from Fox-Hillyer he launched the Gemini and made his way back through the choppy straits towards Ahd Skeir. He looked back and saw the Range Rover reverse and move off along the coast road towards Tarbert.

But it wasn't until he was halfway across that Paulson made a wide turn and headed back towards the mainland of Harris. This time he struck a more southerly course, rounded the point, and beached the craft, some twenty minutes later, on the quay of a small fishing village.

Paulson moved purposefully through the strolling tourists until he found the only bar in the place. There he purchased half a dozen bottles of Scotch, and returned swiftly to the dinghy.

Buechner talked for more than an hour into the tape recorder, at first haltingly and then, coaxed by Eckstein and Greb, with more fluency. It seemed as if some damned-up reservoir of guilt had been breached inside him. Now he couldn't get rid of it fast enough; the atmosphere in the flat had areas in common with a confessional, a headmaster's study.

When he had finished there was a hiatus. Eckstein and Greb dwelt on the huge implications of what they had just been told.

Greb gave the German a stiff shot of brandy and took one himself. Schen, his labours successfully concluded, stared out of the window with an inglowing, slightly complacent smile.

Eventually Eckstein walked across to Buechner.

'You say that you found these documents among your father's effects, and then sold them to Reisener?'

Greb translated. Buechner replied, 'Yes, that is true.'

Greb said with some bitterness, 'Didn't you realise what

you were doing, you bastard—just for a few thousand lousy marks and a job?'

Eckstein said quickly, 'All right, Vic, that can wait.' He continued : 'Do you possess a copy of these documents?'

'Yes, I took a photostat copy of all the documents.'

'Does Reisener know?'

'No,' Buechner said listlessly. 'Herr Reisener told me not to keep any copies, but I did so in case he went back on his promises.'

'Where do you keep this copy? At home?'

'Yes, in a drawer in my study.'

Eckstein said, 'Vic, we're going to need those documents for verification.'

'You think so?'

'I know so. Otherwise who in the world is going to believe this?'

'That could be a point.'

'The question, of course,' mused Eckstein, 'is how do we get our hands on the said documents. Do we request our friend here to telephone his hausfrau and ask her to hand them over when we come to collect them?' The question was hypothetical. They looked at Buechner appraisingly.

'It's too much of a risk in the shape he's in,' Greb said. 'She would know from his voice. By the time we showed up the opposition would be there in force.'

'I wouldn't oppose that theory,' Eckstein said. 'Ask him to give us a note.'

'That's a better idea.'

Greb searched through Buechner's briefcase and found a copy of a letter with the firm's letterhead. He turned it over and placed it in front of Buechner.

'Listen,' he said. 'We are going to your house and we are going to collect those documents. I want you to write a note to your wife on this piece of paper. You will tell her that something has cropped up concerning your father's will, and you need the documents to show them to a solicitor. Understand?'

Buechner nodded.

'So you are sending someone from the office to pick up the documents and you want your wife to hand them over.'

'Please,' the German appealed, 'allow me to come with you. I will give you the papers.'

Greb glanced at Eckstein as he translated. Eckstein shook his head briefly.

'That's not possible. Don't worry, we're not going to hurt your family.'

Greb pressed the ball-point into Buechner's hand.

Eckstein told Schen, 'When we go to pick up the documents I want you to stay here with Buechner. Get him cleaned up and be ready to leave as soon as we come back. We shouldn't be much longer than half an hour.'

Schen's eyes gleamed with anticipation.

'Maybe I should come with you.'

'Not this time. We can handle it.'

Schen seemed disappointed.

Marianne sat outside her tent writing into an exercise book. Some weeks earlier she had decided to keep a diary. It would help with the processes of recollection once her ordeal was over—and besides it was a good way of passing the time.

Paulson had never passed any comment on this activity. He appeared to regard it with cynical amusement.

Now he appeared against the dipping sun and sprawled down heavily beside her.

'Writing your memoirs?'

'That's right.' She continued writing.

'Ever thought of writing a letter to someone?'

She looked up sharply.

'If you wanted to drop a line to somebody just to let them know you're still around . . . you know? Long as you didn't say anything about where you are. I could post it for you next time I go over the water. Course I should 'ave to read it first.'

She was at first hopeful. 'D'you really mean that?'

'Certainly. I'm not supposed to, mind.'

She read in his eyes that he was lying. He would take her letter to Nick, read it, and tear it up.

'I don't think I'll bother, thanks.'

Paulson seemed surprised at this reaction.

He said, 'Look, I'd like to have a chat with you about one or two things. I brought a bottle of Scotch back today—be nice to share it with somebody. Why don't you wander across to my tent a bit later and have a drink?'

Marianne resumed writing.

'Now listen, there's no reason to be unfriendly. I'm just doing a job, that's all.' He stretched across and patted her knee. 'I could make your life a hell of a lot easier while you're here—long as I was getting a bit of co-operation from your side. I mean, we're all human.'

She shifted her position, away from his reach, trying to hide her revulsion.

'I think I ought to make one thing clear,' she said. 'I am not going to bed with you, not now, and not ever.'

Paulson's smile was a supercilious as ever.

'Well, thanks for letting me know—but I don't remember asking you.'

He turned and sauntered off.

Greb opened the gates and Eckstein drove the BMW through them on to the driveway.

Buechner's wife was planting clusters of petunias in a border flanking the lawns.

Greb walked across to her in a businesslike fashion. He stopped beside her and said courteously, '*Guten Tag*, Frau Buechner. What a delightful garden you have.'

'It's a lot of work,' she said, still on her knees.

'I've just come from your husband. He wants me to collect something. Some documents, I believe.'

She stood up. He passed the note over. She dusted the soil from her hands, read it, and gave him a hard look.

'You work with Rudolf?'

'Oh yes, he's the head of my department. I'm Herr Bokel-mann by the way.'

She glanced, to Greb's mind suspiciously, at Eckstein, turning the car. Then walked slowly towards the front door.

Greb walked quickly after her. 'Sorry, I almost forgot.' He produced Buechner's big key ring and handed it to her with one of the keys protruding. 'He said this is the one which unlocks the drawer.'

She took it without comment and walked with painful slowness into the house, stopping at one point to pick up a pair of secateurs.

A few minutes later the school bus disgorged the Buechner twins, who came tearing through the gate. One of them raced up to Greb and stared up at him, round-eyed.

'What's your name?' He demanded to know.

'I haven't got one,' Greb replied.

The boy ran to his brother, shrieking with glee. 'He hasn't got a name.'

The twins produced a football, kicked it against the car in which Eckstein sat, making muddy imprints on the bodywork. They yelled with laughter. They invited Greb to join in the game, rolling the ball towards him. He lunged at it with his foot but the ball merely bobbled off his ankle.

'You're no good,' they yelled. 'Go home, you're no good!'

The mother emerged through the front door, moving more quickly this time. 'How many times have I told you not to play football in the garden?' She commandeered the ball.

The boys looked sheepish. They loped off round the back of the house. Frau Buechner walked to the car and spoke to Eckstein through the open window. 'I'm sorry if they've made a mess of your car.'

Eckstein, who hadn't understood a word, shrugged, spread his hands, and grinned.

She turned to Greb, as he approached, anxiously.

'Those two are real little terrors.'

She handed Greb a deed box, tied with red tape.

'I think this is the one. If it isn't my husband will have to come and fetch it himself.'

Greb smiled. 'I'll tell him. *Vielen Dank.*'

He turned and moved away towards the car.

'Just a moment. What did you say your name was?'

'Bokelmann. Joachim Bokelmann.'

'I think you'd better give my husband back his keys, Herr Bokelmann.'

'Sorry . . . I keep forgetting about the keys.'

He took them from her.

'*Auf wiedersehen*, Frau Buechner.'

As Greb climbed into the car with the deed box he said, 'Let's get the hell out. I think she knows.'

Eckstein engaged the gears.

Frau Buechner watched the car depart with growing suspicion. It wasn't like Rudolf to entrust anything to anybody. She returned to the house and hovered uncertainly beside the telephone in the hallway. She ought to check with Rudolf. On the other hand he had given her strict instructions never to call him at the office except in cases of dire emergency.

As she deliberated, the telephone rang.

'*Hallo, ich möchte bitte Frau Buechner sprechen?*'

'*Ja, es spricht Frau Buechner.*'

'This is Fraulein Loeb, Herr Buechner's secretary. Sorry to trouble you. I just wanted to ask how your husband is feeling after his accident.'

It was a day of real warmth and surprisingly little wind on Ahd Skeir. When the night fell Marianne dispensed for the first time with her sleeping bag and wrapped herself in a single sheet and a blanket. The silence was complete except for the distant sound of the surf.

There were only five hours of darkness on the island at this time of the year and it was well into the second, just before midnight, that Marianne drifted into sleep.

She awoke abruptly about an hour later and was immediately aware of the presence of Paulson. The light was on in the tent, and he was standing over her, stripped to the waist, his sun-tanned skin glistening with oil.

He was flexing the switch which he now carried most of the time during his wandering about the island, a length of 30-amp electric cable, the last foot of which had been stripped of insulation, and the three wires knotted at intervals along this length.

He reeked of whisky. After three months of total abstinence he had drunk a bottle in three hours. He brandished a second in his free hand. As Marianne struggled to a sitting position the face creased into a lopsided grin. 'It's all right, no need to get alarmed,' he said softly. 'I've just come over for a bit of a chat.' He offered the bottle. 'Why don't you have a drink?'

'No thanks.' She was stiff with fear and revulsion.

He paused, apparently reflecting, running the cable through his fingers. Finally he said, 'How old do you think I am?'

'I've no idea.'

'I'm forty-seven. I'm still as fit now as I was when I was thirty. I've always looked after myself.'

The small eyes glittered in the semi-darkness. He sat down on the bed.

'See those abdominal muscles?' He tensed his body, and Marianne saw the stomach muscles stand out like knotted rope. The tendons of his thick neck swelled, and then relaxed. 'Once you let those go soft and slack, you're finished,' he said. He tensed the muscles again, and gave them a solid thump with his fist, without flinching.

'I'm a hard man,' he said. 'I'm very difficult to hurt. I don't feel pain like most people. Pain is all in the mind. Look, I'll give you a bit of a demonstration.' He put the end of the cable into her reluctant hand and squeezed the fingers on it. 'I want you to hit me across the body with this . . . hard as you like . . . and I'll bet you I won't make a sound . . . even if you draw blood I won't feel it.'

An almost unnatural calm settled upon her. She was able to think clearly and rationally about how she was going to handle the situation. She had only one deep-rooted fear—that if she was going to have to struggle against this powerful man her baby might be injured in the process.

Paulson crouched beside her, offering his torso to the switch. 'Come on, don't be afraid . . . you won't hurt me.'

She said, 'I'm sorry, I know what you want, but I can't do it. Why don't you try Sister Ferry?'

Paulson moistened his lips.

'Look, I'm only asking you a small favour. You know what my friend Nelson wants, don't you? I might even let 'im take it if you don't play the game with me.'

Marianne suddenly felt nothing but a contemptuous disgust for this man crouching beside her bed. She said, 'I suppose you know you've got a sick mind.'

The leathery features suffused with anger. Paulson rose slowly to his feet, then he reached out and ripped her pyjama jacket open. His voice quivered with rage. 'You ought to be careful what you say to me y'know. I can make you wish you'd never been born.'

Marianne said levelly, 'I never thought you were the kind of man who needed to bully women.'

He sat down on the bed again, and stared at nothing. The fury seemed suddenly to evaporate. He put a hand to his forehead. 'Christ,' he said, 'I'm pissed.'

'Look, this is getting to be a bit stupid. Why don't you go back to bed?' She began to feel she had nearly won.

'It's not going to do you any harm,' Paulson said.

'It wouldn't do you any good, either.'

'Ah, shut up! You fucking women are all the same!'

All at once the urge seemed to drain out of him, as the booze took over. He stood up, unsteadily, and picked up the bottle of Scotch. At this precise moment Nelson Burr, fully dressed, pushed his way through the flaps of the tent.

'Leave her alone, Paulson,' he said.

Paulson turned his head slowly. He said, 'Ah, piss off! We're just having a quiet chat.'

'I said leave 'er alone.'

Marianne said, 'Nelson, it's all right now.'

Paulson clutched at the central tent pole, steadying himself. He turned to face Nelson.

'Right, I want a word outside with you.'

He picked up the cable and walked outside the tent, shoving the chauffeur before him. They confronted each other in bright moonlight. Paulson said, 'Now listen, Nellie, I'm in charge of this operation so don't start chancing your arm, all right?'

In those last few seconds Paulson had committed three cardinal errors which he would hardly have made when sober. He had first used physical force on the younger man, then called him Nellie, a derivative of his name which had tormented him throughout childhood.

And finally he had dismissed, as an adversary, a man who was six inches shorter, thirty pounds lighter, suffering from a broken hand. The hand in question came from nowhere and smashed into Paulson's head, just above his left ear. It was fortified by a pound of plaster.

The older man tottered back a few paces, then fell across the guy ropes of Marianne's tent. Nelson stooped beside him and clubbed him again, smashing the bridge of his nose. Then he picked up the switch and began lashing Paulson's recumbent body, until Marianne appeared and pulled him away, begging him to stop.

He stood there gasping for breath for a few moments, his rage subsiding. When he was able to speak coherently he said, 'Hurry up and get dressed . . . I'll go and get the others. We've got to get away from here.'

Eckstein drove quickly through the western suburbs of Munich, but not so fast as to attract undue attention.

He arrived outside Greb's flat at 4.27 p.m. Schen was already on his way down with Buechner. A pair of ancient ladies, returning to the flats for tea from their afternoon stroll saw Buechner being helped into the car, and expressed mutual disgust at the sight of such drunken behaviour.

They had now transferred to the hired Fiat and were quickly mobile again. Eckstein drove with Greb beside him while Schen kept Buechner company in the back seat. Following Greb's directions, Eckstein took the road due south from the city, through Benediktbeuern where Schen expressed his awe at the sight of the massive baroque monastery, and his disappointment at not having the time to explore it.

Where the road skirted the Walchen See the lakeside swarmed with tourists. Eckstein had to use his horn frequently. At one point he was forced to wait fretfully while a long white caravan which had got stuck across the thoroughfare was manhandled out of the way by a horde of grinning youths on a hiking tour.

A few miles past the lake Greb indicated a minor road which wandered through a thick pine forest. Eckstein turned on to it, and a mile further on left it for a forest track. The car bumped and plunged up the rising surface until they arrived at a clearing where a wide swath of trees had been recently felled. Eckstein turned the car around.

During the last few minutes Schen had taken from his box of tricks a couple of tubes of industrial glue, and he was now busily mixing them in a palette.

Eckstein turned round. 'What's going on?'

Schen gave a mischievous grin. He briefly touched his ears, eyes, and mouth. 'Hear no evil, see no evil, speak no evil,' he said. He fingered a small brush.

Eckstein had heard of this technique, a fairly recent one. You glued a man's lips, eyes, and ears, with chemicals which set fast within fifteen seconds, so that he couldn't see, hear, or speak until several weeks of painful plastic surgery had passed.

'We haven't got time for that,' he said.

Schen protested, 'Just give me half a minute.'

Eckstein said tersely, 'I said, get his ass out of here.'

'Okay, you're the chief.'

The Israeli got out of the car smartly, moved round to the other door, and pulled Buechner out.

They left him sitting on a tree stump. A man without a future, who would hear nightingales for what remained of his life.

He was to be found dead in his car a fortnight later while travelling alone on company business to Regensburg. The post-mortem revealed a massive overdose of drugs, and the subsequent verdict was suicide.

Eckstein touched ninety on the short stretch to the Austrian border, saying nothing, fuming with impatience as he had to slow to a crawl through the environs of the town of Mittenwald—the home, as a glowing sign proclaimed, of the violin.

But for once he could generate no enthusiasm on the subject of stringed instruments. The operation had been about as tidy as a kitchen after a stag night. At any moment he expected to see police cars charging out of side turnings. He could hear telephones ringing all over Munich.

There was a long queue of cars at the Scharnitz border crossing and it was almost half an hour before they reached the checkpoint.

The immigration check was cursory. It was approaching the height of the tourist season. A trio of Americans travelling in a hired Fiat, registered in Innsbruck. Schen, with the gaily-coloured hatband, smiling in the back seat.

But on the Austrian side a customs man examined Schen's box of tricks carefully. Greb said, 'It's a tape recorder. My friend likes to record the songs of birds.' Schen obligingly played a few snatches of nightingale song.

'Any cameras, watches, bottles of spirits?'

'What, from Germany? At the prices they charge over there? You're joking.'

They were waved on.

At about this moment Reisener was being informed of Buechner's kidnapping by an agitated secretary. He had just emerged from a board meeting, and no one had dared to interrupt him.

The road began to ascend sharply as they approached the mountainous country of the Tyrol. Eckstein drove on for another ten kilometers towards Innsbruck before he eventually slackened speed and pulled into a layby.

'Okay, Vic,' he said. 'Let's have a look at the stuff.'

17

Greb opened the deed box and sifted through the contents. They included a will, couched in the usual legal jargon, and a thick sheaf of scientific notes scrawled on browning paper and clipped into a faded blue file cover.

There was also a green file, on the cover of which was written, in a spidery handwriting, '*For the eyes only of my son Rudolf, after my decease.*' Inside was a letter and some other documents.

Greb commenced to read the letter, translating it in the process, pausing occasionally when the handwriting became difficult to decipher.

'It's dated 6 April 1972.'

My Dear Son Rudolf,
When you come to read this letter I shall be dead. I express no regret about this eventuality. We must all go at some time or another, and it may well be said that there are those who overstay their welcome in this life. If there is another one, about which I have always had the gravest doubts, I can only hope that it is one in which justice prevails.

As I write this letter I am approaching my eighty-first birthday. I can no longer work, I am almost as blind as the door-post, and that vital element known as the will to live has become non-existent, so it's improbable that I shall stand between the mortuary attendants and their fees for very much longer.

My will is enclosed with this letter, together with certain other documents. You will find that I have left a thousand marks to each of my delightful grandchildren and a similar sum to my faithful housekeeper Anna Fettweis; to my old friend Otto Dahne, who is to act as my trustee, I have bequeathed my books. Apart from these bequests you are my sole beneficiary. There will not be a great fortune for you to enjoy, particularly after the vampires from the inland revenue have sucked off their portion; but sufficient, with the house, to allow you and your family some added comfort, much as I have drawn comfort from the support and kindness of yourself and your charming wife during my difficult and doddering old age.

I hope and trust that you will remember me with some affection, as also Heidi and your two strapping sons. One of my greatest pleasures in the last few years has been in watching their development. Don't forget to tell them when they are older what I always used to say to you, and still believe to be the truth: 'Fulfilment can only come through achievement.'

I will not bore you with any more platitudes of this nature. In any case I suppose it will always be the function of the young to learn by experience rather than advice. It should also be the function of the dead to depart gracefully, yet there is one last favour I wish to ask of you.

It is, in effect, to help to restore my reputation as a scientist which was so unjustly taken from me at the end of the war, when I was accused of complicity in atrocities and deprived of all research facilities.

I can imagine you recoiling in horror from this request. What awful burden is this that your departed father is trying to string round your neck?

But all that I am asking, my dear Rudolf, is simply that you should place before the public the evidence which I have already prepared, most of which is contained in the 'certain other documents' which are now in front of you, in the appropriate order.

Perhaps you will read these documents before the final instructions, which I have appended as a footnote.

You may wonder, of course, why a dead man should care a whisker about his reputation. The answer is, that it is for

173

the sake of yourself and your sons that this slander must be removed, so that no one in the future can point to Hans and Rudi and say, 'It was their grandfather who committed the atrocities against the Jews, and got away with it;'—the slur which I have now carried with me for twenty-five years.

Rather let them say, 'This is the family of one of Germany's leading scientists, who was falsely accused.'

You may also wonder why I have not presented this evidence during my lifetime. I have considered this question a number of times and always arrived at the same conclusion: that once a man has been discredited, however unjustly, his testimony will always be rejected.

Greb now laid the two pages he had just read on the seat beside him. He said, 'The next part is headed, "A Public Statement, to Whom It May Concern, by Professor Heinrich Karl Buechner". This document was typewritten rather badly, with numerous errors and corrections. Greb continued to read.

On 12 June 1945, I was arraigned before a tribunal of the Allied War Crimes Commission at Bad Mondorf, on suspicion of being involved in experiments on living human beings during the war. I was subsequently deprived of my career as a scientist at the stage where my work was about to come to fruition, and all my previous achievements were ignored.

The purpose of this statement is to show that I have consistently upheld the highest values of science and guarded them with integrity, even throughout the years when Germany was ruled by madmen who had no respect for values of any kind.

My testimony will include details which were not put before the tribunal and the reason for this is self-evident. At the time I was facing serious and utterly false allegations from the notorious Professor Clauberg who was facing trial for his own part in the atrocities at the concentration camps. In the confused circumstances it is natural that I revealed no more than was necessary to defend my reputation.

In order to illustrate the whole situation clearly, I must briefly describe the circumstances in the years before the war.

In 1929 I was engaged as Research Professor of Gynae-cology at the teaching hospital in Magdeburg. At this period I was engaged in studying the possibilities for the artificial in-semination of women.

The techniques for inseminating cattle were already known at this time, but nobody had yet successfully impregnated a woman by artificial means. The difficulties were both medical and social. Such operations, while not strictly illegal, were socially unacceptable, and regarded with abhorrence by the church, particularly in cases where the donor was not the husband.

Nevertheless I built up a small group of patients, cour-ageous women who desired children of their own but were unable to bear them by the normal process, and were willing to offer themselves for experimentation, despite the stigma involved—I recall one newspaper actually referring to these valiant women as 'worse than prostitutes'.

By 1931 I had succeeded in impregnating three of these volunteers by artificial implantation. Each of them sub-sequently gave birth to normal, healthy children, the first time in history that such treatment had been successfully attempted.

Not surprisingly, when these results were made known I came in for a great deal of abuse from the 'respectable' organs of the press, and sackfuls of letters containing hysterical slanders arrived at my door. One might imagine that I was tearing the morals of the nation to pieces. But the reaction of medical science was warm and congratulatory and the details of my research were published in numerous medical journals. I was referred to as 'probably the world's outstand-ing gynaecologist' by the American publication Quarterly Science Review, *and invited to give lectures in Vienna, Ottawa, and San Francisco.*

For the next three or four years I steadily improved my techniques for artificial insemination and passed them on to others working in the same field. At the same time I was pursuing another line of research—the preservation and storage of human spermatozoa ready for future use in artificial insemination.

There was an obvious need for such a 'sperm bank'. Human sperm begins to deteriorate after four or five hours unless it is adequately preserved—and this caused serious difficulties in finding the appropriate sperm donors at short notice. How much better for a woman whose husband was infertile to be able to choose, from a whole range of donors, one whose characteristics—colour of hair and eyes, docile personality—matched that of her husband. Such things are of the greatest importance to prospective mothers, although there are some who demand more than God could promise. I recall one woman who requested 'a son with green eyes, not too short and not too tall, who never shouts at people'.

During my work on sperm preservation I collaborated closely with Ruben of the United States and Muramatsu in Japan who were involved in similar research. I freely acknowledge my debt to these fine scientists.

By 1934 Muramatsu had developed a batch of samples which showed, over a three-year-period, a loss of twenty-two per cent of motility, and fifteen per cent of viability.

This level of deterioration made the samples feasible for use after short-term storage. During this period I had developed a different method which involved spinning the semen together with a preserving agent, and storing in airtight sterilised containers, frozen in liquid nitrogen at a temperature of −192°C.

The mere recital of these facts should not disguise the volume of work which lay behind them; a process of trial and error running into thousands of each.

By 1937 I was testing sperm samples up to five years old. The loss of both motility and viability proved to be less than five per cent, with the rate of loss decreasing with the passage of time.

The success of my method was substantially due to the

*selection of the preserving agent. The formula for this, to-
gether with details of the entire preserving process, is to be
found in my research notes. Although the techniques of sperm
preservation have been developed appreciably during the last
thirty years, I claim that my own method has never been
surpassed, and is superior to current practices.*

*If this is the case, why didn't I publish my results before
now? A good question to which there is a simple answer. In
1933 Adolf Hitler became Chancellor of the Reich. But it
was some time before the Nazi administration had any effect
on my way of life. Politics had little interest for me. I was
completely absorbed in my work.*

*If I thought about these matters at all, I regarded the Nazis,
like so many other people, like a bad dream which would fade
back into the night when everyone woke up. Such people
were not to be taken seriously. But in the late summer of 1937
I received a directive from the Department of Technology in
Berlin requiring me to give a full account of my line of
research, and the results I had so far achieved.*

*I ascertained that all scientific research in Germany was
to be oriented towards serving the best interests of the country.
We were all, it seems, to be re-directed towards the massive
rearmament programme. I protested to the chancellor of my
university, who told me that we had no choice in the matter.
Already some of the country's leading scientists had been taken
away from their projects and set to work designing bombs. I
therefore sent an account of my work to the department which
was couched in the most general terms, disclosing very little.*

*Nothing happened for six months. Then I got a courteous
letter from a senior official expressing the deepest interest in
my researches, and offering to give any assistance in his power
in order to bring them to fruition.*

*The significance of this was soon unpleasantly apparent. The
new government regarded my work as being of great importance. I was expected to become one of the leading architects
of the theory of the Nordic 'master race'.*

Early in 1938 I received an unsolicited addition to my

staff, a certain Dr Hirsch who was alleged to be an expert on the pituitary gland, but seemed to have no more knowledge of the functions of that organ than a first-year medical student. Officially he had been sent to ' absorb ' my ideas. Unofficially he was on a crude spying mission. He stayed in Magdeburg for seven months, then returned to Berlin, his mind in a state of utter confusion.

It was soon after this that I rceived a visit from Hans Clauberg, now a major in the S.S. He was very affable, having found the perfect niche for his talents, and expressed a great interest in my work, particularly in that part of it devoted to the preservation of sperm. He behaved as if he was an old friend, although I had only known him for a brief period when we were students together.

'You and I, Heinrich,' he said, 'we are about to make a great name for ourselves.'

I found it difficult to disguise my revulsion for this disgusting nonentity. My wife Magda felt such a repugnance for the man that she could hardly bear to remain in the same room with him. Fortunately Clauburg was too thick-skinned to be aware of these feelings.

For several months after his visit he sent me invitations to various junketings in Berlin, attended by his revolting masters—Himmler, Streicher, Rosenberg and company. I never replied to these missives. No doubt Clauberg thought they must have got lost in the post. Who could possibly decline the opportunity to rub shoulders with the great?

After the outbreak of war I was left in peace for a considerable time. I assumed that the Nazi hierarchy had too much on their plate to bother with their Wagnerian dreams. I decided not to undertake further research of the kind which might generate interest in the wrong quarters. For three years I concentrated on the problems of infertility in women and devoted much of my time to teaching students.

I now entered upon the most depressing period of my life. I was completely cut off from scientists working in other

178

countries. I flinched with despair every time the newspapers announced some new triumph of German arms, or the radio blared with fresh calls to duty. (Eventually, Magda banished both these organs of communication from the house.) There was little I could do except to wait until the long, bad dream was over.

There were two consolations during this bleak period: the support and comfort of Magda, and the unflagging trust and loyalty of my research assistant, Johannes Steffen, who joined me in 1939 at the end of his post-graduate studies.

Johannes had not only a first-rate analytical mind, but a sharp wit to complement it. I remember us, all three together, sitting in our small shelter at the height of the bombing raids on Magdeburg. Johannes saw a cockroach scuttle across the concrete floor and picked it up, legs waving.

'I want to apologise,' he said, 'for the quality of the crumbs.'

Thus we endured the war.

By the end of 1943 I had almost lost contact with reality. In comparison with most of my colleagues in the medical profession—respected professors who were now tending the wounded on the Russian front—I had been virtually ignored by the authorities. But I had only been lulled, to use the English phrase, into a position of false security.

This was crudely destroyed on 15th January 1944 when a staff car stopped outside the laboratory and Clauberg emerged, accompanied by a uniformed captain of the S.S.

I hadn't seen Clauberg for almost five years. He had put on a good deal of weight and was fatter in the face. He greeted me with the Hitler salutation, to which I failed to respond. Then he introduced his acolyte as 'my adjutant, Captain Fosse,' and told him, 'This is my old friend and colleague, Professor Buechner.'

Clauberg soon explained the reason for his visit. He was carrying out 'research' at Ravensbruck on a number of Jewish women 'volunteers' with the purpose of making them permanently sterile. He believed that he had discovered the

179

perfect method, but needed my assistance to check his results.

When I expressed my revulsion to this plan and refused to have anything to do with it Clauberg said, 'But my dear Heinrich, you should be only too pleased to be asked to work for the Fatherland. In any case, you have no choice.'

He produced a letter and handed it to me:

'I authorise and direct Professor Heinrich Buechner to collaborate with S.S. Brigade Commander Professor Hans Clauberg in the researches which are taking place at Ravensbruck.'

It was signed by Himmler.

Clauberg then informed me that the women would arrive the following day and that Fosse would arrange their accommodation. Clauberg himself proposed to visit the clinic frequently to see how the treatment was progressing.

After their departure I discussed this distressing situation with Magda and Johannes. I was resolved not to co-operate with Clauberg in any way, although I knew that if I refused an order from Himmler I would be consigned to a concentration camp myself.

But Johannes argued that this would be a futile sacrifice which would not help the Jewish women. We should try to keep them in Magdeburg for as long as possible by appearing to 'go along' with the experiment. It was their only chance of surviving Hitler's 'final solution'. The war was now going badly for Germany. Perhaps it would soon be over. It was even possible that someone would succeed in assassinating the Führer.

Magda supported this argument. I was finally persuaded, with great reluctance, to accept it.

Fosse duly arrived with the women—twenty-four of them, packed into a small horsebox—on the following afternoon, and immediately set about finding somewhere for them to stay. The first choice of this psychopathic lout was a cellar under a bombed-out barber's shop, but I told him that this was too far from the clinic for convenience, and we finally settled them in a vacant wing of the nurses' quarters. The captain wanted them to sleep on the floor and be fed on slops, but I persuaded him that unless they were kept in reasonable conditions the value of the treatment would be lost. He was not too difficult to convince, being seriously deficient in reasoning powers.

The women were in a pitiful condition, beaten and half starved, many of them suffering from drug addiction. Their ages ranged from forty to a girl of fourteen who had not yet reached puberty. Most of them had been raped to see if they would conceive in the 'normal fashion'. They were all in a hysterical condition, wondering what was going to happen to them next.

I discovered later that Clauberg's sterilisation theory had been derived from a paper by an Italian psychiatrist who had noted that among drug-addicted women he had treated very few were able to conceive, and he suggested that the drugs may have damaged their capacity to ovulate. Thus Clauberg had injected his subjects with varying amounts of opiate drugs, usually with fatal effects. The women he had sent to Magdeburg were the survivors.

They were to be guarded by Fosse and two soldiers of the S.S. he had brought with him. They quickly found amenable accommodation for themselves in the vicinity.

For the next few months Magda applied herself unsparingly to the welfare of these captives, despite the continual interference of Captain Fosse and his minions, who seemed genuinely appalled that a woman who was so obviously a 'pure Aryan' should treat their charges with humanity. She treated him with such fierce contempt that I was constantly in fear for her safety.

She insisted that the women were given the same meals as the hospital patients—now mostly wounded soldiers and air-raid casualties. She provided them with a gramophone and records, and even 'fiddled' a supply of extra clothing from an organisation of German women who thought they were helping war widows.

Clauberg returned within a fortnight and inquired how the treatment was progressing. I had to explain to him that I could not make a viable test of fertility until the immediate effect of the drugs had worn off, since this alone would seriously diminish the chances of conception.

If Clauberg wanted to find out if the drugs had permanently affected ovulation, he would have to wait until the women had been restored to something like the normal physical condition. I suggested that it might be possible to begin inseminating some of the women after another month.

Clauberg was full of hostile suspicion. But he knew that he had no option but to accept my prognosis. Which was in fact accurate. Some of the Jewish women—at least half a dozen—were suffering the agonies of massive drug withdrawal, and I was treating them for this condition.

Two of them died in the process, including the fourteen-year-old child, despite all the efforts of myself, Johannes, and Magda to keep them alive.

It was on March 1 that I began to give artificial insemination treatment to the captive women, assisted by Johannes Steffen, with Clauberg in attendance. For this purpose I had decided to use stocks of sperm samples which I had preserved in deep freeze over the course of the preceding six years.

It was the most distressing experience of my professional life. Although the women had come to trust Magda by this time, they were terrified by the treatment, believing that some loathsome experiment was involved; the presence of their arch-tormentor, Clauberg, lurking in the background, did nothing to alleviate their fears. Some of them became so hysterical that they had to be given a sedative drug before the treatment could be given.

During the next four weeks, all of the remaining twenty-two captives were artificially inseminated.

Clauberg returned to Ravensbruck to await results. For the next few weeks he was frequently on the telephone asking for news, becoming more and more unbearably exultant as the weeks passed and I informed him that there was nothing to report.

'Are you now prepared to accept that they are all permannently sterile, my good doctor?' he would ask.

I would stubbornly reply, 'I can't confirm or deny it at this stage. I need to take further tests.'

It was one way of playing for time. But it couldn't go on for ever. On the 5th May I told him, 'I've just confirmed the first pregnancy.'

There was a long silence at the other end. Then Clauberg shouted, 'You're lying!'

'Why should I lie on such a subject to a fellow physician?' I asked.

He returned to the clinic on the following day and insisted on having the unfortunate girl brought before him. She was a dark-haired wisp of a thing, about eighteen, with very large eyes. She cowered away as Clauberg bawled questions at her. I had to inform him, 'She's Hungarian. She doesn't understand a word of what you're saying.'

Clauberg still couldn't believe it. During the following fortnight I was able to give him further news—another five of the captives had conceived.

But this time his reaction was different. He told me scornfully that the women who were pregnant hadn't received the full sterilisation treatment, and declared that the pregnancies would never complete their natural course. Either the mothers would miscarry, or the children would be stillborn, or idiots.

I couldn't resist the response: 'Are you sure that isn't just wishful thinking?'

I wish to repeat here, categorically, that the treatment I gave to these women was carried out solely for the purpose of trying to keep them alive.

I denied treating them to the tribunal, for the reasons I have already given.

Moreover, this treatment was exactly as prescribed for childless women who came to see me in the normal way. It cannot be described as 'experimentation'.

Yet as a scientist I made two important observations during the treatment of the Jewish women. One was that all the six who conceived were among those I treated with a combination of mild tranquillising drugs. These drugs (which are listed in my notes) must therefore help to produce the ideal emotional background for conception.

The second was that the preserved sperm samples, previously untried, proved to be entirely effective, even in these appalling circumstances.

Simply to dwell on those days—to recreate the atmosphere, the nadir of the human spirit which prevailed over the whole country, to consider that the abominations in which we were involved were just an infinitesimal part of a millennium of human suffering crammed into a few short years—this is an agonising experience in its own right.

On May 26 Clauberg again visited the hospital. No further pregnancies had occurred, and he insisted that the women who had not conceived should be taken back to the concentration camp.

I resisted as strongly as I could. I claimed that I needed further time to test his 'theories'. But Clauberg was unmoved by this argument, although he conceded that the six pregnant women should be kept at Magdeburg under my care for the time being. The remainder were herded together on the following day, and driven away by Captain Fosse.

As I watched them go, I reflected that perhaps I should go with them, and die with them. But something within me dictated otherwise—I had so much still to offer, so much to contribute to the welfare of a future society.

After this there was a strange and almost unnatural silence. One month followed another without any communication from Clauberg. It was as if he'd forgotten all about us.

By the end of September 1944 we had seriously begun to hope that the six remaining women, now six or seven months into pregnancy, would survive. The end of the war was already in sight. The whole of the Russian front down to the Black Sea had collapsed, and Bulgaria had fallen. The Wermacht was in retreat on every front.

Perhaps Clauberg was having second thoughts about his experiments.

Then, on the 22 September, out of the blue, as I was crossing the yard of the clinic after a consultation I saw an army truck parked outside the nurses' quarters. A few moments later the six women appeared, shepherded by S.S. men. Fosse had been sent to collect them.

I argued with him fiercely, but Fosse coldly informed me that he was acting on Clauberg's instructions.

As I continued to protest, Magda came running from the house and attempted to grapple with the S.S. soldiers who were pushing the weeping women into the back of the truck. She was quite berserk. Eventually one of the guards clubbed her to the ground with a pistol butt.

The women were never seen again. Clauberg claimed later that they gave birth to deformed children before they were sent to the gas chambers.

It was his final attempt to justify his sterilisation theory— and to destroy my reputation.

The loss of the remaining six women had a traumatic effect on Magda. She had grown very fond of them. From this period she began to suffer from serious depressions.

Seven years after the end of the war she took her own life.

Greb paused, lit one of his small cigars, and drew deeply on it, stretching his cramped legs as he did so. Schen lay back in his seat with a frown of concentration. He seemed troubled. Eckstein watched a Boeing 707 climb steeply from Innsbruck airport towards a range of peaks in the distance, glinting like a silver fish in the blue haze.

What in the world was there left to suffer, but a painful death? [continued Greb]. *I apologise for the misquotation, but the truth of the matter was that we had not reached the end of our nightmare—it still had one or two kicks to deliver.*

Seven months later, on the 20th April 1945, another uniformed visitor appeared at the hospital, this time a major with the distinctive flashes of the cavalry. He arrived unheralded while I was eating a quiet supper with Magda and Johannes, punctuated only by the distant rumble of artillery fire. The Russians were now only eight miles from the city.

'Professor Buechner, excuse me . . . I would like a word with you in private.'

'Have it here, in public,' I suggested. 'We are beyond having secrets in this place.'

'I am Major Hochheimer of the intelligence section of the General Staff,' he said with a courteous bow in Magda's direction. 'I have been assigned to take the professor to the Führer in Berlin.'

'What does the Führer want with me?'

'You will find out in due course.'

It sounded like a death sentence which was for some curious reason meaningless.

'All right,' I said, 'give me twenty minutes and I'll come with you.'

The major was sensitive enough to wait outside in the annexe until we had finished eating. I packed an overnight bag, then took leave of my wife and my faithful assistant. I don't think either of them expected to see me again. Nor was I particularly optimistic about the prospect. We had all become fatalists.

I was driven to Berlin in the major's staff car. He didn't say much during the journey. He was rather a taciturn fellow.

At some time he had incurred serious facial injuries and there was a knot of scar tissue on his left cheek. He wore numerous medal ribbons, and oak clusters. No doubt a brave man, and from his manner a representative of the old tradi-

tion of Prussian militarism. He was at least an agreeable improvement on the odious Captain Fosse.

'Does this summons have anything to do with Clauberg?' I asked him.

'Who's Clauberg?'

'A doctor of sorts.'

'I wouldn't know,' said Hochheimer. 'There are two kinds of people I avoid like the plague—doctors and lawyers.'

'I feel the same about soldiers and politicians,' I said.

The major smiled.

The sixty-mile journey to Berlin took more than five hours, the road being jammed with military convoys moving in both directions.

As we got closer to the capital I saw squadrons of tanks deployed by the roadside, along with batteries of artillery and anti-aircraft guns, and soldiers digging slit trenches, and jawing to each other in little groups. The situation looked quite chaotic. I wondered if there was a general somewhere who had a grasp of everything that was happening, and could transform the scene with a few crisp orders. Just outside Potsdam we were waved down by a staff colonel. His own car had broken down and he wanted to commandeer ours. But the major was equal to this. He flashed his pass, signed by the Chief of the General Staff and curtly ordered his driver to proceed.

Although I hadn't been to Berlin for more than a year I was prepared for the scenes of destruction through the reports of others. Still, it was sickening to see the acres of rubble, the shells of great buildings sticking up like giant fingers of accusation. I found it difficult to believe that I was being taken into the presence of the prime architect of all this devastation—and so much more.

While I was in the Reich Chancellery—or rather in the bunkers beneath it, where I stayed for three days—I kept a diary. Since this gives an accurate description of events as they took place, I now present extracts from it as part of this testimony.

20 April 1945

We park outside the ruined façade of the Chancellery. It's like an ant-heap, officers scurrying in and out, sentries prowling around with machine guns.

In the adjacent grounds young men putting up tents, digging positions. The major tells me they are members of the Hitler Youth, preparing a last ditch defence of their Führer. He speaks with pride of the guts of these fifteen-year-olds, itching to throw their frail bodies against the hulls of the Russian tanks when the great moment arrives.

Although Hochheimer is obviously well known, we get stopped at the entrance to the building by the N.C.O.s of the S.S., the major's papers examined and myself searched. Next we go through a long passage, a pall of dust hanging inside it although there are still pictures on the walls, and arrive at a steel door leading to the bunker complex.

The process of interrogation all over again. This time I'm issued with a 'temporary' pass, for which I'm grateful. How would I ever get out of this place without one?

The door opened and slid back into its slot behind us. A steep flight of concrete steps. A long corridor, then another at right angles, Hochheimer stalking ahead with the assurance of a man who knows exactly where he is going.

We passed small locker rooms, the size of broom cupboards, crammed with sleepy-eyed soldiers sitting on kitbags, weapons stacked in heaps, waiting for a millennium of some sort to goad them into frantic action.

A hum, which the major explained came from the ventilators. But it was stuffy and there was a stink of new paint mingled with stale tobacco smoke.

We turned into a fresh corridor marked with the sign, 'Generalstab: Ausschliesslich Offiziere'. The walls here were less crudely finished, shining pink in the fluorescent light.

I had never suffered from claustrophobia before I entered these forbidding tunnels. Now I felt like a rat in a drainpipe.

Eventually Hochheimer halts in front of a door with the number 28 on it. It is opened by a sleek-haired man of about forty.

'Dr Stumpfegger—Professor Buechner.'

The customary click of heels from the major as he bows, and departs.

I follow Stumpfegger into the cell behind the door. It's not much bigger than a railway compartment. A pair of bunks built into the walls, a small table and a couple of chairs, the walls and ceiling a pale dove-grey.

Stumpfegger, who is Hitler's personal doctor, is to look after me during my stay.

I've heard something about this man through the medical grapevine. Once a popular 'society doctor' and until recently one of Himmler's court favourites. Not exactly the finest of references. But he seems to want to be friendly, puts himself out to make me comfortable, exudes charm and a certain amount of respectfulness.

We sit down to dinner in the room, brought in from the kitchens by Stumpfegger's personal servant, together with a bottle of brandy. He informs me that the Führer will probably see me on the following day.

'Do you know what he wants to see me about?' I ask.

'I have a pretty good idea, but I can't discuss it,' he says. 'Hitler wants to be the first to broach the subject.'

He also tells me that he has been attending Hitler for six months, under the instructions of his physician, Professor Morell. Also that his predecessor, one Dr Brandt, had recently been condemned to death by the Führer.

Clearly a difficult patient. But Stumpfegger seemed devoted to his task.

After the meal he excused himself. It happened to be Hitler's birthday, and all the Nazi bigwigs were dropping in for a celebration.

A few moments later he left for this bizarre occasion, leaving me alone in the room.

I turn in about eleven. Stumpfegger still hasn't returned.

Sound of distant laughter merging with the rumble of guns which never ceases. Some drunken singing in the corridor. I'm not too optimistic about the prospect of a good night's sleep, feeling distinctly uneasy. Perhaps a drop more brandy will help.

The bottle is half empty already.

21 *April 1945*
Woke late, suffering from a headache. Am grateful for the coffee which arrives.

Stumpfegger is already up and about and tackling a good breakfast. While I am dressing he tells me that Hitler is in a very poor state of health, although there is no evidence of organic disease. It's largely psychosomatic, Stumpfegger thinks, brought about by emotional exhaustion and depression, caused by the military defeats, and the attempt upon his life. Although the Führer is a vegetarian and neither drinks or smokes, he can only keep going with drugs.

Stumpfegger gave me a list—coramine, vitamultin, omnadin, septoid, mutaflor, and eupavarin to name but a few. Most of these injected.

After breakfast Stumpfegger goes off briskly and eagerly to attend to his patient's medication.

I decide to wander about a bit, get my bearings in this hell hole. As I emerge from Stumpfegger's room I'm almost knocked down by a group of five children, goose-stepping and swinging their arms in a parody of military pomposity, chuckling with glee. Two women follow, one grey-faced and middle-aged, the other younger, a plumpish blonde in a gay flowered frock.

These, as I learn later, are Frau Goebbels and her children whose quarters are further along the same corridor, and Eva Braun. I wander further afield. Am stopped three times, asked to produce my pass. A situation I am sure Kafka would have appreciated. On the third occasion the sergeant is quite friendly. I ask him where I can get a breath of fresh air. He says he feels like one himself, hands over to a corporal, and conducts me to an exit which leads on to a concrete court-yard about the size of a tennis court.

There are about sixty people in this small space taking an airing, mostly soldiers, many of them eating out of mess tins, snatching a short period off duty.

Intermittent sunshine but a cold breeze. At the far end of this compound is a long bank crowded with thousands of daffodils, but their yellowness corrupted, most of them dying and the rest trodden down.

The sergeant, wanting to unburden himself to this apparently sympathetic stranger, shows me a photograph of his wife and child.

He tells me there are about sixty rooms in the bunker complex and about six hundred residents, mostly guards, sentries, kitchen staff and orderlies who live in the corridors and sleep on top of each other. He confides that he wishes the war, which he knows to be lost, will soon be over, but doesn't want to become a prisoner of the Russians.

He fears they will castrate him. He is only twenty-two years old and maintains, reasonably enough, that if he had to live the rest of his life without his balls he would rather not live at all.

He also tells me the story of his colonel who was in charge of the bunker guard, but suddenly disappeared. He was found a few days later living peacefully in the bosom of his family at Potsdam.

He was brought back to the Reich Chancellery and ceremonially shot in the garden in front of his officers.

He was shot by his second-in-command, who succeeded him on the spot. It was a good time for rapid promotion, the sergeant said. The new colonel was only nineteen. The dead one twenty-six.

We stayed in the compound for fifteen minutes, then the sergeant decided to return to duty—before his corporal reported him as a deserter.

After we parted I again took a wrong turning, blundering through a corridor which was stacked with loaves, racks of *vegetables, sacks of potatoes and boxes of ammunition. There was hardly room for a midget to pass. Eventually a white-overalled cook, himself a midget, gave me vague directions towards the 'General Staff' block, looking at me fearfully in case I exploded and condemned him to death for his stupidity. Instead, I gave him my watch as a memento. It was not a generous gift, since time had ceased to have any importance.*

By the time I arrive back at Stumpfegger's room the doctor is in a state of near panic, and is about to report my 'disappearance'. He thought I'd escaped from the bunker, an event which would clearly have had serious repercussions for all and sundry.

'Martin Bormann is waiting to see you,' he announced, after he'd managed to cool down a little.

He took me to see Bormann, who operated from a large office. We had to wait outside for a while, as the Führer's deputy was involved in a heated discussion with a general, Jodl, who had just returned from a reconnaissance of the battle front and wanted Bormann's support for a new tactical plan.

To judge from the raised voices he wasn't getting it. Eventually he stalked out of the office, white with fury, and Stumpfegger ushered me inside.

Bormann seemed completely calm, however. He has large bulging eyes which tend to wander when he talks. According to Stumpfegger nothing that happens in the bunker escapes his notice.

'How good of you to drop in and see us, professor,' he said. 'Is the doctor looking after you properly?'

I said I had no complaints.

'Herr Hitler is most anxious to meet you as soon as he can spare the time. He has a great admiration for your achievements as one of our greatest surgeons. I think he's got a few ideas of his own that he wants to talk to you about.'

He smiled and nodded dismissively, then walked across to his secretary and began to give her instructions. I followed Stumpfegger out of the room.

As we returned to our own corridor I asked Stumpfegger, 'Does he seriously think I'm a surgeon?'

Stumpfegger: 'No, of course not. He knows exactly who you are and why Hitler wants to see you. Unfortunately he seems to detest scientists and intellectuals and always pretends that he doesn't know what they do.

'When I first appeared on the scene he congratulated me on inventing a new kind of torpedo.'

The day begins to drag interminably as I wait for the summons which might come at any moment.

Is the Führer about to make some final, loathsome demand of me which I will be obliged to refuse? I imagine being taken up the steps to the compound, stood against the wall below the bank of crushed and bruised daffodils, and shot.

Whatever is going to befall I hope it won't be delayed for much longer.

Stumpfegger is hanging about all the time. Obviously he's decided not to let me out of his sight. His constant presence is irksome.

He confided that after the war he expected to be treated like an ordinary citizen. He was, after all, merely a doctor exercising his honourable responsibility towards his patient. The identity of that patient was immaterial.

It seemed to me a highly optimistic viewpoint, unlikely to carry much weight with the Russians, but I didn't bother to tell him so. No point in upsetting the fellow.

The message finally came—that Hitler was ready to see me—at seven o'clock in the evening.

Stumpfegger led me up two flights of narrow stairs, then through another corridor where there was a smell of cooking, and knocked at another steel door. We had passed by this time two other sets of sentries and satisfied their professional suspicions.

The door was opened by Fräulein Braun. We entered and Stumpfegger introduced me before he withdrew.

She said, 'Adolf is having a bath, he'll be here in a few minutes.' She moved away towards the kitchen. 'Would you like a cup of coffee?'

The room was puce-coloured but still couldn't escape the aspect of a dungeon. From the next room came the sound of piano music—one of the Beethoven bagatelles, played on a gramophone. As it finished she emerged and went through to switch it off. She wore a knee-length orange-coloured dress, and her movements were deliberate, almost to the point of being theatrical.

She returned, carrying a wriggling alsatian puppy, and sat down opposite. The puppy squealed. She released it and it ran under a sideboard.

'That one's full of mischief,' she said. She got up and began to arrange some tulips in a vase. But before she had finished this exercise she came back and retrieved the puppy, dragging it out by the scruff of the neck and scolding it, then went back to the kitchen to organise the coffee. A woman who could never keep still. 'Do you like dogs, Professor Buechner?' she shouted.

'I've got a little terrier,' I shouted back.

'Good for you!'

Shortly afterwards Hitler came into the room, pulling on his jacket.

Like most of my countrymen I had become familiar with the cast of this man's features. They stared out everywhere from hoardings, flickered from newsreels, the trim black moustache, a hank of hair falling across the forehead.

Since it may be of interest, the Führer I now saw in the flesh for the first time was a pale flabby man with greying hair, unkempt moustache, the features blotched with red.

There was no lustre in his eyes. His whole manner expressed an intense weariness.

As I rose to greet him he gestured for me to remain seated, and sat down himself on a settee opposite.

'You are Professor Buechner?'

'That is so.'

194

'I understand you've been helping Clauberg with some of his experiments.'

I replied, 'It's not possible for me to collaborate with Clauberg. Our aims are completely different. Mine is to preserve life.'

He seemed surprised. 'Well, there's something to be said for both points of view. Don't you agree with Darwin about the survival of the fittest?'

'Yes, but I prefer to let nature take it's course.'

'We have to interfere with nature when it is seen to be inefficient.'

'But who is to be the judge of that?' I asked.

He replied impatiently, 'Man must adapt nature to suit his own development, through the medium of science.'

'Isn't there a danger that he might destroy himself in the process if he ignores natural laws?'

'That's a fallacy. There aren't any natural laws. You don't destroy yourself if you cut the diseased parts from your own body.'

Fräulein Braun placed a cup of coffee in front of me, and what seemed to be a glass of carrot juice at Hitler's elbow. He didn't seem to notice her presence. She perched herself on the arm of his chair.

'However, I haven't asked you here to discuss philosophical problems,' said the Führer. 'Have you any children?'

'Yes, I have a son of thirteen.'

Hitler said, 'It may seem strange to you—I've always wanted to be a father, but in my position it hasn't been possible to raise a family. Fräulein Braun has also wanted children of her own. Now it's far too late.' He paused and looked into the eyes of his mistress. 'We shall be dead very soon.'

She reached out and gripped his hand.

He said, 'I understand from Clauberg that you are able to preserve human sperm for long periods.'

'I have succeeded in storing some samples,' I said cautiously.

'I wish you to preserve some of mine. Would that be possible?'

It took me a few moments to digest the implications of this request.

I said, 'May I ask for what purpose?'

I saw the colour rise in his face. His eyes bulged.

'By your own admission, Buechner,' he rasped, 'you have a child to succeed you. Are you denying me the same privilege?'

Fräulein Braun said, 'Sei still, Liebling. Rege Dich nicht auf.'

At this moment, I had never felt in greater peril. I decided to proceed with the greatest caution.

'I would be glad to help, but there are practical difficulties.'

He glared at me with contempt.

'You as well, Buechner? Everyone in this place talks of "practical difficulties". What sort of practical difficulties?'

'I can't be sure that the sperm in question is active enough to survive a long period of preservation.'

'The sperm in question has been tested by Professor Morell. He says it is well above the normal potency. Any more of your practical difficulties?'

'The sperm must be processed within four hours, otherwise it will deteriorate—and my laboratory is in Magdeburg.'

His stare was unwavering. 'I will get you to Magdeburg in two hours.'

'In that case, Führer, I will do my best.'

This seemed to pacify him. He rose and prowled around the room.

'I understand from Morell,' he said, 'that a single ejaculation contains enough sperms to make every woman in the world pregnant.'

'That is true in theory, perhaps,' I told him.

'How true is it in practice? How many women could you successfully inseminate with a single sperm sample?'

Fräulein Braun's eyes never left his face.

'Given ideal conditions, perhaps two hundred.'

A telephone rang. He picked it up and said, 'Yes, yes, tell them to wait for me.'

He sat down again, wearily. He said, 'You will be ready to return to Magdeburg tomorrow. In the morning I will give you instructions.'

Fräulein Braun went back to her tulips. The interview was clearly over. As I left I noticed, for the first time, a row of oil paintings on the wall. They look like the Italian school. Tributes from Mussolini?

As I write this, late at night in Stumpfegger's cell, the ground shakes with reverberations. A bombing raid, or shell-fire? Who knows. Boots clump in the corridor.

22 April 1945

I awake with Stumpfegger shaking me by the shoulder.

'Get up!' he shouts. 'You've got to leave in ten minutes.'

'What's the time?'

'Seven-twenty.'

I stumble fuzzily out of bed, dress, and start throwing my few belongings into the holdall. Stumpfegger is very animated. 'You won't have time for a shave,' he says, as I pick up a razor. 'The Führer's waiting to see you.'

I am hustled round to Hitler's suite before my eyes are fully opened.

Hitler was standing fully dressed in the centre of the room surrounded by Bormann, Eva Braun, Major Hochheimer, and a man I recognised as Goebbels, who was in the act of signing a document on the table.

Hitler said, 'Professor Buechner. Listen carefully, I will tell you exactly what I want you to do.

'In a few moments you will be given a sperm sample from my own body. You will take it immediately to Magdeburg and preserve it in storage in the presence of Major Hochheimer, who is my trustee in this matter.' (Hochheimer gave a slight bow, as if to confirm this.)

'If you do not carry out this task to Hochheimer's satisfaction, he has been authorised to shoot your wife and child in front of you.

G* 197

'You will retain the semen in storage, under your control, until Hochheimer calls for it. This may not be for a period of years, but when he asks for it you will hand it to him immediately. Do you agree?'

I considered this for a few moments, with all their eyes on me. Then I said, 'Yes, I agree.'

Bormann now handed me two papers to sign. The first read:

I, Professor Buechner, agree to preserve and retain in cold storage the sperm sample given to me on the 22nd day of April 1945, and to deliver the said sample to Major Hermann Hochheimer on demand, at a date to be specified.

The second:

I, Adolf Hitler, Chancellor of the Reich, declare that the sperm sample given into the custody of Professor Buechner on the 22nd day of April 1945 in the presence of the undersigned, is the seed of my body.

This certificate was already signed by Hitler, Goebbels, Bormann, Eva Braun, Hochheimer, and Stumpfegger.

I signed both documents in duplicate. They were typed on Reich Chancellery notepaper. Bormann handed me one copy and gave the other to Hochheimer.

A moment later Stumpfegger handed me a phial containing the sample.

It was with huge relief that I ascended from those abominable tunnels into the light of day.

Hochheimer had his car standing by and we drove at reckless speed through the ruins of the city centre, turning into the vicinity of the Siegessaule.

A little later we were confronted by a remarkable sight—a long straight avenue with all the trees chopped down, and lamp-posts lying prone on the pavements.

At the eastern end, two aircraft—Junkers 52s—were being loaded with stretchers from a long line of army ambulances. It transpired that the planes had just landed in the avenue to evacuate wounded, all the air strips in the Berlin area being out of action or under fire.

We stopped beside one of these converted bombers. Hochheimer jumped out and went straight over to the pilot who was supervising the loading operation.

He was a civilian, wearing a shabby grey flying suit which looked nearly as old as its owner.

Hochheimer imperiously ordered him to stop loading the wounded and get ready to take off immediately. 'On whose orders?' asked the pilot.

The major flourished a signal, signed personally by the Führer.

I heard the pilot shout, 'These men are dying. Fuck the Führer.' Hochheimer instantly drew his pistol. I'm sure he would have shot the unfortunate man if he had been able to fly the aircraft himself.

But faced with this intractable situation the pilot had to submit. The hatches were shut, the ramps pulled away, and I climbed aboard with Hochheimer.

My companion ensconced himself in a turret formerly occupied by the air-gunner. I elected to sit in the body of the plane which was equipped with racks to accommodate about sixty wounded men on stretchers.

Only about a dozen of these were occupied, their sole attendant being a medical orderly who was scarcely more than a schoolboy.

When we took off the aircraft bumped along the road for what seemed miles—then somehow we became airborne.

It was only a fifteen-minute trip to Magdeburg, but it seemed like a year!

The pilot was hedge-hopping—or rather, in this case building-hopping—to escape the attentions of the Russian anti-aircraft guns.

One of the wounded men was screaming in agony. I found

199

the orderly trying to inject morphia into his right forearm which was almost completely stripped of flesh. I took the syringe from him and injected into the buttocks. It wasn't too easy with the aircraft lurching and juddering all over the place.

We landed at Magdeburg airfield on the only runway which was still in action. A car was waiting there for Hochheimer and we got away in a veritable hail of shellfire.

I was to learn later that the Junkers 52 was hit and put out of action before it could take off again, but some of the wounded men were safely evacuated.

When I arrived back at the hospital Magda threw her arms around me and burst into floods of tears. Yet she knew from the presence of Hochheimer at my shoulder that the bad dream was not yet over.

Before we proceeded any further with the business in hand I called Johannes Steffen, whose assistance I needed with the processing of the sperm, into the consulting room, while Hochheimer waited outside. I explained the circumstances briefly and asked if he would be prepared to assist.

He thought about it for quite a while. Then he gave his small, wry grin and said, 'Well, if it's all right with you, Professor, it's got to be all right with me.'

We then walked across to the laboratory and subjected the Führer's sperm to the preservation process. It took about twenty-five minutes, during which time Hochheimer hovered over us like a falcon. Johannes and I went through the motions just as if we were immortalising the sperm of Joe Smith. Hochheimer, who had no knowledge of science whatsoever, had a keen nose, and had he smelled any chicanery, would have blown Magda's head off, being a man without compunction in such matters.

Eventually I showed him the stainless steel container, hermetically sealed.

'I am now going to place this in a deep-freeze cabinet,' I told him.

He produced a reel of sticky tape, stuck it round the container, and signed it—Hochheimer—across the join.

He said—this man of few words—'Professor Buechner, I leave this in your custody. I shall return for it. I will know if the tape has been removed, and if this is the case I will kill you. Heil Hitler.'

Major Hochheimer left at about two-thirty that same afternoon. He informed me before he got into his car, that he was going to surrender himself to the British or the Americans.

Since the whole area was now encircled by the Russians I didn't give too much for his chances.

'That seems to be the end of the diary,' Greb said. He continued to read.

I hereby state that at no time did I intend to allow Hochheimer to take possession of Hitler's sperm. This for two reasons. First, I did not want to be responsible for a proliferation of Hitler's progeny at some future date. Secondly, since the Führer had been taking massive quantities of drugs during the final days of his life, I would under no circumstances have considered him a suitable donor for artificial insemination.

Steffen wanted me to destroy the sample, but for some reason—no doubt the instinct of a scientist—I couldn't.

Soon I had other things to consider. Within five days the Russians had taken Berlin and Magdeburg, and the armistice was signed.

For the next few months, it was all remorseless questioning. The bad dream still had not ended. I must admit to a certain slight feeling of satisfaction at the secret knowledge that my Russian inquisitors never succeeded in dragging into the open.

The nightmare finally reached its conclusion at Bad Mondorf.

In April 1945 the Russian military authorities published their first list of war casualties. It included the name of Major Herman Hochheimer among those killed in action.

In January 1946 Johannes Steffen disappeared from the clinic in Magdeburg. I heard later that he had escaped to the West, and was practising in Osnabruck.

In 1945, after repeated applications, I was allowed to emigrate to West Germany with my son, Rudolf. I took with me my research notes and scientific equipment, including the sperm samples.

Rudolf and I settled in Stuttgart, where I practised as a gynaecologist until my retirement in 1958.

I declare that the foregoing is a true and sincere account of the tragic events in which I was involved during the Nazi régime.

I maintain that I did not at any stage betray my principles as a scientist, despite the most intense pressure on me to do so.

I further maintain that my real achievements as a scientist have never been accorded their deserved recognition.

As a gesture of reconciliation, I bequeath the living proof of those achievements—the phial of Hitler's sperm—to any respected institute of medical science which is prepared to endorse my own contribution to that science, to the satisfaction of my son and executor, Rudolf Buechner.

The importance of this sample may well be incalculable to the future study of genetics. It is well known that personality characteristics are passed from one generation to another through the sperm cells although the exact nature of this process is still unknown.

When further research has found the key to this mystery, the genetic scientists of the future will be able to study the living sperm cells of the man who encompassed more of the capacity for evil in his own personality than any other single human being throughout history.

This concluded Professor Buechner's 'public statement'. He had signed it on the final page.

Eckstein gazed through the windscreen and puffed thoughtfully at his pipe as a squall of rain smeared his vision. Greb picked up the next sheet, which was handwritten. He glanced at it briefly, then said, 'I guess this is a continuation of the letter to his son.'

I am hoping and praying as I write these words, my dear Rudolf, that this re-creation of the ghosts of the past will not cause you too much distress, particularly in respect of your dear mother. She was a woman of the highest quality, of a stature that I could not hope to match. But it is only through experience and understanding of the past that we can hope to tolerate the present, and survive the future.

To return to the pragmatic: what I ask of you is this. That as my executor you will have my statement reproduced in some responsible organ of the press. This, I have no doubt, will arouse considerable interest in scientific circles.

You will then, at your discretion, transfer the sperm specimen mentioned into the custody of the appropriate medical institution for the benefit of future research.

You will find it in the deep-freeze cabinet located in the small laboratory adjoining my study. It is contained in a stainless-steel cylinder marked with a green band, and sealed with a white tape signed 'Hochheimer'.

God bless you all, and may our family flourish! Auf Wiedersehen. Heinrich Buechner, your devoted father.

Thus the letter ended.

Greb fished about among the remaining papers. These included copies of the two certificates signed by Professor Buechner in the presence of Hitler. The rest were technical notes relating to Buechner's research.

'I guess that is it,' he said.

The three men sat in silence for a while.

Then Greb commented, shaking his head, 'The things some people will do for money!'

Eckstein said, 'Let's go home.'

He started the engine and drove on towards Innsbruck.

18

When Paulson came to, it took him several moments to become fully cognisant of the almost unbelievable thing which had happened to him.

He rose to his feet groggily, feeling the pain from his crushed nose, putting a hand to it and discovering the mask of congealed blood on his face.

He became swiftly inflamed by a murderous rage.

From across the straits the wind carried the faint puttering sound of the Gemini's engine as it headed for the dark mass of land opposite. He could just about make out the dinghy bobbing in the moonlight, and ran back to his tent for the carbine. But after loosing off a few shots in the general direction of the small craft he recognised that it was hopelessly out of range.

Paulson's mind raced through various possibilities. He needed urgently to contact Fox-Hillyer and warn him of this disaster. But his chief, now sleeping peacefully at the hotel in Tarbert, ten miles away, would not be in radio contact until noon.

By which time . . .

He guessed that Nelson Burr and the others would leave the dinghy at the nearest point on the island of Harris, then continue on foot across the island on their way to the Scottish mainland. But they would have to cross on the morning ferry from Tarbert.

Paulson consulted his watch. It was 3.25 a.m. and already there was a flush in the sky where the dawn was due to break.

He adjudged that he still had about five hours in which to contact Fox-Hillyer.

He decided to swim across to Harris.

He first collected his wallet—he might need money—and thrust it into the back pocket of his trousers. Then he slipped on a small life-jacket, one of several which was part of the dinghy's equipment, and inflated it.

The sea, looked at from the distance of Gleann Chillidh, was an expanse of liquid graphite, the surface no more than mildly granulated.

When Paulson reached the landing stage he was slightly perturbed by the swell, slurping and slopping against the rocks. But he was a powerful swimmer who had formerly represented the army at the sport, had more than once swum five mile across open sea, and it was not much more than a mile to his present destination.

He lowered himself into the water and struck out. The coldness made him gasp, and he had to fight fiercely against the currents and eddies which swirled round the island.

Eventually he emerged into calmer water and began to forge ahead with a low, economical crawl stroke, towards the centre of the channel.

Paulson was already aware, from his trips across the strait in the rubber dinghy, of the strong tide which ran south-west from the Sound of Taransay, and he compensated for this by striking hard into the prevailing current. He could see a buoy light winking off the point of Rubha Romagi and he made this his target.

Paulson put his head down and swam.

Some fifteen minutes later he struck the mainstream of the tidal undertow. At this point the water became intensely choppy, with small wavelets smacking uncomfortably into Paulson's face as he strove to surmount them.

He felt he was making rather slow progress and wondered if he should jettison the rather cumbersome life jacket, but decided against this.

He rested for a few minutes, treading water.

When he resumed swimming he found he could no longer see the light.

But the brooding mass of the heights of Rubha Mas a'Chnuic comforted him—they seemed almost within spitting distance. Yet he had to get round them into the bay before he could land.

Paulson struck out fiercely for the final lap, and soon he was out of the choppy water and into a heavy swell.

He had changed to breast stroke now, but still seemed to be making little headway.

For the next ten minutes it was as if he were swimming on the spot—or was the peak slipping slowly away to the north? He now decided to make for the nearest landfall, and try to get ashore at the foot of the cliffs around Toe Point.

Paulson got to within a hundred yards of this prospect and then saw that it was an impossible one. The waves were thrashing and boiling through the rocks, and surging against the cliff face. At one point he felt himself being sucked towards this maelstrom, and had to fight his way back to less turbulent conditions, further offshore.

It was at this juncture that Paulson began to think exclusively, and with increasing desperation, in terms of survival.

He had been swimming for just under an hour, was about three miles from Ahd Skeir, and even further from his original objective.

It was now broad daylight. He decided to swim along the south-westerly coastline of Harris and look for a beach of some sort.

Yet as he attempted to follow this course, he became aware that his puny arm strokes were having little or no effect upon his progress.

A ferocious ebb-tide was pushing him further and further into the mainstream of the Sound of Harris.

This stretch of water between the large islands of Harris and North Uist, some fifteen miles long and five miles wide, dotted with rocky crags and islets, acts as a bottleneck between the Atlantic and the Scottish coast.

It is probably the most disturbed seascape in the British Isles, and for long periods unnavigable by smaller shipping.

At this time, approaching midsummer, the sound was usually at its most amenable. But on this occasion a stiffish north-westerly breeze was blowing against the outgoing tide.

Despite his most desperate efforts the shore continued to recede from Paulson. When he was close to exhaustion he gave up swimming but kept calm, recalling his army survival training.

But in those days there was always a boat waiting alongside ready to pull him out.

After another fifty minutes the tide seeping out from the sound had pushed him four miles into the Atlantic.

He could still see land in several directions as he wallowed in a gigantic swell, but only remotely, inviting yet unavailable.

Several small ships passed, mostly incoming trawlers, one or two coasters, a small passenger liner on a Hebridean tour.

Nobody at that time of the morning spotted the man in the life jacket.

After another hour the tide had turned.

Paulson, lying on his back, gasping in air and blowing out water was sucked fiercely, a piece of human flotsam, back towards the Sound of Harris. He recognised the outline of Toe Head as he was swept past it like a baulk of timber.

The wind had freshened, and was now driving billions of tons of seawater through the bottleneck.

Unknown to Paulson, a storm warning had been broadcast to shipping in the immediate area some forty minutes previously.

A number of smaller craft had anchored, or run for shelter, at either end of the Sound of Harris.

Paulson's experience was far more dramatic, and immediate.

Again and again he rose inexorably on the crest of a wave, only to find himself staring into what seemed a three-acre chasm of foaming water, thirty feet below. He then plunged into this, tossing like a cork, with a massive wall of water hurtling towards him. Somehow he rose in front of this wall, through the frothing crest of it, and was swept down once more into the seething depths below.

All he was capable of doing now, in terms of survival, was to try to close his mouth when he was engulfed by water, and to gulp in air when he was not. Other senses, of sight and sound, were still operative. He heard nothing but the whine of the wind and the turbulence of the water. But sometimes he saw birds, guillemots and razorbills, riding the waves beside him. Once a flight of gannets passed across his line of vision.

As Paulson was swept past the small island of Killegray he was driven through an outcrop of rocks, just above the surface, well marked by buoys. His body was flung mercilessly from one to another. It was soon after this that he finally lost consciousness.

Promptly at noon Fox-Hillyer spoke into the microphone. 'Calling Pima . . . Sunray to Pima . . . Are you there, Pima? Pima, are you receiving me?'

After ten minutes Fox-Hillyer drove down to the small stony beach where Paulson landed when collecting supplies.

He gazed through binoculars at Ahd Skeir, enticingly green in the morning sun, birds wheeling around it. But he could see no sign of a human presence.

Then he noticed the beached dinghy, a hundred yards away. The encroaching tide had just reached it, and it was about to drift away.

He jumped out of the Range Rover, hurried across and rescued it, dragging it further up the shore. He checked it for petrol. A little later he started the engine and set off across the straits.

19

'The thing that bothers me,' said Coulman, 'is that thing ticking away.' He pointed to the bland face of the electric clock on the wall of his office. 'That woman . . . what was her name?'

'Marianne Seal,' Eckstein provided.

'Is now more than three months pregnant. So we've got less than six months to find her. If we don't, we'll have to start looking for one Nordic infant somewhere in Europe, which doesn't look too different from around two hundred million others.'

'You're being unduly pessimistic,' Eckstein said. 'A lot can happen in six months.'

'Am I? I don't think so. I mean, six months is all.'

'What do we do when we catch up with her?'

'I've been in touch with head office on that one,' said Coulman. 'The short answer is, we destroy the embryo.'

Eckstein asked, 'What happens to what's outside it?'

'We'll think about that when we find her.'

'I'd rather think about it now, Richard.'

Coulman was patently surprised by this persistence.

'We feed her a pill,' he said, 'which will kill the embryo, but not the mother.'

'So what happens to a mother who is carrying around a poisoned, half-grown child?'

'That is not our responsibility. Maybe if she got to a surgeon inside a couple of hours . . .' he shrugged. 'Barry, this is something big.'

Eckstein said drily, 'You mean, bigger than both of us?

209

Maybe I'm being a bit simple-minded, Richard, but there's a theory going the rounds that people get as much from their environment as they do from their genes. So let's suppose that Marianne gives birth to the son of Adolf Hitler, and the kid grows up? What sort of evidence do you have that the lad is going to be a chip off the old block? Suppose he takes after his grandmother?'

'That doesn't enter the argument,' Coulman said. 'If Reisener gets hold of the kid, he's going to try to turn it into what he wants it to be, and it's going to inherit everything he's got. Whichever way he turns out this kid is going to become the Messiah of every twisted right-wing anti-Jewish organisation in the world. And he's going to be brought up to believe it.'

'That could be some load to carry,' Eckstein observed. 'I'd hate to be responsible for this guy's security. And it could be a girl.'

'Sure. You ever hear of Joan of Arc. Okay, there's a load of imponderables. Who knows what the world is going to be like in twenty years time. Let's just make sure it doesn't happen.'

He switched off the tape recorder, and stood up. 'By the way, I've given Vic a couple of weeks leave. He had it coming, and his wife's getting a bit neurotic, so he's taking it back in the States. Which means we're going to be short-handed for this operation. D'you want me to ask for Schen?'

'For over here? He'd stand out like a pork chop in a synagogue.'

'I guess so. We'll see how it goes, but I may have to pull him in later. Let's talk again at eleven tomorrow morning . . . and I'd be grateful for a few ideas.'

Eckstein nodded, and wandered downstairs. As he left Coulman assumed an anxious frown. He was a long way from liking what he had just heard. But that wasn't the only thing that bothered him.

It was now early in June, some three months after the blonde English girl and her captors had disappeared from the clinic, and still there was no hint of a clue as to their whereabouts.

Eckstein strolled into Durandt's office where Angela Stringer was opening the mail, largely art books and catalogues of forthcoming sales. He perched on the corner of her desk. 'How does the world seem from your point of vantage, sweetheart?'

She looked at him with a quizzical frown. 'Oh, I'd say it looks a bit battered, but I think it's going to make out.'

'Business good?'

'It's a bit quiet at the moment, thank heaven. Last month everything went haywire.'

'Is the master still flourishing? I haven't seen him for a while.'

'Mr Durandt's round at Christie's at the moment. We've had some lovely things in recently. Would you like to take a look?'

'I would indeed.'

She gave him the keys to the store room. He kissed her hand. 'I'll definitely take you to dinner, one evening this week, followed by a concert.'

'Mr Eckstein, you've been saying that for months,' she scolded.

'Each time, business has intervened. This time, I really mean it.'

The door of the store-room was triple-locked and intricately burglar-alarmed. On the other side lay works of art which were insured for a total of £750,000. Eckstein locked himself in, and gazed around.

The wall at the far end was given over to the more recent acquisitions; on this occasion a set of six exquisite pastel and charcoal sketches of dancers by Degas, a blaze of Kokoschka landscapes. He gazed at these pictures for some considerable time.

It occurred to him that he was looking at the work of men who had given something of immense value to their own society and to successive generations.

This compelled him to brood upon the paucity of his own contribution. Someone had claimed that if intelligence agents had never been invented, the history of the world would not have changed by one iota.

He considered this to be a simplification. There was little doubt that they had added appreciably to the more unpleasant aspects of life throughout the centuries.

He strolled around the room, looking at the other exhibits. Durandt had arranged these in three sections.

There were the 'accumulators', works whose market value was steadily rising. These included some early bronzes by Henry Moore, several Miros, a good blue-period Picasso, a pair of Gaudier-Brzeszka door knockers, two portraits by Modigliani.

Next to these were the 'seconds'—works which, though unlikely to fall in price, were waiting for slight changes in fashion to move up-market. Stanley Spencer, Giacometti, Ben Nicholson, and some of the early surrealists were represented here.

Finally there were what Durandt referred to as 'occasional errors of judgement', which were awaiting the first reasonable offer—several landscapes by Sydney Nolan, a dozen early Augustus Johns ('Why did that man go on churning out rubbish for thirty years after his talent had died?' Durandt had complained) and three copies of a portrait of Winston Churchill by Epstein. The dealer had acquired these a fortnight before it had been discovered that there were more than a hundred on the market.

It was all too much to take. Eckstein found himself as captivated by the blazing scarlets and yellows of the Johns as anything else on display. As he peered closely at a study of gipsies he heard the muffled thump of an explosion.

He moved rapidly to the door and unlocked it, cursing at the intricacies of the unlocking device, managing to set the burglar alarm going in the process.

When he got to Durandt's office he saw there was a hole a foot wide in the desk and Angela was slumped beside it. She was making a small whimpering, blubbering sound through the blood which was beginning to choke her.

Eckstein rang for an ambulance.

It took fifteen minutes to arrive during which time he crouched beside her, an arm round her shoulders. He said, several times, 'Oh Christ!'

The ambulancemen arrived and took her away on a stretcher. Eckstein went with her to the hospital. She was dead on arrival.

Coulman blamed himself. He had frequently suggested to Angela that he should monitor the mail. She had always refused. 'If there's anything wrong I'll be able to smell it, Mr Coulman,' she had said. But he knew he should have insisted.

The forensic experts from Scotland Yard spent two days in the office. An inspector told Coulman that there was no evidence concerning the source of the package, and asked if there was any special reason why anyone should sent it.

Coulman replied that he didn't know of any, except that Heller Art International was a company with strong Jewish associations.

When they had beached the dinghy, Marianne, Dr Stephen, Alison Ferry and Nelson Burr walked the twelve miles along the coast road to Tarbert, reaching that town soon after eight in the morning, and passing the entrance to Fox-Hillyer's hotel as he was complaining to a waitress that his breakfast had been served on a cold plate.

They caught the first ferry, to Oig on the island of Skye, then climbed into a tourist coach which crossed to the mainland at Kyle of Lochalsh, fifty miles away, in the early afternoon.

From there they headed south, by way of other coaches, through mountainous country, staying overnight at a youth hostel, where they slept the sleep of exhaustion.

At first Marianne found it hard to believe that she was really free again. She fully expected Paulson to thrust his way forward from every knot of tourists clustered on the quays and coach stations. 'All right, you've had your fun. Let's get back to where we belong, shall we?' It was only after they reached the mainland that she dared to hope that the illusion was about to become a reality.

By noon on the following day they reached Fort William, and held a brief conference in a small café outside the railway station. Nelson Burr, wiping egg from his plate with a wedge of bread, said, 'Well, I don't know about you lot, but I reckon it's about time we split.'

Stephen said, 'Yes, I agree we can't afford to stay together for much longer.'

'Right, I'll be on my way then.' He rose, grinning at them like a guilty schoolboy, and slung his haversack over his shoulder. 'See you some time. Watch yourselves.' Marianne took both his hands. 'Thanks Nelson,' she said with sincerity. 'I shall always remember you.' He glanced away, almost with shyness. 'I wouldn't do that if I was you.' He glanced around them. 'Hey, let's have your signatures.'

Alison Ferry produced a ballpoint. They all signed their names on the filthy plaster.

He walked away, head held back, stiff-legged, let 'em all come, and fuck 'em. A few yards further down the street he started walking backwards, jerking his free thumb at passing trucks.

They sat silently for a few moments, finishing coffee. Marianne said, 'Why don't we go to the police?' Stephen glanced at Alison, then looked gravely at Marianne.

'Miss Seal, there are a number of very good reasons why that would not be very wise. For example, we should have to implicate young Burr, who has just made it possible for us to escape—yar? Then again, we have no evidence against the people who actually sent us to the island.'

'You mean Mr Harrington and the German.'

Stephen nodded.

'What about Paulson?'

'My dear, you can be quite certain that Paulson is miles

away by now. The important thing is to try and put all this unpleasantness behind us.' He smiled. 'Are you willing to trust me?'

After a slight hesitation she said, 'Yes.'

'There are some other things I want to explain to you, but not at this moment. Just now I'd like to talk privately to Sister Ferry. Would you leave us alone for a few minutes?'

'Yes, of course.'

She strolled out of the café and wandered across the sunlit street, stood aimlessly examining the property advertisements in the window of an estate agent's. Now and again she glanced back at the café where she could see, through the plate glass window, Stephen and the nursing sister huddled together, deep in conversation. At one point he handed something across to her which looked like money. She gave them twelve minutes, then walked slowly back. As she re-entered the café they drew apart. She thought she heard the doctor murmur, 'I'm afraid we have no choice.'

As she sat down Stephen said, 'Miss Seal, we've decided it might be best if you and I go on to London by train, while Sister Ferry continues by coach.' He spoke with some urgency. 'Are you agreeable to that arrangement?'

She said, 'Yes, if you think it's best.'

'Good. We can talk on the train.'

'I haven't got any money.' All her personal belongings had been taken from her at the clinic.

'I've got enough for both of us.'

Alison Ferry said, 'Aye well, I'd best get round to the coach station.'

She got up quickly. Stephen gave her a light embrace and kissed her forehead.

'I'll be in touch,' he said.

She went out rapidly, eyes behind the spectacles welling with tears. For the first time, Marianne felt sorry for her.

An ageing white-coated waiter with a rubicund complexion engineered his features into a professional smile. 'Seven minutes

215

late out of Crewe? That's not like Derek at all. Now what would madam prefer? The turbot is not to be despised, they tell me.'

The sheer speed of the express pounding towards Euston, landscape cantering past, gave her a feeling of real security, with each racketing over points moving her further from the nightmare of Ahd Skeir. Stephen had booked dinner in the first class dining-car, a table for two, secure and private, comforting mur-mur-mur of relaxed voices. 'The sole bonne femme I would think.'

Yet she had difficulty in saying it: 'Why are they so interested in me? Is it because of my baby?'

The doctor evinced a special interest in his British Rail napkin.

'I think I can tell you something about that.' He paused, twined his fingers, looked through the window at a grove of racing trees. 'First of all I was born in Germany, but I have been naturalised British for twenty years. When I was a young doctor I worked with a professor in Germany who was one of the world's leading scientists in gynaecology, yar?

'During the war the Nazis tried to force my professor to help with experiments on Jewish women. He refused to do so . . .

'He was also asked to preserve the sperm of a number of S.S. men, ready for future use in producing the master race. You have heard of this concept, no doubt?'

'Yes.'

'The professor agreed to do this, intending to destroy the sperm later. But for some reason or other, probably scientific curiosity, he failed to do so. When he died, last year, the sperm was still in existence together with some documents, and these fell into the hands of the man called Schultz.'

Her eyes began to widen with alarm. 'But you didn't . . .'

'Please allow me to finish.' He dropped his eyes, picked up a soup spoon, fiddled with it. 'Schultz and his British colleague, the man Harrington, called on me and tried to force me to implant the seed in one of my patients to discover if it was still active. They threatened me, that if I didn't co-operate, they would publish the documents, which would ruin me professionally, since I was named as the professor's principal assistant. At first I refused absolutely, but then I pretended to agree. I wanted to get enough evidence to convict them of blackmail. This was of more importance to me than my own reputation.'

A small, anonymous station fled past in a blur of faces, coloured clothes, posters, old brown pillars.

'I think I could have managed it . . . but your friend Nick discovered too much. That is why we were all taken to the island. You see my dear . . . they want your baby. They believe he will be a true son of the Fatherland . . . and the first of many more.'

'What . . . happened . . . to Nick?'

The wine waiter poured a finger of Niersteiner into Stephen's glass. He sipped, and nodded. Both glasses were filled.

'I regret to tell you that the night before we were taken from the clinic he telephoned me and asked me to tell you that he wanted nothing more to do with the baby and he had decided to return to the United States.'

'Oh no,' she whispered. 'Poor Nick.' She hid her face in long, tapering fingers for a few seconds, then: 'Please tell me. Am I really carrying Nick's child?'

Dr Stephen ruffled his hair, longer now, and unusually slicked down with water. An anxious gesture.

'Of course you are,' he said gently. 'Do you think I would pollute your body with that filth?'

'I'm sorry,' she said. 'I shouldn't have asked.'

He picked up his glass. 'Why not? Why should you trust me? I got you into the situation.'

On June 16 the body of Paulson was found drifting face down in a small creek on the island of Benbecula, some forty miles south of Ahd Skeir, by a corporal of the Royal Artillery's rocket-firing detachment on that island.

It was badly battered, the features unrecognisable, but the wallet still clung to the pocket of the shredded trousers, and thus its owner was identified.

Paulson, who had twice been divorced, had lived alone in a small flat attached to the offices of his firm, Apex Inquiry Services. His junior partner, an ex-C.I.D. man called Dunning, told the police that Paulson had been on holiday in Western Scotland.

Dunning didn't know offhand of anyone who had a grudge against him—although private detectives inevitably had enemies—and he could think of no possible reason why he should take his own life.

The inquest recorded an open verdict.

'I chose you because I was informed you were the best man available in this country. You have proved yourself to be entirely incompetent.' Reisener squashed another cigar butt, his third in twenty minutes, in the porcelain ashtray.

'Yes, I dare say. On the other hand we haven't reached the end of the operation.'

Fox-Hillyer spoke equably enough but he was finding it difficult to disguise his contempt for the raging old man pacing up and down his study like a frantic orang-outang. 'As you must be aware,' he continued, 'from your own recent experience, Herr Reisener, we can't expect to win every battle. The important thing is to win the war.'

'Well, what are you proposing to do next in order to win the war?'

'I confidently expect to find the lady in the very near future, and this time I will take personal charge of her security.'

'And Doctor Steffen? No doubt he has already spoken to the police?'

'I rather doubt it. He's much too deeply involved . . . don't you think?'

'And the Jewish vermin, who seem to know everything about us?'

'Let me get you another brandy.' Fox-Hillyer took the glass from the German's unprotesting hand, and warmed it in his palms before he lifted the decanter. 'With regard to the Jewish vermin who seem to know everything . . . well, as you know, we have already given them a warning. No, I wouldn't expect any serious opposition from that quarter. After all, we know all about the er . . . whatsit . . . the Heller Art International.'

The disappearance of Greb from his Munich flat had not escaped notice.

After a further twenty minutes of fuming and stomping Reisener returned to the airport for his flight to Munich. Fox-Hillyer, as he courteously closed the door of the taxi, was glad to see him go. While he respected the old man's principles, he regarded his fanaticism towards Hitler as the fantasy of a diseased imagination run riot.

Every political genius was of his time, could never come again. Yet Reisener wanted the Führer's child to be reared under his own senile wing, he saw in the growing infant the whole apotheosis of his own frustrated ambitions—he would inherit them together with all of Reisener's wealth and power —or so the old fool fondly imagined. What if he (or she), had different ideas, took a fancy to left-wing politics, got married too early, became a homosexual, or simply, and most obviously, lacked the frantic energy of its parent? The chances were that under Reisener's guidance, the child would become a raving schizophrenic before it reached puberty.

As he returned to his study, Fox-Hillyer reflected upon his own ambitions which were, by contrast, much more pragmatic and viable. He simply wanted to take charge of his own country, and restore it to the tight discipline of its former colonial glory.

He loathed and detested not Jews (who had their uses), so much as the Marxists, the trade union leaders, the feckless and devious politicians of the left who had brought his country to a permanent brink of economic ruin, and more importantly whittled away the will to work, killed the conscience and the self-respect, and destroyed the incentive and the morale of his fellow-countrymen, at every level.

For some years now, Fox-Hillyer had regarded a military take-over as the only solution. In 1971 he had begun to form a loose organisation of area commanders, all of them retired senior officers, who had in turn recruited their men, mostly ex-regular N.C.O.s of the sort who regularly attend their regimental reunions.

These men were simply asked whether, in the event of a national emergency, they were prepared to form a militia to back up the armed forces. Over nine thousand, up and down the country, had expressed enthusiasm for the idea.

Reisener had offered Fox-Hillyer a million pounds to take charge of the Pima operation, and he had already received a quarter of this sum. The money would provide arms and ammunition for Fox-Hillyer's militia, to be stored at a number of convenient sites, ready for the great day.

When that day arrived there were seventeen hundred names on Fox-Hillyer's list, including five cabinet ministers, marked down for immediate extinction.

Just over an hour after Reisener's departure Fox-Hillyer held another conference in his study.

Ginger Dunning had succeeded Paulson as head of Apex Security. Once a Detective-Sergeant in the C.I.D., he had become one of the first casualties of Sir Robert Mark's AIO squad, formed by the Commissioner to root out corruption in the Metropolitan Police. Dunning's weakness had been for taking backhanders from the peddlars of pornography. Still in his late thirties, he had a habit of cocking his angular features to one side while listening, and frowning, as if dealing with a suspect. A habit which did not commend itself to Fox-Hillyer.

'Well, have you got anything to report?'

'I've just had a look over Miss Seal's cottage, sir. One or two small items of interest.' He threw these down on the desk, Marianne's passport, a couple of photographs of herself, her bank statement, a few letters from friends. Fox-Hillyer leafed through them. 'Good. You'd better check on these right away. She could be staying with a friend, but I'm inclined to think she'll stick with Dr Stephen, probably here in London. As she has no passport she won't be able to leave the country, at least not for a while.'

'Yes, I think we're safe there.'

Fox-Hillyer took a sheet of paper from a drawer. 'Here are some details about Stephen . . . his accountant, bank manager, solicitor, professional colleagues. He's bound to get in touch with one or other of them sooner or later.'

'I'll keep tabs.' Dunning folded and pocketed the document.

'I'd like you to do more than that,' Fox-Hillyer said crisply. 'I want their telephones bugged.'

'That's just what I had in mind, sir.'

'Keep an eye on the abortion clinics, especially those run by Dr Stephen's friends. He may persuade her to get rid of the foetus . . . if it's not too late.'

'I will certainly do my best.'

'I want all your people working on this full-time, Dunning. Is that perfectly clear?'

'That's already been arranged, sir. We've dropped everything else.'

'You're probably going to be watched by the Israeli security people from Parlane Close.'

'No problem there sir. There's only a couple of 'em.'

'Yes, but there could soon be a lot more. Right, you'd better get cracking. Don't forget I want you to report to me every evening between 1800 and 1830 hours, wherever you are, either personally or by telephone.'

20

The death of Angela Stringer cast an atmosphere of deep despondency over the household at Parlane Close.

Durandt was mentally shattered. After the funeral he returned to the United States for an indefinite holiday. He never came back. The Israeli intelligence chiefs considered that Heller Art International was no longer a useful cover, and that Durandt was now too exposed to continue his fund-raising activities.

Eckstein moved to a hotel in Tavistock Street. Coulman borrowed a flat in Kensington from an executive of the First National Bank of Chicago who was on a six-months' tour of the European financial centres.

The last week had thrown up only two items of interest. Eckstein, browsing through the newspapers, came across a report on the drowning of Paulson. Coulman had checked on Fox-Hillyer's house in Bloomsbury, and was able to report that the ex-Brigadier was back in residence.

Eckstein, for want of a better idea, decided to take another look at the Grasspool Clinic. Slim chances being an improvement on no chances at all.

In order to explore the place under cover of darkness he arrived at a quarter past eleven and parked the grey van in precisely the same spot as before. Once more it was sheeting with rain. He felt dismally as if he was back where he started.

Like a losing game of snakes and ladders.

A large board just inside the entrance gates announced that the property was for sale. Intending purchasers should apply to Knight, Frank, and Rutley, at Hanover Square.

Eckstein walked up the drive, prowled round the dark silent shell of the house, and made for the chalet where he knew Marianne had stayed.

The door was padlocked, but he easily forced a window.

Inside he switched on his flashlight. It revealed nothing but the naked delineations of a hut, stripped of furniture and fittings.

He searched for half an hour, groping around on the floor for some remote evidence of the former occupant. He discovered only a small coin—sixpence—which could have come from anywhere.

He emerged from the chalet and walked back across the lawns.

Something grabbed the fringe of his attention in passing—the half-open door of a summerhouse. He stopped, came back, and looked inside.

A newish ladies' bicycle was leaning against the wall.

Eckstein examined it with the aid of his torch. The insides of the mudguards were wet. There was fresh mud adhering to the tyres. And there were wet tyre tracks on the concrete floor.

It had been used very recently, almost certainly within the last two or three hours.

Eckstein approached the house again, this time with a greater sense of urgency.

The front entrance, as he expected, was securely barred and bolted. He walked all round the building again, looking up at the windows for a chink of light. He saw none.

He tried each of half a dozen outside doors. They were all bolted on the inside.

Eckstein smashed a pane in one of the kitchen windows, opened it, and entered.

He wandered through the kitchens and followed a flight of stairs leading up to a wide carpeted corridor.

He emerged at the head of the great central stairway. The tall Palladian columns gleamed in the torchlight.

Arrowed signs were still everywhere: *Gymnasium: Physio-*

therapy Department: Heat Treatment: Rest Room.

Eckstein tried a battery of light switches. The current had been turned off.

He walked on. At the end of the corridor he turned up another staircase where the sign read, *Residents Only.* This led to a dark passageway running the length of the house, with rooms on either side.

From under the door of one of these a thin shaft of light percolated into the passage. As Eckstein approached it he heard the faint tinkling notes of piano music.

He stopped outside, trying to identify the piece—a Scarlatti sonata definitely, but which one? It bothered him a little that he had got so out of touch.

He rapped on the door. The radio was immediately switched off. After a few seconds a woman's voice called out tremulously, 'Who's that?'

'The name's Eckstein. I want to talk to you.'

'What about?'

'There's no need to worry. I'm a private detective. I'm looking for a missing person, Marianne Seal.'

'I've never 'eard of 'er.'

Eckstein pondered for a few seconds. Then he decided to play what had become a fast-breeding conviction.

'It's Sister Ferry I'm talking to, is it not?'

An appreciable pause, then—'Aye, that's right.'

Eckstein said, 'Okay. I know that Miss Seal disappeared from here nearly four months ago, and you left at the same time. Now are you going to talk to me or do I have to call the police?'

There was a brief hiatus. Eckstein heard her shuffling about behind the door. He guessed that she had been in bed when he knocked.

Eventually she said, 'I can't help you. I don't know where she is.'

Eckstein said, 'I'd still like to talk.'

After a further interval he heard a key turned cautiously in the lock. 'You'd better come in,' she said.

He pushed open the door and entered. It was a large room, elegantly furnished in the Regency style, dimly lit by a single tilly lamp.

Alison Ferry, wearing a grey dressing-gown over green pyjamas, was sitting on the bed with a double barrelled shotgun resting on her knees. Eckstein also observed a bottle of Burnett's White Satin Gin and some tonics on the bedside table next to the radio.

'Sit down over there.'

She motioned with the gun towards a chair in the corner of the room. Eckstein sat on it.

'What do you want to know?' she asked in a flat voice. She looked jaded and a little drunk.

'It might be a good idea if I told you what I know already,' Eckstein said. 'I know that Miss Seal came here about four months ago for infertility treatment.

'She was artificially insemniated, against her will and knowledge, with the preserved sperm of Hitler. This treatment was carried out by Dr Stephen, with your assistance.

'I also know that Dr Stephen was once the research assistant to a Professor Buechner who acquired the sperm and preserved it. After he died his son sold it to a man called Reisener, who was here at the clinic at the time the treatment to Marianne Seal was carried out. There were two other men with him named Fox-Hillyer and Paulson. Now would you like to carry on from there?'

She said nothing for quite some time, taking off her spectacles, rubbing her eyes as if in disbelief, blinking myopically at Eckstein. Then, awkwardly trying to prop the shotgun between her knees, she poured herself a drink.

'They called 'emselves Schultz and Harrington,' she said. 'You know a lot, don't you?'

He waited for her to resume.

'I'll tell you something. Doctor Stephen didn't want to have ought to do wi' it. They offered 'im a lot of money to begin with, but 'e refused. Then the German said if 'e didn't co-operate 'e'd make it public. If 'e 'ad of done it would 'ave ruined 'im. That's why 'e left Germany in the first place, to get away from it.

'So in the finish 'e pretended to go along wi' 'em. 'E was trying to play for time. 'E thought 'e could switch the sperm they gave 'im, with the sample from Marianne's boy-friend. Only it didn't turn out that way.'

'What way did it turn out?'

'The German watched 'im all the time . . . 'e seemed to know something about gynaecology . . . at least 'e'd read all Professor Buechner's notes. So in the end Dr Stephen 'ad to use a mixture o' both samples.'

'You mean the father could be either Hitler, or Marianne's boy-friend?'

'Aye. The boy-friend most likely. The other stuff were thirty years old and Dr Stephen said it were nearly inactive.'

'But you've only got his word for it.'

The nursing sister shrugged.

'You must have known that what Stephen was doing was wrong. So why did you help him?'

'For 'is sake I suppose. I wish I 'adn't.'

Eckstein said tersely, 'It's a bit late for expressions of regret. Somebody I was really fond of got killed the other day because of this.'

She became increasingly nervous, stumbling over words.

' 'E was very good to me, you know. 'E was the only one who gave me a job after I was struck off the nursin' register.'

'How could that have happened?' he inquired cynically.

'If you really want to know, I was nursin' a woman with multiple sclerosis. I 'ad to visit 'er every day for injections at 'ome. Anyway, I 'appened to fall in love 'wi 'er daughter. She found us in bed. Would you like to put that in your records?'

She savagely picked up her glass and drained it.

'So the doctor knew about this and he still gave you employment?'

'Aye. He got me put back on the register after a couple o' years. Pulled one or two strings.'

'Where is he now?'

'I've no idea. I left 'im with Marianne. 'E said 'e was going to try to get 'er out of the country. 'E said I was to keep in touch with 'is solicitor, and 'e'd send for me as soon as 'e'd got settled.'

'Did Reisener pay you anything?'

She gave him a fierce glance. 'D'you think I'd take 'is disgustin' money?'

She said this with strong conviction. He believed it.

Eckstein said, 'All right, tell me what happened after Marianne Seal first arrived at the clinic—like they say, in your own words.'

She told him. About the involvement of Fox-Hillyer who was being paid a huge sum by Reisener. About the suspicions of Nick and his subsequent fate. About their incarceration on the island and their escape.

At the end of this recital Eckstein said, 'So Reisener still believes that Marianne Seal is carrying Hitler's child?'

'Oh yes. Dr Stephen never told him he'd mixed up the sperm samples.'

'Which means that Fox-Hillyer will be out there looking for her.'

She said, 'Why are you so interested? Who are you working for anyway?'

'Right now, I'm not sure I know.'

Eckstein's lackadaisical manner, his total absence of aggression, had caused her to forget about the shotgun which had now toppled on to the carpet.

'Is there anything else you want to ask me?'

He seemed miles away. 'Sure, fifty thousand things. But just now I can't think of one.'

'Would you like a drink?'

He appeared to consider this seriously, then shook his head. 'No thanks. You finish the bottle.'

As she poured herself another he took a half-finished pipe from his pocket and lit it.

He said, 'What's your Christian name?'

'Alison.'

'Listen, Alison, these people are not playing for matchsticks. You could be—how would you say—disposed of because of what you know. Could be the next character who walks in here . . .'

She interrupted with bright confidence. 'Oh, I've already thought of that. I've made a full statement and given it to my solicitor and if anything should happen to me . . .'

'I've heard about that one before, Alison. I have also heard of several methods of dealing with the problem.'

He stood up, stretched himself, puffing at his pipe which was giving trouble. On his way to the door he picked up the shotgun and examined it.

'Any time you want to use this,' he said, 'it's a good idea to take the safety catch off.' He showed her. 'Forward is ready to fire, backward is safe.'

He tossed the gun on to the bed beside her. She turned her head to the pillow and began to sob. He patted her on the shoulder.

'Look after yourself,' he said.

He closed the door gently behind him.

A bluebottle circled lazily around the blank screen of the television set.

'There are a few matters of practical importance which I would like to discuss with you.'

An italianate boy of perhaps fifteen, dressed as a waiter, emptied ashtrays. It was now July. The sun glared on a broken child's tricycle on the strip of lawn outside.

'We can't go on living in hotels, they will find us eventually.'

Marianne said, 'Yes, I realise that. I'm going out to look for a flat tomorrow. We'll be safer there.'

'That isn't a bad idea, but I'm thinking about the long term prospects. What we have to do if you want to bring up your child in safety is to go abroad. I've got some contacts in East Africa. Would you like to go there?'

She considered this prospect. 'I wouldn't mind—if you want to go.'

'I wouldn't object to a change of scenery.'

'I left my passport in the cottage.'

'We'll have to get another. Of course there is one other possibility. You could have an abortion.'

She sat up straight. 'What me? I think my child deserves to live, don't you. After all he's been through already.' That same morning she had felt the infant kick inside her for the first time.

Dr Stephen said, 'I appreciate your feelings, my dear. But I thought I ought to mention it.'

'All right,' she said cheerfully. 'You've mentioned it.'

The boy collected their teacups. He coughed, wanting them out.

'You know, I've always been a coward, and a very selfish one at that. If I wasn't, I'd have got married. I would have liked someone like you for a daughter.'

'It looks as if you're going to have both of us for a while.'

It was the first time she recalled hearing him laugh.

21

On July 6 Ginger Dunning paid a further visit to Russell Square. 'I've got something rather interesting this time,' he told Fox-Hillyer.

He placed a tape recorder on the desk. 'We managed to get a bug inside the accountant's phone. This came through about eleven this morning.'

He switched on the machine and cocked his head to listen with a small, gratified smile.

'Henry Whichelow here.'

'Henry . . . this is John Stephen.'

'John, hallo . . . I've been . . .

'Listen, I'd like you to make a few arrangements for me. I've decided to take an extended trip to Zambia. I believe there may be a good opportunity for me to open a clinic there. Anyway I want to look around. But I shall need some money over there . . . I think about twenty thousand pounds to begin with. Can you arrange the transfer to a bank in Lusaka?'

'Ahm . . . no reason why not. It might take a week or two. The currency regulations are a bit stiff in that area at the moment.'

'Also I shall need two visas. I have my niece travelling with me as secretary.'

'I see. Well, I'll try and get that organised.'

'One other thing . . . my niece has lost her passport. Could you arrange a replacement?'

'Well, er . . . that might be a bit tricky. No reason why

they shouldn't give her another if it's a genuine loss. But she'll have to apply personally.'

'Right, I'll put the details in the post today, with the authorisation.'

'Where can I get in touch? I hear you've closed down your place in Suffolk.'

'That is true. I'm in the Islington area at the moment, but I'm still moving around. I'll ring you in about a week and perhaps we can arrange to meet.'

'Yes, why don't we do that.'

The bank clerk, finishing his shepherd's pie in a pub in Ipswich, was nearing fifty and had known over the course of some years now that he was never going to become the manager of his own, or any other branch. He comforted himself with the thought that even if he had already reached that exalted position, his income would be in no way superior to that which he enjoyed already.

He was an abstemious man but as usual on such occasions he downed a schooner of dry sherry before leaving the premises and finding his way to a call box situated in a conveniently quiet side street.

He dialled a London number.

'Am I speaking to Mr Coulman . . .? Ah, splendid, the agency gave me your name, sir. With regard to your inquiry, your Dr Stephen has been drawing rather heavily on his credit card recently . . . thirty pounds on four occasions last week, at our branches in Pentonville, City Road, and twice at the Angel, Islington . . . the last occasion was the day before yesterday . . .'

A few moments later he was dialling another London number. 'Am I speaking to Mr Dunning? Ah, splendid, the agency gave me your name, sir. In answer to your inquiry . . .'

When he returned to the bank some five minutes later, there was nothing in his demeanour to suggest that he was richer by forty pounds, to be delivered in cash, by unregistered post.

She was preparing something for lunch on the electric cooker, now divested of its coating of grime.

Pilchards on toast. With coffee.

The Borough of Islington was at this time the most over-crowded district in London, due to a huge influx of young people from the provinces, living two or three to a room in the bulging tenements.

Marianne had found the place, a first-floor flat, after a fruitless round of agents. Eventually someone referred her to the Ceylonese, and showed her the dim restaurant where he was consuming his evening curry. She waited patiently for him to emerge and accosted him on the pavement. He first of all claimed he didn't have any flats, then said they were all fully occupied and anyway he wasn't interested in short lets, and finally admitted that he did have a small flat in Almeida Street which was empty. But the previous tenant, a successful middle-aged actor, had a fetish for living alone and in total squalor and the place needed cleaning up. She could have it for a month, unofficially and rent free, provided she tidied the place.

When Marianne first entered the flat she saw what the landlord meant.

The floor was carpeted with old newspapers, fag-ends, crushed beer cans. In one corner were four crates of milk bottles, many of them half-full and growing a fungus. One wall was covered with graffiti over a bilious yellow. There was a thick rime of filth round the bath.

On one boisterous occasion the actor had painted his feet green and, supported by his friends, left a trail of footprints up one wall and halfway across the ceiling.

The bedroom reeked of stale sex.

They had now been living there for three days, during which Marianne had spent most of her time clearing out the rubbish, scrubbing the floors, washing the blankets. The place was at last beginning to look habitable.

She rather enjoyed the domestic role, liked looking after

the doctor, who had quickly become dependent on her for the practical necessities of life. In return he treated her with an old-fashioned civilised courtesy which pleased and intrigued her—she was unused to being deferred to, as a woman, by the men of her own generation. She looked forward to the new experience of Zambia, to having her baby in new and exciting surroundings, completely divorced from the prickly fear of kidnap which still occasionally gripped her.

Marianne still had the odd twinge of suspicion as to whether Dr Stephen—perhaps for her own sake—had withheld the true facts about the child's fatherhood, but she had already decided with true feminine logic that this was of no consequence.

There was one thing she knew for sure. The child which was slowly developing inside her body was her's, and her's alone. It had ceased, in her mind, to have a father.

Stephen came through the front door into the small sitting-room and sat down heavily in a sagging settee. She put her head through from the kitchen. 'Something to eat in about ten minutes,' she called out.

'I've bought some fish, as you said. But I forgot the name. I got some turbot I think.'

'I did say haddock but turbot'll do nicely.'

'Something you might find useful.' He held out a bunch of carnations.

'Oh, they're gorgeous.' She was enchanted as she took them. 'Wait a second, I'll find something to put them in.'

When she reappeared Stephen said, 'I talked to my accountant on the telephone. We have arranged to have lunch together next Thursday. He hopes to have the documents ready by that time.'

'That sounds great. Oh, something I forgot to tell you. I rang up about my passport. I've got to go and see them the day after tomorrow.'

'Please be careful, my dear.'

She perched on the arm of the chair. 'Ooh, I should think

233

they've given up hope by now. How long do you think it will be?'

'Before we leave for Zambia? Well, with a bit of luck I should think about two weeks from now.'

Dunning rang his chief promptly at six the same evening.

'It's beginning to move, sir. Dr Stephen rang the accountant again this morning. They're meeting for lunch at the Gay Hussar next Thursday.'

'Good. But don't relax. Keep on looking.'

'I'm doing that very thing. I've got two men in Islington and another at the passport office. It won't be long now.'

'I hope not. Now I'd like you to come in tomorrow for some detailed instructions.'

'Right you are, squire.'

Fox-Hillyer frowned as he replaced the receiver. The man was getting unpleasantly familiar. He would have to strangle this tendency at birth.

Coulman and Eckstein had been involved in a certain amount of to-ing and fro-ing without much tangible result.

Coulman, watching the offices of Apex Inquiry Services from a discreetly parked car, had been able to provide photographs of Dunning and three of the other detectives working for that establishment, and had checked on Dunning's visits to Fox-Hillyer.

He had once shadowed the ex-C.I.D. man all one evening, from his flat at the Oval, to several pubs in the area of the Elephant and Castle, to a Chinese restaurant, and back to his flat again. From this exercise Coulman gathered nothing except that Dunning allowed himself the occasional night off.

For ten days Eckstein had wandered around Islington's pubs, supermarkets, Wimpey restaurants, Chinese food take-aways, lonely bus stops, shattered call boxes, fish and chip counters, laundrettes and park benches, looking for a blonde with a bulging waistline whose features had become engraved in his memory. He also carried around with him a conviction which was growing to monumental proportions.

An innocent woman had died already in the course of this operation, and he was not going to let it happen to another— and still less to her unborn child.

Greb returned from his leave in good spirits. He had, or so he claimed, demolished the backlog with his wife, and left a six-months' forelog in the bank. He moved in with Coulman at the Kensington flat and the following day, after Greb had been briefed from the tapes, Eckstein was called in to discuss progress. Which wasn't impressive. Coulman was fretful and anxious.

'I've checked out all the clinics which specialise in abortions in the London area,' he said. 'They don't have any recent patients that fit.'

'Maybe if they did, they wouldn't want to part with the information,' Greb suggested.

'I did meet with some light resistance.'

'It would sure solve some problems if she got rid of it,' said Greb.

'Sure, but I don't think she will. Anyway, it must be too late now.'

Eckstein said, 'Richard, nobody seems to know exactly who the father is. I'd say it's more likely to be the boy-friend. So, when we find Marianne, why don't we just tell her the score, and send her some place Reisener won't find her.'

'You think I could sell that to Tel Aviv?'

'It was just a thought.'

Coulman looked at him.

It was arranged that Greb should go on looking in the Islington area, while Eckstein kept a permanent watch on Fox-Hillyer's residence. After Eckstein left Coulman confided to Greb, 'Barry is beginning to bother me.'

On the day following this meeting Alison Ferry received two visitors—one a soft-spoken Irishman with prematurely grey hair, the other a woman.

She was easily dispossessed of the shotgun, but confidently

referred to her statement with the solicitor. The Badger searched the flat and eventually found a letter from the solicitor confirming the deposit.

He then casually ripped her heart to shreds with the saw-toothed bayonet while Mrs McCombe pinned her screaming to the bed. She was wrapped in her own blankets, and buried some two hundred yards from Nick.

Later that night two of Dunning's colleagues broke into the solicitor's office and blew the safe. Since they took the whole contents, including many items of value, the loss of Alison's document caused no undue concern by comparison. In any case no one knew what was in it.

After a decent interval the solicitor wrote to Alison, expressing his sincere regrets. He wondered if perhaps she would care to send him another copy, which he would deposit at a bank.

French and Japanese tourist voices chuntered around her, excitable, on the top deck of the bus which lumbered towards Victoria through a moving peninsula of traffic. When she got out, rain imprinted itself on shafts of sunlight but failed to damp her spirits. Well, there was just one small niggle of anxiety as she approached the passport office in Petty France. She was about to perjure herself, commit an actual offence moreover for which one could, she supposed, be heavily fined, sent to prison, even. Her. A social worker. It didn't seem possible. Lips silently recited the rehearsed facts of the story.

The immigration official who interviewed her—after the statutory forty minutes spent sitting in a bleak waiting-room—put mechanical questions in bored tones and seemed disinterested in her replies, which came out much too pat, she thought. Yes, she had gone to Colchester to draw some foreign exchange from a bank there. What currency. Spanish. Why did she need Spanish currency. She had arranged to visit her father in Benidorm for a holiday and so she had taken her passport to have the money entered and a friend and herself had lunch in a little restaurant near the castle well not really

236

a restaurant what you might call more of a sort of tea shop, and she had a bit of shopping to do afterwards and it wasn't until . . . What was the name of the restaurant. The Copper Kettle. So after about ten minutes she went into a shop and couldn't find her handbag, with the money and the passport in it, she thought it was in the shopping bag but it wasn't and she suddenly realised she'd left it on a chair in the restaurant and she ran all the way back but nobody remembered seeing it. When the manageress . . .

He jotted down bits and pieces on a pad . . . had she informed the police. Yes, it was one of the first things . . . please God, don't let him check that . . . what was her father's address in Benidorm . . . well, at least that was easy. Eventually he said, 'We'll have to make a few inquiries, Miss Seal, but I see no reason why you shouldn't get a replacement in due course. But I must ask you to be very, very careful in future. You must understand that a passport is the property of Her Majesty's Government and it is not burr-burr-burr-burr.' She was terribly sorry . . . she certainly wouldn't let it happen again . . . how long would it take to get another one only she was thinking of . . .

'I'll try to get it ready in about a fortnight, but you'll have to collect it in person.' She gushed gratitude and left, light-headed and blushing with retrospective shame. But thought, with an inward giggle, looking preggers had its advantages now and again. Dunning's man, who had scanned about twelve thousand faces, had picked her up instantly when she went into the building, and he was five yards behind her when she came out. He had no trouble tracking her back to the flat in Almeida Street. Marianne didn't once look back.

Eckstein was sometimes the American tourist, hair lank and long, tee-shirted, jeaned and sunglassed. At other times he affected the overalls of an engineer, or a denim suit with black bargee's cap pulled well down over rimless spectacles. Yet always the real Eckstein, the thoughtful manner, hunched shoulders of the professional student, struggled through.

He wandered perpetually around the square, sat on the public benches, or watched from a distance, cramped inside the cab of the mini-van. He noted the comings and goings of Fox-Hillyer, and the visits of the detective, Dunning. He observed, with keen interest, workmen fitting wire-mesh screens to the inside of the basement windows.

'Ah, there you are, squire. Got some news for you. We know where they are now. One of my fellers managed to . . .'

'Dunning, if you have any serious information to impart, I suggest you come round immediately rather than discuss it over the telephone.'

'Oh, sorry about that, squire. See what you mean. Right, I'll nip round straight away.'

'Just one other thing. In future you will address me as "sir". Is that perfectly clear?'

'Er . . . yes, sir.'

Dr Stephen enjoyed a satisfying lunch with his accountant. He had a particular liking for Hungarian food and especially for tokay, of which he had drunk the best part of a bottle. Apart from a small query about his financial resources from the Zambian embassy—easily settled by a letter, Whichelow had said—everything was in order, the visas stamped and in Stephen's pocket, the money safe in Lusaka. All that remained was to book the flight as soon as Marianne received her new passport.

It was a quarter to three when he emerged into Dean Street and walked through Soho Square towards the underground station at Tottenham Court Road.

He had always wanted to work in Africa. Now, he reflected, events had brought Marianne—a perfect ally for the venture. She would grow into his adopted daughter, her child his grandchild.

Whoever the father.

But there remained another fortnight in the shadows. He decided, as he stepped on to the escalator, that it might be a good idea to move on, perhaps get out of London, keep on the move.

On the Northern line platform a fair-sized crowd—well over a hundred—had built up. Stephen, filtering among them, found a yard of space. He let his eyes drift across the advertisements on the hoardings across the tunnel.

'Excuse me, would ye tell me how to get to Hampstead?' The polite enquiry, couched in a pleasant Irish brogue and accompanied by a courteous smile, came from a man with spiky blackish-grey hair standing on the edge of the platform.

'I'm afraid I couldn't tell you without a map,' Stephen said.

'I have one here, but I can't understand the damn thing.' The Irishman produced it from his pocket and opened it for Stephen's inspection. 'Would ye be kind enough to show me where Hampstead is?'

Stephen moved forward and studied the diagram of the underground network.

'Ah, here we are,' he said finally, pointing. 'You need an Edgware train.'

'I'm much obliged to youse.' The Badger glanced at the indicator board. 'Sure and that looks like the next one.'

He put the map away.

'It's the first time I've been in this city for seven years,' he confided.

'Really? That's quite a long time.'

'D'ye happen to know Dublin?'

'Not very well, I'm afraid.' Stephen wished the man would go away and leave him to his thoughts.

'I know the place like the back of me hand. I could show you everything in Dublin. There are things goin' on in that city would surprise ye.'

Stephen began to feel vaguely irritated. Was the fellow about to offer him a conducted tour? 'Yes, I've no doubt,' he murmured.

'There are things goin' on over there which ye'd never find in London.'

'I'm sure you're right.' Stephen heard a distant roar and felt the welcome rush of air which presaged the arrival of a train.

'But ye have to know where to look.'

The train hastened towards them, braking hard as it approached the platform. The crowd stirred, manoeuvred into small clusters.

Stephen saw the Irishman take a pace backwards, then felt a violent shove between the shoulder blades. He lurched forward into unavoidable space, saw glittering metal rush to meet him. As he sprawled across the track he made a frantic effort to push himself from under the wheels, grabbed at the live rail, felt a huge force drill through his body, then nothing.

The train, when it stopped, was already well-filled. More than half the waiting passengers climbed in. The rest, aware of something, hung about on the platform.

Subdued voices.

'Oh my Christ!' Faces turned away.

A woman, white-faced with shock, stared at the Badger. 'You . . . you pushed him. I . . . I . . . saw you.'

A younger woman, slight, dark, pushed between them.

'No, he jumped. I was standing right behind him. He said something, then he jumped.'

The Badger said, 'I'll go for an ambulance.' He hurried away through an arch which stated *Way Out and To Street*. The guard appeared, looked, turned away. 'All right, stand back, everybody stand back!'

He went to a cabinet set into the wall of the platform, took out a telephone.

Marianne, feeling rather lazy, lunched on a liver sausage sandwich with coffee, heard with satisfaction the dustmen, at last, trundle away the three loaded dustbins outside the window and discharge their odoriferous contents.

She would have loved to go out and wander around the warm streets, see people around her, but caution forbade it.

She settled into a chair to read a battered Solzhenitsyn paperback she had found while clearing up.

After an hour she heard a baby cry in the flat above, and its mother's comforting voice. She had heard this before. She wanted to talk to that mother, exchange notes as it were, but Dr Stephen had warned her against getting involved with any of the other residents.

By four o'clock in the afternoon she had become unsettled and restless, longing for the doctor to return, with news to discuss and ponder.

The next couple of hours were the longest she had known.

Nothing out of the ordinary had happened to him, she kept insisting to herself. The accountant had left a document in his office, and after lunch Dr Stephen had gone back there to collect it. Or he had gone round to the Zambian Embassy to clear up the final details. He would be back any minute.

Or the minute after . . .

She tried to get back into the book.

By six o'clock the house began to fill up as the occupants returned from work. There were six flats, most of them occupied by young people, secretaries, teachers, office workers, drifters, male and female, living three or four to a flat, doing their own thing, the sexes mixed, few thinking of marriage.

Doors slammed, feet thudded on stairs. Cries and shouts. Domesticity. She felt increasingly alone and afraid. Amplified pop music pounded up loud from the basement. From above the baby wailed, a man's voice complained. Somebody, somewhere, began to practise Spanish guitar.

By nine she was almost frantic. Several times she'd been on the point of going out, there was a pub round the corner, she needed a stiff drink to pull her nerves together. But she was sure that as soon as she left Dr Stephen would arrive and worry about her absence. It began to grow dark. As she switched the lights on, a knock on the door. She opened it. A man and a woman.

'Excuse me, would you be Miss Seal by any chance?'

The man spoke gently, politely, with an easy assurance.

'That's right.'

'The name's Patrick McCombe. This is my wife. Dr Stephen gave us the address. He's been involved in a slight accident.'

'An accident?' She was dry-mouthed.

'Nothing very serious. He was knocked down by a taxi just outside our place in Bloomsbury.'

'Just crossing the road,' the woman added.

'I think he's broken his ankle,' the man said. 'But he's a stubborn man. He wouldn't let us call for an ambulance. He insisted on sending for his niece.'

Marianne felt a surge of relief. 'I've been waiting for him for hours.'

'He's sitting in our front room,' the woman said. 'He says he won't go to hospital. And him a doctor? I must say I'm surprised.'

'I have the car outside,' the man said. 'If you'd like us to run you over, maybe you could persuade him.'

Marianne was looking at the woman's eyes. The pupils wavered a little, all the time, one side to the other.

She tried to recall where she had seen such eyes before, and suddenly remembered. A woman she had visited as a social worker. Who had killed her baby.

She struggled to quell the rising panic. She said, 'All right, I'll get my coat.'

She went to the wardrobe, fumbled for a long time with her coat. Then she said, 'You'll just have to excuse me a minute, I promised to babysit for the couple upstairs. I'll just go and tell them I can't make it.'

'Don't worry,' the man said. 'My wife will tell them for you.'

'No, I think I ought to tell them. They'll think I'm rude.'

But the woman had already slipped through the door. The man stood in front of it as it closed.

She slowly pulled on her coat, despairing inwardly.

The woman came back. 'I've told them,' she said. 'They quite understand.'

242

Marianne said, almost calmly, 'What have you done with him?'

The man and the woman exchanged glances. The man said, 'Well, why don't ye come over and see for yourself? Don't ye think that's the best idea?'

'How do I know he's with you?' she said defiantly.

'Oh, he came to see us this afternoon, after having lunch with Mr Whichelow.'

Pink Floyd pounded up from the basement. From miles away.

22

A blue-overalled Eckstein knocked out another pipe against the door of the van, and watched the spiky-haired man pass by on the other side of the square, walking the dog, a large alsatian, muzzled on a short leash.

Eight in the morning. Not too many people about.

It was the third time he had watched this performance. The dog-walker had moved into Fox-Hillyer's house four days earlier. Also a woman. Man and wife possibly? Servants—housekeeper and caretaker? In which case why hadn't they been there all the time? Just returned from holiday . . . perhaps. Except that neither of the pair looked remotely servile, and their arrival on the day of Dr Stephen's death was too much of a coincidence.

Eckstein was ninety-five per cent sure that Marianne was behind those sealed-off windows in the basement, but badly needed the other five.

In anticipation of that eventuality, he had already made certain plans and arrangements which had not been confided to Coulman or Greb.

At ten minutes past nine Fox-Hillyer came out and drove off in the Rolls. Some twenty minutes later the woman emerged with a bag of washing.

Eckstein followed her to a nearby shopping centre, and stood in the doorway of a laundrette as she pushed the garments into a machine. Something red, a jumble of things together, what looked like a green sweater. Marianne was wearing one when he saw her at the clinic . . . but inconclusive, his trained mind warned.

Later, he stood beside her as she checked her purchases at

the pay desk of a supermarket. Fairy liquid, dog food, corn oil, instant coffee, pork chops, a chicken . . . nothing to latch on to there.

He didn't much like the look of the woman . . . like an experienced professional whore who needed a refresher course in the basic principles of the craft.

Eckstein walked back to the mini-van and drove to Kensington where he was due to report back to Coulman and Greb at 10.30.

'Just get rid of the imponderables,' Coulman said, 'we can safely assume that Marianne Seal is in the custody of the opposition. She is either here in London—maybe at Fox-Hillyer's place—or she is somewhere else.'

'If she isn't I guess she soon will be,' Greb suggested.

'Right. They're not going to keep her around here for very long, and the next place they take her is going to take an awful lot of finding—if she's not there already. Barry, what do you say?'

Eckstein shrugged. 'I wish I knew.'

'D'you figure she's over at Russell Square?'

'It's a possibility.'

Coulman said, 'Well, there's one way to find out. We're going to take a look in there. By the way, I've asked for Schen. He's arriving by El Al tomorrow. I think we're going to need him on this operation.'

Eckstein seemed about to question this statement. But he said, 'When were you thinking of moving in?'

'Tomorrow night. We can't afford to wait any longer.'

'Suppose she's not there?'

'In that case we pretend it's a social visit.' Coulman's voice had an edge of impatience. 'Barry, do I detect a certain lack of enthusiasm in your approach?'

Eckstein grinned. 'Just natural caution, Richard.'

'Maybe you could tell us something about the security of the place.'

'Sure. There's a rear entrance which is never used. The

245

front door is always locked whenever anyone goes in or out. Also there is an expanding metal barrier across the front door which is closed and locked at night. The basement and ground floor windows have bars or mesh on the insides. The place has iron railings round the outside about six feet high and the surroundings are lit up at night. There is also a guard dog and burglar alarms, and it wouldn't surprise me if the residents carried weaponry.'

'You mean it's no problem?' Greb said.

'We could always dig a tunnel,' Eckstein suggested facetiously.

Coulman's impatience began to blossom into irritation. 'I would appreciate a few sound observations.' Eckstein and Greb grew thoughtful and serious again.

Greb said, 'Maybe the best idea would be to grab one of the servants in daylight and grab the keys.'

Coulman said, 'It's a thought, but I would guess they have that one covered.'

Eckstein said, 'There are ways into the place. I've got a few thoughts. But I'd like to spend another night around there. If it's all right with you Richard, I'll grab a couple of hours in the sack and get back around midnight.'

'You wouldn't care to elaborate?'

'Not just now. It could wreck my concentration.'

Coulman and Greb exchanged glances. Coulman said, 'You want to take Vic with you.'

'Not tonight. I don't think it would be a good idea. They haven't picked me up yet. Two of us could complicate the issue.' He turned to Greb. 'Vic, you appreciate that.'

Greb smirked. 'Okay Barry, tomorrow I try a different deodorant.'

Coulman hesitated, then said, 'All right with me, if that's the way you want it.'

'Okay, I'll talk to you about this time tomorrow.'

An hour later Coulman and Greb lunched together at a small trattoria across the street.

As a bottle of chianti arrived Coulman was saying, 'Barry seems to be playing this one very close to the chest.'

'That's his habit. He usually comes up with the stuff.'

Coulman filled his glass.

'Vic, I suppose you wouldn't like to take a wander over there some time tonight, see what he's doing.'

'You don't trust him?'

'I didn't say that.'

'Richard, once we start checking each other out . . .'

'It was just off the top of my head. Forget it.'

Eckstein did not snatch any sleep when he left Coulman and Greb, although he began to feel the need of it. Other things were more important and he had less than twenty-four hours left. He returned to Russell Square and continued his inspection of the Fox-Hillyer premises.

The house was the end one of a Georgian terrace three stories high, flat-roofed, squarely and solidly built of Portland stone. Beside it ran a small alleyway flanked by an office block of much more recent origin.

From a previous inspection of lighted windows Eckstein knew that there were bedrooms on the first and second floors, both with windows facing across the alleyway, although he wasn't sure who occupied which. He also knew that these windows, of the sash variety, were left partially open at night for purposes of ventilation.

There was just one snag. Below the windows the precincts of the house were guarded by six-foot iron railings topped by a further four feet of tautly-strung steel wire, the strands three inches apart, stretched between insulators. Electrified no doubt, and attached to alarms.

Standing in the alleyway, Eckstein reluctantly discounted the simple expedient of a ladder. He now turned his attention to the office block. The first floor was hopeless, but the second offered a frosted-glass window which looked fairly adjacent to one of the bedroom windows opposite.

He made a rough assessment of the distance between the

two buildings. About eleven feet, from wall to wall.

Realising that he had not eaten that day, Eckstein retreated to a pub opposite the British Museum and thoughtfully chewed a sausage and a beef sandwich.

He returned to the minivan just before two, pulled on his blue overalls, and equipped himself with the bucket and wash leather of a window cleaner.

He walked across the square to the office block and studied the name plates for a few moments . . . Studely and Wilson, industrial architects . . . Morris Weiner, stained-glass consultant . . . Peter Wenham and Co, auditors. He entered, walked round a small knot of people waiting for the lift, and climbed the stairs to the second floor.

Walking through a corridor flanked by offices on both sides, Eckstein concentrated on trying to get his bearings. It would be either the end window in the auditor's outer office, or the one next door which was marked 'Ladies'. He tried the latter and was in luck. The long window above the washbowls was almost directly in line with the bedroom window of Fox-Hillyer's residence, but he noticed, as he briskly wiped it with his wash leather, that the other window was about a yard higher.

Difficult, but not impossible.

A girl came in, stopped, said 'Oh er . . .'

He grinned. 'I'm just going.' He wrung out the wash leather and departed.

Half an hour later he drove into the yard of a builder's merchant some three miles away. Eckstein ordered twenty yards of nylon rope and a scaffolding plank of as near to sixteen feet as possible. He got one of precisely that length and lashed it to the roof of his van before returning to Russell Square.

It was now just after half-past four. Eckstein reached into a small compartment under the passenger seat and took out a box of plastic nerve gas grenades. They were the size and shape of cakes of soap, had been designed to resemble these to the eyes of the uninitiated. Eckstein stuffed five of these into various pockets in his overalls. He deliberated whether he should also take the Walther automatic pistol from its compartment but decided against it. He had not so far killed a man during his career as an intelligence agent, and he was particularly anxious not to start now. He untied the rope and hung it round his neck, picked up the scaffold board and the window cleaning equipment, and went back into the office block.

Inside the hallway a trio of young executives were holding an animated discussion beside the lift cage. Eckstein said, 'Would you excuse me?' They moved aside politely as he put the scaffold board down beside a wall and tucked the rope behind it.

Picking up his bucket, Eckstein made his way up to the second floor, entered the ladies' washroom, and locked himself in one of the cubicles.

At five the washroom began to fill with home-going typists and secretaries, animated by the release from the daily grind, putting on a dash of make-up for the tube journey home. Eckstein listened to the bright chit-chat . . . plans for the evening, somebody's boy friend who had changed affinities, somebody's party, a barbecue but you had to bring your own booze . . .

By six o'clock the washroom was empty again, the last footfall had died in the corridor. Eckstein gave it a further half-hour, then made a wary reconnoissance.

He seemed to have the place to himself. But there was a long time to go. He picked the lock on the door of the architect's office, helped himself to a dry sherry from the drinks cabinet, and sank gratefully into a comfortable armchair.

He slept fitfully for what seemed no time at all but when he awoke fully it was dark. He looked anxiously at his watch. Twenty minutes before midnight. He emerged into the corridor and turned into the ladies' room. There was a light in the window of the bedroom opposite, behind drawn curtains.

Beside the lift shaft he found the scaffold board and rope where he had left them. He carried these items awkwardly

249

upstairs. When he reached the washroom, he studied Fox-Hillyer's window again. The light was still on. A shape, indeterminate, passed across the curtains. Alcohol-induced laughter pealed up from the alleyway.

He noticed with some satisfaction that the top section of the window was open about six inches.

It was another twenty minutes before the lights went out. Eckstein decided to give it another hour. He knew that the deepest level of sleep occurs at an early stage, but it was also possible that whoever was on the other side of that wall suffered from insomnia.

A whiff of stale scent hung in the air above the wash-basins. He had nothing to do but examine his motives for the absurd risk he was about to undertake . . . for a pregnant woman, and her infant . . . whom he had met for a couple of minutes beside a goldfish pond. And in doing so betraying his loyalties to the Jewish race, to his friends and colleagues.

All he had to do was walk out of the front door, get stoned in a club, ring up Coulman in the morning, tell him to find somebody else. What happened to Marianne Seal afterwards would be no concern of Barry Eckstein.

He strolled back to the ladies' washroom and looked almost reluctantly at his watch.

Ten minutes to two. Time.

Eckstein picked up the rope and tied each end securely to a waste pipe on either side of the window. Then he opened the window and pushed the scaffold board out over the alley-way for over half its length.

He was obliged at this point to wait an agonising couple of minutes while an elderly dosser, muttering to himself and hanging on to the railings, negotiated the short passage below.

He now sat astride the board—one man on a see-saw—took hold of the ropes for anchorage, and slowly worked it further forward with his thighs, using the window-sill as a fulcrum. He needed about another five feet to make the ledge of the window opposite. The ledge itself was about a foot wide, but the higher level made the task more difficult. He was grateful for the illumination provided by the lights at each corner of the house.

Over the final six inches the plank seemed to weigh a ton, but finally he managed to place the tip, almost soundlessly, on the opposite ledge. He was now able to push the board further up until there was an overlay of about six inches, and lash it firmly into position.

Still time to withdraw. He clipped on a small gas-mask and adjusted it.

He had originally planned to walk across, but a glance down at the stone flags and the railings suggested a more cautious approach. He eased himself out of the window, straddled the board, and began to push himself forward by his hands.

Half-way across he was uncomfortably aware that with each thrust of the hands the board was slipping back, straining against the rope. A yard from the end and he could see that the overlay had been reduced to less than an inch. He glanced down. The spikes of the railings were directly below. Eckstein knew that this way he wasn't going to make it.

Slowly and cautiously he stood upright on the plank, then leaned forward, tensed himself, and sprang.

As he gained the ledge and grabbed the top of the window, the scaffold board fell away under his feet. Still anchored by the rope, it yawed in midair over the alleyway.

He froze for quite some time, crouched awkwardly on the ledge. He had rattled the window hard. But he was reassured by the sound of deep and regular breathing from inside the room.

Eckstein groped in a pocket for one of the gas grenades, stripped off the seal, activated the valve, and dropped it gently inside the window. The gas, a refinement of the nerve gas commonly used by riot police, was invisible and had no smell. In a confined space, it was effective within ten seconds.

He waited for almost as many minutes. Still the regular breathing. The inside of the room was obscured by net curtains. Eckstein leaned forward to pull these apart. In doing so he leaned heavily on the top section of the window, which suddenly lurched downwards several inches with a harsh clatter.

The breathing stopped, was succeeded by a grunt. Bedsprings creaked. Eckstein, peering into the room, was suddenly blinded by light. He saw Fox-Hillyer, green-silk-pyjamad, reach in a drawer for a gun, come round the bed towards him. He was half-way to the window when he hit the gas.

Fox-Hillyer reeled back, as if seeking the security of his bed. He got off two shots, one shattering a pane a foot from Eckstein, the other hitting the ceiling, before going down on the carpet. He made an attempt to crawl towards the door before he passed out.

Eckstein clambered gingerly through the opening in the window, dropped on to the carpet, and briefly examined the unconscious form of Fox-Hillyer. The gas would rise fairly quickly, allowing him to inhale clean air—but he would offer no further opposition for at least eight hours.

He turned out the light quietly, crept through the bedroom door on to the landing.

The other bedroom would be almost directly below. Presumably the couple slept there. Eckstein could hardly believe that they hadn't been roused by the shots. But he heard nothing for some time as he waited for his eyes to get used to the dark. Then from somewhere below the dog whimpered and yapped.

Eckstein quickly prepared another gas grenade and moved stealthily down the wide carpeted stairway.

When he had descended about half-way to the landing below, velvet darkness suddenly turned to violent light.

'Right, stay where y'are.'

The Badger was standing outside the door of the bedroom, one hand on a light switch, the other levelling a Browning automatic.

As Eckstein froze, he saw the woman emerge from the bedroom and slip downstairs.

'Let's have a look at youse . . . take that thing off ye're face.'

Eckstein removed the mask.

'Now put ye're hands on top of ye're head.'

He did so, dropping the mask and the grenade uselessly on the stairs.

The dog barked and whined.

The Badger grinned, thinking about the immediate future. He proposed to incapacitate this intruder with a couple of shots, then finish the job with the bayonet. But first he was curious about the identity of the man he was about to slaughter.

'Now tell me who y'are, and who sent ye.'

The alsatian gave a triumphant bark and came scuttling up the stairs from the ground floor. The Badger glanced round momentarily. 'Who told youse to loose the bloody dog,' he shouted down at the woman. It was clearly a complication he could do without. As the animal approached him he tried to bring it under control . . . 'Sheba . . . heel, lass . . . goo' bitch . . . stay lass!' But the alsatian, which had been reared and trained by Fox-Hillyer, took commands from that source only. It bounded past the Irishman's outstretched arm and made straight for Eckstein, who thought rapidly as he saw it coming. He had been taught how to handle guard dogs as a CIA cadet, but the ones he had trained with wore muzzles. But this one at least had a collar on, which was a small point in his favour.

Yet he was taken by surprise at the speed of the animal as it leaped at him and fastened its teeth in his left arm, just above the elbow.

Eckstein slipped his right hand under the collar and squeezed his knuckles hard against the alsatian's windpipe, using the collar for leverage, leaning forward at the same time and biting hard into the bitch's ear.

She began to gasp, and the grip on his arm relaxed.

Eckstein now began to twist the collar, forcing the bitch on to her hind legs. He next thrust her quickly backwards down the stairs and literally hurled her on to the landing.

The Badger, still covering Eckstein with the Browning, kicked at the bitch as it sprawled, snarling, in front of him. 'Get out of it!' He was a man who considered himself the natural master of any four-footed beast. This was a grave error. Sheba, now thoroughly confused in the absence of her only master, turned on the new enemy, the Badger. She hurled herself straight at the hand holding the gun, seized the wrist, and shook it like a rag.

The Badger dropped the pistol, but as Eckstein dived for it, he contrived to kick it through the stair rails.

The alsatian tore at the Irishman, seeking his face, as he backed against the wall and whipped out his bayonet, lancing and stabbing at the animal's body. Finally, when the bitch was savaging his thigh, he buried the weapon up to the hilt in her throat.

Sheba backed away, blood gouting from her mouth.

The animal walked, drunken-legged across the landing, whimpered, rolled over, and died.

Eckstein stood apart, watching this performance, very much aware that he was probably going to have to kill this man. He felt a certain regret, a sadness almost amounting to a sense of failure, yet the prospect of the encounter left a salty taste in his mouth.

The woman watched them from the bottom of the stairs as they confronted each other on the landing.

Eckstein crouched, arms low, waiting for the Irishman to lunge with the bayonet. He seemed in no hurry to do so, making little taunting remarks . . . 'Ah so ye want to try ye're luck . . . come on then, come on . . . I'm going to have a good time wid youse, so I am . . .'

Eckstein assessed the thick, muscular body opposite and decided to play it at long range.

He moved almost towards touching distance and stretched out an arm, tentatively.

The Badger slashed at his proffered hand and grinned as it was swiftly withdrawn. Eckstein withdrew a few hesitant paces towards the stairs. He turned his eyes despairingly around him, as if seeking some hypothetical sanctuary. His adversary moved forward, stalking him, expecting him to turn and run, relishing the subsequent chase.

Then—and very swiftly—Eckstein came straight at the Badger, grabbed the hand holding the bayonet with both hands, twisted it sharply until the arm was rigid, crouched a little, turned, and smashed it down on to his shoulder, like a green branch, tearing out the tendons of the biceps muscle and dislocating the elbow. He crouched still lower, and used the same arm as a lever to throw the Badger over his back on to the carpet.

As he moved in, the Badger, grunting with pain, attempted to lunge at him with his feet. But Eckstein stepped aside nimbly, caught one of the feet in both hands, and twisted it.

The Badger whimpered with agony as he tried desperately to turn his body to keep up with these revolutions, but Eckstein continued turning until he heard the tibia crack.

He then reached down, almost tenderly, lifted the heavier man on his shoulder, staggering a little under the weight, leaned him against the stair rail, and toppled him over on to the parquet floor some fifteen feet below.

Mrs McCombe retreated before Eckstein as he stepped over the alsatian's carcase and came downstairs. She ran to the pistol, was was lying a few feet away from the Badger, and tried to fire it at Eckstein, but the impact had jammed the mechanism. She tried to slip past him as he approached but he easily intercepted her, gripped her by the collar of her dressing-gown.

'Where's Marianne Seal?'

The pupils wavered. 'I don't know . . . it's nothing to do with me . . . it was him . . . he took her away somewhere . . . honestly.'

Eckstein whacked her hard across the mouth with the back of his hand. 'Let me repeat the question,' he said patiently. 'Where is Marianne Seal?'

She pointed towards the mound of tattered flesh and clothing under the stair well. 'He's . . . got the keys.' There was an edge of hysteria in her voice.

'Get them!'

He followed her across to the body, turned it with his foot, glanced briefly at the features. The Badger had broken his neck during the fall and must have died instantly.

Mrs McCombe fumbled in one of the trouser pockets and produced a key ring.

'Now show me where she is,' Eckstein commanded.

The woman led him through an annexe in which the dog had been confined, unlocked a door above a flight of steps, and another at the bottom which led directly into the basement.

'Switch the lights on!'

The woman did so. Eckstein saw a bleak, bare cellar containing a small iron bed on which Marianne was sleeping. Beside the bed a table supported a wash basin, the remains of food, a hypodermic syringe, phials of drugs. The place reeked of disinfectant, as if someone had spilled a bottle.

'Who's been doping her?' Eckstein asked savagely.

'It was him . . . upstairs.'

'You bet.' He saw a length of chain attached by a padlock to the bed post, pulled away the blankets at the bottom of the bed, and found the other end attached to a pair of handcuffs, one of which was locked around Marianne's ankle.

'Get it off!'

At this point Marianne stirred, then slowly raised herself to a sitting position, blinking against the light.

She gave a vague smile. 'What's happening?' she asked.

Eckstein said, 'We're getting out of here.'

'Oh, where are we going? Is it somewhere nice?'

The large eyes squinted at him from chalk-white features.

'Does she have any clothes?'

Mrs McCombe went across to a cupboard and took out an armful of clothing.

'Put them on the bed.'

He said to Marianne, 'Can you walk all right?'

'Yes, I'm perfectly all right.' She climbed out of the bed, took a few paces, and staggered. Eckstein caught her, led her back to the bed. 'Help her to get some shoes on,' he told the woman.

A few minutes later he helped her to slip a coat over her night-dress, and they were ready to leave. He said to Mrs McCombe, 'Lay down on the bed.'

'I had nothing to do with it,' she said. 'It was him up-stairs . . . that's God's honest truth.'

He forced her on to the bed and snapped the handcuff round her ankle. Then he picked up the pile of clothing and guided Marianne, an arm round her shoulder, towards the stairs.

Eckstein switched off the lights as he left. He paused at the foot of the stairs, took out a gas grenade, activated it and tossed it into the basement. Then he closed the door.

23

She woke up.

Slight, but developing feelings of panic. Where am I? What's happened? Recent vague recollections struggled with the urgency of now. Right, let's get now sorted out to start with.

She was lying in a narrow bunk of what was quite clearly a caravan, under a sheet and a couple of blankets. Wearing her nightdress. In the opposite bunk, still sleeping, lying on top of the bedclothes in his underwear was a man whose features in repose looked vaguely familiar.

She sat up, parted a chintzy curtain, and looked out at other caravans in the full light of day. Washing lines. People about. Children bickering around a sandpit.

Current situation established—a caravan site. Now examine vague memories. Yes, that terrifying cellar, the horrible woman . . . and . . . well at least she wasn't there any more . . . but how in heaven's name . . .?

She sat up straight and looked at the man again as he grunted and stirred in his sleep. One of his arms was injured, pitted with small dark holes and caked with dried blood.

Marianne noticed a heap of her clothing dumped on the floor by the foot of the bunk. She crept out quietly and investigated what was there. No bra . . . Christ . . . still, never mind. A smock . . . good, the bulge was getting huge . . . a couple of skirts, tights, sweaters . . . she crept behind a curtain dividing the segments of the caravan and hurriedly dressed, then looked in a mirror. Oh my God! She found a headscarf and knotted it round her matted locks, slipped on her shoes.

Now for a quick recce.

She tried the door of the caravan. Locked. Oh, so that was it. She tiptoed back through to the sleeping quarters, saw the crumpled overalls dumped on the floor beside the sleeping man, and went through the pockets . . . a pencil torch . . . something that looked like a piece of plastic soap . . .

'Looking for something?' She glanced up. He was looking at her with a faint, lackadaisical smile.

'Yes,' she said fiercely, 'the key. Why have you locked me in?'

'I guess I was locking everyone out.' He propped his head on a hand. 'You'll find it hanging on the door if you want it.'

'Thank you.' She went and checked. It was there. She opened the door, looked out, closed it again, and returned.

'Who are you, anyway?'

'The name is Barry Eckstein. You have got to be Marianne Seal. We met by a goldfish pool once.'

Her eyes widened. 'Oh yes, I remember. But that doesn't explain . . .'

'Could we leave the explanations until later. I have just woken up.'

'All right. What have you done to your arm?'

'I had a misunderstanding with a dog.'

She looked appalled. 'Not that alsatian that was . . .'

'Right.'

'You'll have to see a doctor. It might be rabid . . . anyway you definitely need an anti-tetanus injection.'

'I'll risk it. That bitch looked a fine healthy animal to me.'

'Is there any hot water in this place?'

'Should be. The brochure promised every modern convenience.'

She heated some water on a calor gas cooker, found a medicine cabinet with a few supplies, and washed and dressed the wound. As she bandaged it she said, 'You haven't told me who you're working for.'

'Let's say I used to work for the state of Israel, but as of now I'm unemployed.'

Afterwards she brought a suitcase full of Eckstein's clothes from the van and he got dressed.

It was now nearly half-past twelve. 'There's supposed to be some kind of a restaurant around here. Why don't we go and eat?' he said.

Marianne, who had been rummaging about at the far end of the caravan, put her head round the curtain. 'Could you give me half an hour? I've just found half a bottle of shampoo and I'm going to wash my hair.'

The café was about a hundred yards from the foreshore, overlooking a muddy creek. Teenage girls wore inadvisable bikinis. Thin spidery grandmothers chuntered together, commenting and nodding. Children shrilled demands, sandy-haired fathers acquiesced, but with reservations. Elton John reverberated. Sausage, egg, beans, chips, ice cream with chocolate sauce. No dogs. Open to non-campers.

They talked for a long time about recent experiences and arrived at a joint conclusion—that Marianne had been the intended subject of an unpleasant experiment, which had been thwarted by Dr Stephen. That Nick was the true father of the child growing inside her, but those who had initiated the experiment believed otherwise, and she was still in considerable danger.

Eckstein felt it unnecessary to mention the involvement of Professor Buechner and Adolf Hitler. It would have been an obscene irrelevance. Nor did he refer to the small cachet of pills he had carried for the last three weeks, and had recently flushed down the caravan's toilet.

Marianne already knew of Dr Stephen's fate. The Badger had told her about it with considerable relish.

Eventually Eckstein said, 'I'm about to go back to the States. Would you like to come with me?'

It took her several moments, and a mouthful of cold coffee, to digest this possibility.

'I don't know anyone in America,' she said at last.

'You know me.' He produced a pipe and fiddled with it.

260

'I could find somewhere over there where you'd be pretty safe. It's a big place . . . plenty of room to get lost.'

'I couldn't. I haven't even got a passport.'

'That did occur to me.' He felt in his pocket and took one out. 'You are now a Mrs Sandra Wharmby,' he said. 'She's not quite as tall as you but you could try flat heels. Also she is a brunette but women have been known to change in that respect. All you need is your own photograph in the space provided.'

She gazed at him with wonder. 'How did you manage all this?'

'Some people sell their passports,' he said, 'for money. Then claim to have lost them. I also have a visa for a four months' visit.' He passed it across.

They were now alone in the restaurant. An elderly kitchen hand rattled trays and plates behind them.

'When were you thinking of going?'

'We are about five miles away from Southend airport. They run a lot of charter flights to the continent at this time of year. We could be in Paris tonight, Washington tomorrow morning.'

'I can't believe it. Barry . . . why are you doing all this for me?'

He considered the question carefully.

'Well, I suppose you could say I've been taking orders from other guys for some years and I've recently begun to question the wisdom of those who are dishing them out.

'Or alternatively you might say that I've decided to become the founder, president, and only paid-up member of the International Society for the Preservation of Unborn Children.'

A green-overalled harridan approached. 'Can we have you out now, please?'

Marianne said, 'Are you actually going to smoke that pipe?'

Forty minutes later Eckstein handed in his keys at the site office, paid for the week he had booked, and left with

261

Marianne for Southend Airport. He managed to find a couple of seats on an Air France Caravelle which was leaving for Paris just over an hour later. In the interim he telephoned the Berkeley Square branch of the Chase Manhattan Bank and asked the manager to put into operation certain arrangements he had already made in writing concerning the transfer of his account. These arrangements to be absolutely confidential.

He also addressed a brief letter to Coulman, announcing his immediate resignation from the Israeli Intelligence Service. He had decided, he wrote, to take up a teaching career in Africa.

There was no need for Coulman to pursue the current operation. He guaranteed to make himself personally responsible for the welfare—and complete anonymity—of the child in question.

Like, Eckstein wrote, a kind of godfather, in the original sense of the word. He concluded by giving Coulman explicit instructions where to pick up the grey mini-van.

When Coulman received the letter the following day he at once wrote a personal report on the situation with a strong recommendation that the case should now be closed, and sent it by coded cable to his chiefs in Tel Aviv.

He received a reply two days later. The committee had decided that the operation should be vigorously pursued until it was satisfactorily concluded. Schen—who had spent the time since his arrival in England fruitlessly watching the arriving passengers at Heathrow Airport—was to be indefinitely committed to finding the mother and destroying the child.

Hugo Reisener suffered a severe heart attack in Munich in January 1975. Although a team of specialists managed to keep him alive for a week, he succumbed on the 22nd of that month. His impressive funeral was attended by prominent industrialists and right-wing politicians from Germany and abroad.

Among them was Charles Moresby Fenton Fox-Hillyer, who had just been appointed a Commander of the Order of the British Empire in the new year's honours list, for his services to military science.

There is a town somewhere in the mid-western states of America which has a population of between thirty and eighty thousand people. It contains a high school, co-educational and fully integrated, catering for some six hundred pupils.

On the morning of 7 May 1977—a Saturday—Shirley Delgardo, the head of the school's music department, had a lunch appointment at the home of her newly-appointed deputy, Mr Barry Brownrigg, and his wife.

Although there was a newly-built ranch-style bungalow available on the staff site next to the school, the Brownriggs had elected to settle for a country cottage some seven miles out in the country. Mrs Delgardo, a brisk-mannered and still pretty divorcee of thirty-four, drove out there in a state of pleasurable anticipation.

She had already liked what she had seen of Mr Brownrigg at the interview and had enthusiastically supported his selection. He had played a technically difficult violin piece with total accuracy.

She was sure they would quickly strike up a good working relationship. Perhaps even something a little deeper in the course of time.

She drove through a valley flanked by rocky foothills and stopped the car outside the cottage—a small, eccentric-looking clapboard dwelling—and picked her way towards the front door over a broken footbridge which crossed a bubbling stream.

As she approached the house she saw Mr Brownrigg bending down beside a hedge. He was hacking away at a root with a spade.

She called out. He straightened up and came towards her, grinning, trousering his hands.

'The garden's running wild,' he said.

He glanced around him. 'Marianne's around somewhere.' He shouted, 'Marianne!'

After a few moments Mrs Brownrigg appeared from the back of the cottage, brushing away long strands of dark hair which were blowing across her face.

She was wearing a pair of torn yellow trousers, a man's red sweater of some antiquity. But beneath these coarse habiliments, Shirley was enviously conscious of the sort of body she had prayed for ever since her breasts had started to develop. And those eyes to go with it. Some women would never know their luck.

The other woman stretched out an arm and propped herself against her husband, with a friendly smile for the visitor. Brownrigg kissed her gently on the ear.

'Darling, this is Shirley Delgardo, my boss.'

Shirley protested, 'Oh, please don't call me that. I'd much prefer the word colleague.'

'Hallo,' said Marianne. She went over and gave the guest a sisterly kiss.

The idea of anything but a professional relationship with Mr Brownrigg had now vanished from Shirley's thoughts. With this one at home, there was no way. Instead, she began to dwell on Marianne's obvious potential as a social asset.

'Would you like to have a look round the garden before lunch?' Brownrigg asked.

'Sure, I'd love to.'

As they strolled towards a straggling rose bush Shirley noticed the child playing with a trike on the stretch of lawn beyond.

'Hey, you never told me you had a baby.'

Brownrigg said, 'Sorry, I guess I forgot to mention it.' He called: 'Amanda.'

The little girl turned and glanced across, then toddled over and stood beside her father, gazing curiously at the intruder. Shirley had never been a 'baby person' but felt she had to go through the motions.

'Aren't you beautiful?' In fact, she had seldom seen so

strikingly attractive a child, or one which bore so close a resemblance to its mother. She bent down and diggled the bare, plump little chest with a finger. 'How old are you then?'

The child said nothing, but gazed at her with its huge blue eyes, brushing a hand over the point where her finger had landed. Marianne volunteered, 'She's two years and three months.'

'What's your name?' the child inquired.

'This is Mrs Delgardo, darling. Say hallo.'

Amanda moved forward and clutched at the crocodile-skin bag which hung from the teacher's shoulder. 'What's in there?'

Shirley smiled. 'I'll show you if you like.' But as she opened the bag the infant grabbed it and ran off across the lawn. Cosmetics, money, showered on the grass.

'Amanda, come here at once.'

Brownrigg ran across and grabbed her, brought her struggling back.

'Now you just say sorry to Mrs Delgardo.'

The features wrinkled into a scowl. The eyes now glared at Shirley with undisguised hostility. The features reddened. The dimpled fists opened and shut.

'No, I won't, I won't. Go away, I hate you!'

The mother said, 'You're going straight up to your room until you apologise.' She picked up the child, who began kicking and struggling, yelling with rage as Marianne carried her back to the house.

Mr Brownrigg began picking up the contents of the bag.

'I'm sorry,' he said. 'She is not usually like that.'

'She is sure grown-up for her age,' said Mrs Delgardo. 'I think she is going to be something special.'

On the way back to the school Mrs Delgardo passed a rather dusty Opel estate car with a Texas plate driven by a large, swarthy man wearing a Caribbean shirt and a fedora with a striped band.

The car turned off about half a mile from the Brownrigg's

residence and turned up a rough track over steeply rising ground. The driver parked beside a clump of scrub and small, scrawny firs.

A jay protested harshly at this intrusion.

The man seemed in no particular hurry, seeming at perfect peace with his surroundings as he sat on the tailboard and opened a flask of coffee. After a while he picked up a pair of binoculars and scanned the valley below.

The clapboard cottage was clearly visible through a gap in the trees.

A rotary mower started up with a clatter. Brownrigg came into view, attacking the long grass on the lawn.

It was another fifteen minutes before the child appeared and began swinging in a motor tyre suspended by a rope from a pear tree.

'Daaaa . . . ddy . . . look at me! Daaaaaaa . . . ddy!'

From a small selection of weaponry lying in the back of the vehicle Schen selected a pre-war Mannlicker sporting rifle— a collector's item—and clipped on the telescopic sight.

He paused, as if a thought had struck him, then smiled wryly to himself and adjusted the range to four hundred and fifty yards.